MAXIM: SUBMIT

A CLUB XXX NOVEL: BOOK ONE

LANA SKY

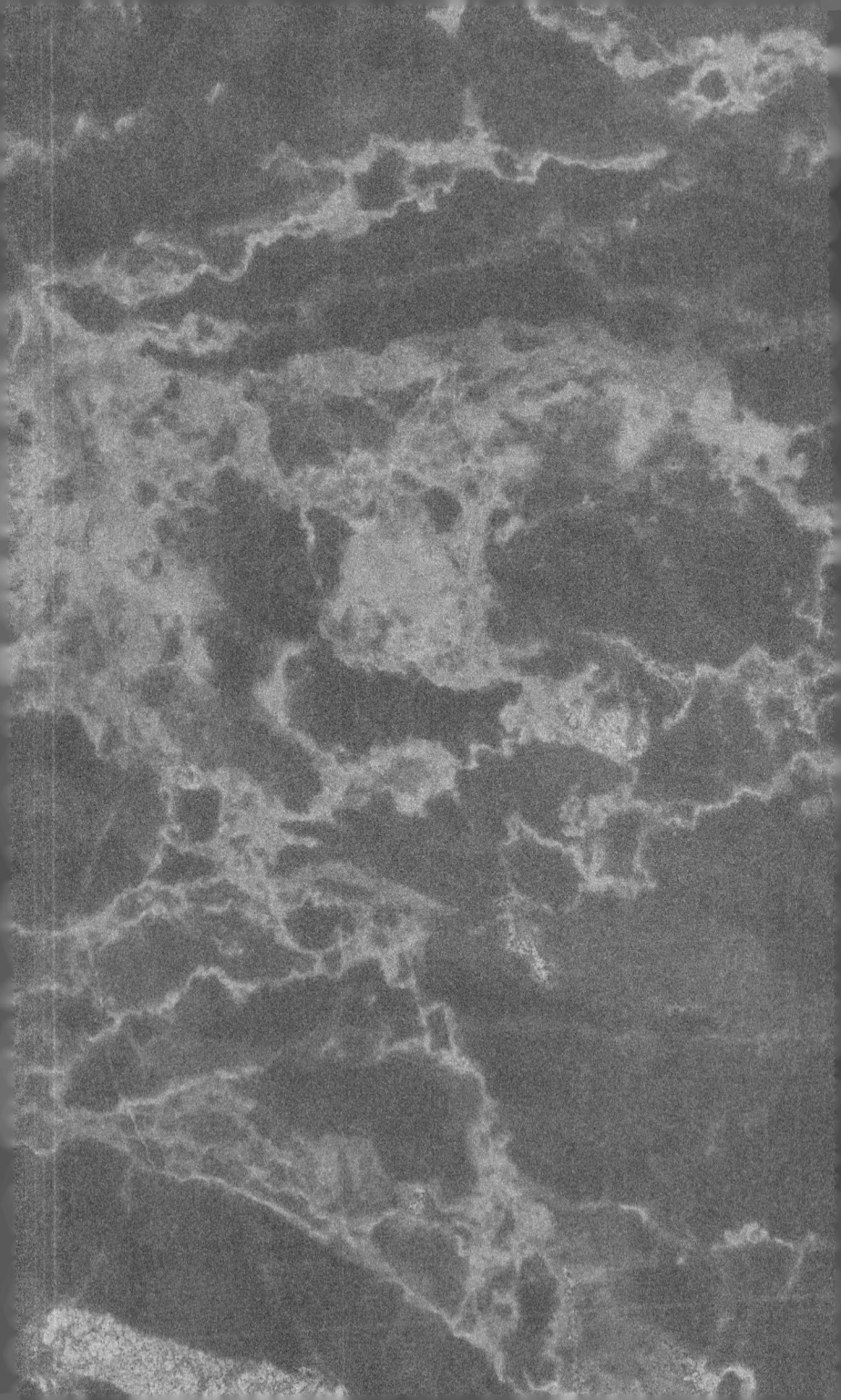

Maxim: Submit

Maxim: Submit By Lana Sky

Cover Design and Interior Formatting by Charity Chimni
Editing by Mickey Reed Editing
Proofreading by Charity Chimni

ACKNOWLEDGMENTS

Thanks so much to everyone who supported this draft along the way! Please keep in mind that this story includes dark, graphic and explicit content matter that is not suitable for readers under the age of 18—or for readers who are uncomfortable with the following subject matter: explicit sex, mentions of sexual abuse, mentions of child abuse, graphic depictions of violence, and mentions of self-harm.

CHAPTER ONE

$375. That number is the only thing on my mind as Fuckface #3 rails me from behind.

That's what he calls it: *railing*.

If only he were actually good at it.

Damn near bored out of its skull, my brain takes his stupid term and spins it around, making a game out of it. *Rail. Railroad.* There are train tracks not too far from here, actually. I can hear the distant howl of the siren riding the still night air—the de facto theme song of a small fucking town like Mayer. The lonely whistle drowns out Fuckface's final groan as he thrusts deep, pinning me flat against an icy brick wall.

Thank fucking god. My palms are rubbed raw and sting as I let them fall to my side. Then I wait. The bastard knows the drill: in and out. But, instead of going for his wallet, he runs a meaty hand over the back of my head, gathering my hair in his fist.

"That was so fucking good, baby. I've never come so hard."

"Likewise," I choke out. I even sound nice. Ish. Kinda. After all, I still have to keep the act up until I get paid. The truth is, I don't orgasm. Ever.

Especially not with a man who smells worse than the overflowing dumpster a few blocks down.

When he doesn't move, I brace my hands flat against the wall and try to shimmy out from under him—but Fuckface must have drunk more liquid courage than usual tonight. His breath fans my neck, reeking like the toilets at Barney's after happy hour.

"You want to show me how good it felt?" He grinds his hips against my ass, showing off his flaccid, not-much-to-brag-about-even-when-hard dick. "How about a kiss?"

"How about an extra fifty?" I shrug him off and wrench the hem of my dress down while he staggers against the opposite wall. No more Miss Nice.

"Pay up." I stick my hand out.

He spits at it. "Bitch."

Ugh. Considering how many "frequent flier miles" this douche-wipe has racked up over the past six months alone, one might think he'd have learned some manners by now. Or at least the common fucking decency to pay upfront.

"You know the drill," I tell him, making my voice hard, the way Benny taught me to. I bet no one else's johns ever gave them this kind of shit. "Pay up."

Fuckface runs a hand over his gray stained t-shirt before fingering the pocket of his still open jeans. Considering what he did with those fingers only minutes ago—sloppily, I might add—it's disgusting fucking imagery. I hope the electric company doesn't mind the extra germs on their blood money.

"I don't know, baby," Fuckface says as he reaches for his wallet and thumbs through a stack of bills. "Have you really earned this?"

I crane my neck before I can help myself and catch a peek: fifties, fifties, fifties... He fishes out two and offers them to me.

Fucking asshole.

I snatch the money before he can pull it out of reach and snap my fingers impatiently. "*Baby*, you're a little short."

Fuckface chuckles. "Why don't you come and get it, you little bitch?"

Well, he did ask for it. I turn and take a few steps toward the mouth of the alley. The extra distance gives me enough time to reach along my hip and draw the knife strapped to my right outer thigh.

The dumb bastard didn't even notice it.

"Come back, you bitch," he tells me, laughing. I sense him behind me, his footsteps heavy and slow. "You know you need the money."

He's right. I do.

So I stop, letting him come up behind me. I wait until he palms my ass and tries to push up against me again. After tucking the handle of the knife into my palm, I turn and jam the butt of it into the fucker's beer gut with one hand while grabbing the wallet with the other.

"Nice doing business with ya," I tell him, snatching out the full amount he owes—along with a little extra for "service fees."

I drop the wallet while he groans behind me and leave the alley. Even on heels, I make it to the bus stop in ten minutes flat. I'm already on my way back to the city before the bastard can get his pants back up.

The money in my hand isn't anywhere near enough. But I'll make it last.

I don't have a fucking choice.

CHAPTER TWO

Everyone likes to think that their soul doesn't carry a price tag—and sure, some lucky sons of bitches never become desperate enough to find it. The first step is having to look at yourself in the mirror and no longer seeing a person, just an object with pretty eyes. She's worth about fifty a lay, you tell yourself—a hundred dollars tops.

Cha-ching.

When Benny first "scouted" me for a place in his business, the only question to leave my mouth was, "Will I get the money upfront?"

That's the way the cookie crumbles in this world. You'd sell your ass for a dime the moment the rent is due. Just as long as you could smell it first, feel the telltale promise of money in your hand. Hopefully it's enough so that the rabbit-eyed kids shackled to you don't have to eat their Cheerios on the street corner tonight. Let's say that the kids aren't even yours.

That's my life.

There's no use crying about it. To be fucking honest, I don't think I have any tears left. So, when Benny calls me into his office for a "special" assignment the moment I get back from Mayer, I don't let myself think through the potential cons. I just accept.

"What's the job?"

Good old Benny wrings his fingers together. Though it doesn't take much to make a man like him nervous. Why the hell he chose pimp as a career, I will never know. At least he doesn't beat his girls. Sometimes, a few of us *don't* try to take advantage of him—like me.

"It's…a little fucked up," he says, staring down at the peeling tile floor of his office. It's really just a spare room in a laundromat on Fifth, but he put a desk in here and even has a secretary, Grace, who answers his burner phones and sometimes keeps the police off his tail with on-the-house blow jobs. "It's not exactly legal…"

I raise an eyebrow. "Benny, my outfit isn't legal." I gesture to the black, skintight dress I "borrowed" from JC Penney's the other night. As long as I keep the tag intact, I can have the bastard smuggled back into the store before the next inventory.

Any other night, the joke would have drawn a chuckle out of him. But Benny just sighs and drags on the lit cigarette perched at the corner of his mouth. "Not like that. This is some freaky shit, Frankie."

I roll my eyes. "Freaky shit? Getting fucked in an alley butt-ass naked because you can't afford to get a drop of some loser's cum on your dumbass dress is freaky shit." My elbows still sting from the friction of being pressed against the brick wall while FuckFace #3 did his business. "How much does it pay?"

Benny Ireland never shies away from talking about money. His entire profession is built upon it, for chrissakes. But, rather than lay out any solid figures, he sighs again. "There's this guy I want you to meet. Tomorrow. Noon. It's at a café downtown on the south side. Don't you fucking dare be late." He reaches into the pocket of his faded gray suit and pulls out a business card, which he places within my reach on the desk. "He can tell you more than I can."

"He the John?" I pick the card up between two fingers, eyeing the front of it. It's plain. There is no wording on either side: just a single silver letter X and a phone number.

"Don't know," Benny says, drawing another hit of his cig. "Don't think so. He's kinda old. Bald. Though it's not like you have a type."

"That's right. My *type* comes out of a cash register. Bills and quarters," I say, "You know me, Ben."

"Damn right I do." He puts his cigarette out in the ashtray, but his hands shake and he winds up getting more ash on the table than anywhere else. "Ever heard of the name Koslov?"

"Is that like a country or something?"

"I'll take that as a no," Benny says, rolling his eyes, but I think I hear him sigh. "Good. Trust me, you don't want to have heard of it."

"Why?"

"No reason." He shrugs and darts his gaze to the opposite end of the room. Any other night, I'd press harder. Make him squirm.

A night when my arms weren't scratched to shit.

"So what's this guy into for you to pick me?" I demand, tucking the business card beneath my bra strap. "Brunettes? Baby faces?" It's not like I have low self-esteem, but I do have two perfectly working eyes. Eyes that reveal a girl who is not too bad to look at, but nothing special either.

"You want the truth?" Benny leans back against his ratty armchair and cracks his knuckles one by one. "The bastard just came in and asked me to give him the most desperate, money-hungry girl I've got." He glances me over, frowning at what he sees, the prick. "You, baby, fit the bill in every fucking way."

"Thanks for the vote of confidence, Ben." I turn on my heel and kick the door to his office. There's no latch on it, so it flies open against the adjacent wall. The thud startles Grace, who's perched on the edge of a washing machine, painting her nails pink.

"Yikes, Frankie," she chirps in the high-pitched drawl she uses to lure in customers. Her shtick is that creepy Lolita shit, pink baby doll dress and all. "Benny do something to piss you off?"

I just look at her sideways and shrug. "Everybody pisses me off."

Grace nods slowly like I've just given her the answer to some million-dollar question. "Oh. Well, see you around, Frankie."

Well, isn't that the truth in a nutshell: I have no choice but to come around.

After working for a week straight, I'm still five hundred dollars short. Daisy will have to miss that fucking field trip she's been talking about—*again*. All because I'm too damn tired to tack on an extra blow job or waste an extra five minutes of my goddamn life for a few more bills.

I'm too tired.

Too hungry—once I eat, I can think. I can plan a way to score more cash in time.

I'll make it up to her.

I wonder if there's anything left over in the fridge. Some bread to make a goddamn sandwich. A piece of toast.

I'll make it up to her.

I don't even realize I'm already home until I stagger through the front door and catch the tail end of what seems to be World War III.

"You touch my doll again and I'll put my fist through your damn mouth—"

"Hey!" I slam the door behind me, marshaling all six rug rats to attention.

The threat came from the youngest, Ainsley, who stands barely taller than my knee. It's not too hard to see what pissed her off this time: a decapitated Barbie doll at her feet.

The culprit appears to be Eric, the second youngest, who keeps flashing Ains his middle finger when he thinks I'm not looking. *Great.* Standing between them are the four oldest. Mikie's been smoking again—I can smell him from here. Daisy has her shirt on backward, while Ollie and Ray are in the middle of a silent shoving match.

Sighing, I throw my head back, stare up at the ceiling, and count to ten out loud. Meanwhile, the bickering dies down. Without looking, I dig into my bra and fish out the wad of cash tucked inside. Then I snap my fingers and gesture in my general direction.

"Line up." I look down and find Mikie, the oldest at sixteen, standing in front of me with his hand outstretched and I quickly rip off a few fifty-dollar bills. "Electric," I tell him, pressing the money into his hands. "Drop it off on your way to school tomorrow. There's a ten in there for lunch. Don't forget to turn in your homework from last week too, and if I get a call from the principal tomorrow, I swear to God—"

"Got it," Mikie huffs, snatching for the money. "Damn it, Frankie. Chill." Then he steps aside.

I wave up the next two: they come as a packaged deal. "Heat," I tell Ray and Ollie. "Don't forget to pick up the neighbor's recycling on the way home, either. Whoever gets the most cans gets the extra slice the next time we order pizza."

"Oh holy shit!" Ray exclaims before shoving Ollie out of his way.

I have to sidestep them both in order to continue with the dispensing of the household chores. "This is for the rent stash," I tell Daisy, shoving some of the last few bills into her hands. "Take the ten for lunch."

"Um, Frankie?" She looks at me, her brown upturned eyes shining and hopeful. "About the field trip…"

Something in my chest feels tight. Fuck. I tug at the strap of my dress, but the damn sensation doesn't go away. "Hold on." I pry the money from her hands and count it. One hundred and fifty—every bit of the extra I stole from Fuckface # 3. To make up for it, I'll have to work my ass off —literally—tomorrow night in order to have enough left over for the bills due at the end of the week. But what the fuck. It's not like having *almost* enough matters. "Take it," I say, tucking the money into her hands.

She frowns. "Are you sure we can—"

"I'll work something out." I wave her off and dig out my final few ones. "Milk money," I explain while the two

11

youngest look up and nod. The moment I hand the cash over, they immediately start shrieking over who owes who what.

Ah, the rat race of life. It never ends. Not even here.

"Bed. Everyone," I command, jabbing my finger at the stairs.

They hustle off after ten minutes of whining, and I savor the silence composed of wailing sirens and the shouts from the neighbors next door. The place is a fucking wreck. Daisy must have made dinner tonight because there's a pan with something burned onto it soaking in the sink. The living room is a sea of book bags and loose pages of homework. Without any money to spare on bug spray, I find the roaches out in full force.

It feels like I wear out the bottom of my heels attempting to stomp on as many as I can while I tear through the house, picking shit up. Shoving shit somewhere else. Scraping shit off more shit.

When I'm elbow-deep in the middle of washing the dishes, my fingers slip on a knife and I cut myself on my wrist. Accidentally. Twice. As the blood-colored water circles the drain, only then can I finally fucking think. I hear shouting. Someone's threatening to blind someone else with toothpaste. Someone's crying. Someone's slamming doors.

The peeling walls around me form a prison. A hellhole.

It's all I've got.

So I just keep scrubbing until the dishes are clean and the water runs down the drain. Then I take the couch for the night, facing the door just in case that bitch decides to come walking through. I consider taking the dress off, but it's safer on me than it would be in the morning rush once the kids get up for school.

Besides, a little blood never hurt anyone.

CHAPTER THREE

I wake up after everyone's already gone—something I don't do too often. The house is silent when I finally crawl out from beneath the open sleeping bag someone draped over me. I find a lukewarm Pop-Tart beside a shitty cup of coffee on the end table near my head.

Daisy.

With a sigh, I haul myself upright and strip the dress off. Then I climb upstairs and wander through the maze of clothing spread across two bedrooms in search of a clean pair of jeans and a tee shirt. The jeans might be mine or Daisy's. The shirt is probably Mikie's.

When I start to brush my teeth, I notice that it's already wet courtesy of Ainsley, who doesn't seem to like using her smaller, pink toothbrush. I make do anyway, and I almost feel semi-normal after a belly full of sugary pastry and one of the beers I keep hidden at the back of the fridge in a bag marked *veggies*.

The buzz has only just kicked in when I finally glance down at my watch and then bust my ass racing across town to reach Penney's before my shift starts. I sneak in through the main entrance and drop the dress off at the fitting room rack. By eleven, I'm already three hours into a measly eight-hour shift that, when all is said and done, won't even net me half of what I need to make rent. Tomorrow, it's a night shift at the diner. My only prayer of getting by is scoring enough tips from the truckers who might stop in—any way I can.

"Hey, Francesca!"

I glance over my shoulder and find Meryl, the manager, shuffling across the store, her hands shoved into the pockets of her pants where she keeps her "totally prescription" pain meds.

"I'll take over the register," she tells me, coming around to my side of the counter. "You go home for the day. Terra needs the extra overtime. Her damn husband's in jail again. The poor girl's gotta put up bail."

It doesn't seem to faze her that a line of customers hears this little exchange. Dumbass Terra, her cousin twice removed, needs to steal the money out of *my* mouth in order to get her ass beaten for a few more nights before her husband winds up in a cell again.

Go figure.

My fingers shake, but I curl them into fists. Deep breaths and shit. "I was supposed to get thirty hours this week—"

"I'll give you priority on the schedule next month," Meryl assures me as her meaty fingers dart for the register.

Fuck this shit. I leave through the back entrance, nicking a sweater on my way out. This time, I don't justify it as being "borrowed." Instead, I pull it on in place of Mikie's shirt and rip the tags off.

Then I head south, digging my nails into my palms. *Good job, Frankie girl.* I'm on a goddamn roll—at least five hundred dollars in the hole already with no real way to make up for it. I could always head to Benny and see if he has any extra work, but…

Wait. I bite my lip and fish through my pockets, finding the crumpled-up business card stuffed inside one of them. I don't even remember grabbing it. Benny told me a time too, I think. Noon. For a meeting. Shit, where was it? I'm moving before I even really remember.

I don't show up at the address until close to one: a little café on the south side. Even at this time of day, it's not exactly hopping with activity. There's just one man inside, seated at a corner booth. He's oldish and bald like Benny said. He must be the client.

I plaster a fake smile on my face and run a hand through my hair. My fingers get stuck halfway and I have to tug them loose. Shit. I look down and find that the sweater I stole has deodorant stains on the side. My jeans have a hole in them. I have Pop-Tart breath.

And this man is wearing a tailored suit. He smells fancy. A silver pen rests between two of his fingers, and the leather notebook open in front of him is probably worth at least six shifts at JC Penney's. When he sees me, his eyes narrow and he runs a hand down the front of his black suit jacket. "Are you Francesca Marconi?"

I shrug. "Frankie."

The man nods once to himself and jots something down with his pen. "Have a seat."

I join him at the table, already weirded out by the place. It's quiet. Something tells me that it shouldn't be empty, even during a weekday. Then I happen to glance out the window and find another man in a black suit standing just beyond the main doors. When a smiling couple approaches the entrance, he shakes his head and points toward another café just down the street.

Alarm bells go off in my head.

"Did you rent the place out or something?" I ask the bald guy.

I'm not given an answer right away. He takes his time to rip open exactly four packets of those diet sugars and pours them all into a steaming cup of coffee beside him. Carefully, he stirs it up with a spoon. When he takes a sip, I notice the silver ring on his right hand. It looks real. It looks expensive. I can't take my eyes off it as he sets his mug to the side.

"My name is Lucius," he says, extending his hand toward me.

I take it and shake it once. His ring feels cold—*super* expensive.

"How old are you, Francesca?"

I look up and find him observing me, but it's not the kind of stare I'm used to. It's the way my mother's parole officer looked whenever he came by the house and I spun whatever lie I could to explain why she hadn't shown up that morning. He's searching for something.

"Nineteen," I say.

He nods again and scribbles something else down into his book. "Do you have HIV, hepatitis, syphilis, or any other STD?"

I cough to smother my shock. "Not that I know of."

"We'll do a blood test, to be sure." He glances over at the man standing outside and scribbles something else. "Now, allow me to ask the most pressing question."

I'm holding my breath. So, what will it be? Maybe he wants me to wear a little girl costume to get him off. Spank me. Do anal? Thinking about it creeps me out to the point that I shudder. But money makes the world go 'round and my universe is already about a million spins behind the starting line.

"Okay?" I prod when he doesn't spit the proposition out fast enough. "What's the deal?"

"My client is an unusual man, Francesca."

"*Your* client? I thought—"

"Let me just cut to the chase," Lucius says, folding his hands in front of him. "My client is an unusual man, Ms. Marconi. A man with very unusual tastes."

"Like what?" I ask. Benny said that this guy wanted someone desperate. Luckily for him, my goddamn picture was probably in the dictionary under that word by now.

"I won't mince words," Lucius says. "A lot more involvement than the usual tryst. You would be his *exclusive* companion."

Now, I have an idea of what this guy must want: some bitch to wear a collar and crawl around while he pretends to be Christian Grey.

Sounds weird, but I'll bite. "How much?"

It's funny how a year can change people. I used to tell myself I'd never give in to that sort of shit. And that I'd only give blow jobs just once a month if that bitch Meryl cut my hours short. I used to tell myself a lot of dumb lies.

"It's a compensatory payment system, to be sure," Lucius admits. He flips through the pages of his notebook and pulls a slip of paper out. It has wording printed on it. A list, I find as he slides it over to me.

Make that a contract.

Well, fuck me. I don't know whether to laugh or sigh. This guy really does think he's Christian Grey.

"The sixteen thousand is just the base salary," Lucius says as I drag the paper closer.

Then I stop thinking after that. My brain fucking short-circuits at the sight of a few zeros. Way too many. Enough for rent. Enough for food. Enough for a million fucking field trips.

But it's funny. The words that follow kill any excited butterflies that came alive in my stomach: *The aforementioned party will hereby agree to a base salary consisting of $16,000 per monthly quarter, barring any injury.*

My eyes skip down to read the rest and those cold, dead butterflies turn into stabbing scorpions.

Clause 1: *In the event of a burn, wound, cut, or any similar injury greater than ten inches in length or diameter, the aforementioned party will receive $1,000 per inch.*

Clause 2: *In the event that the aforementioned party is rendered unconscious and unresponsive—no pulse and/or pupil reaction—for a period of documented time extending more than one minute in duration, the party will receive $5,000 for each additional minute and $500 for each remaining second of.*

Clause 3: *In the event of accidental death...*

"What the hell is this?" I lunge away from the table, nearly knocking myself over in the process. My fingers shake. I have to curl them into fists to hide how badly.

Lucius takes another sip of his coffee. "I understand that this might seem overwhelming."

"You're not serious." I don't know what seems more insane or what disgusts me more. That a man might actually write a contract with seriously *maiming* a woman in mind or the fact that I'm already fucking considering it.

"If you are not interested, Ms. Marconi, then I thank you for your time and—"

"Would I get paid upfront?" The question is out of my mouth before I can stop it. My sweater itches. The taste of dried Pop-Tart lingers in my throat. I swallow it down.

"Well, of course." Lucius cocks his head and runs a hand over the pages in his notebook. "There is a one-thousand-dollar signing bonus. After you meet my client, of course. He will decide if you fit his requirements."

I nearly fall out of my chair. One thousand dollars—just for *meeting* someone. I've considered doing a frat party for less.

"But I'd get the money when?"

"After your first encounter. In cash," he adds.

Cash. I brace both hands flat against the table and drag myself forward until the rim of it digs into my chest. "S-so I just sign here?"

I jerk my chin to the paper, already reaching for the silver pen. I can think about the consequences later. I can *think* later.

"No." Lucius reaches into the breast pocket of his suit jacket and pulls out a different sheet of folded paper. It's crisper. Official. "You sign here. Please keep in mind that it includes a confidentiality agreement. You breathe a word as to the identity of my client and I can assure you that no expense, legal or otherwise, will be spared in ensuring that you sorely regret that decision."

His soft, professional tone takes on a hard edge as a hint of darkness peeks out from behind the blue in his eyes.

I don't say a damn thing in response. I just hold my hand out and he places the contract onto my palm, followed by the silver pen. The smart thing to do would be to read the damn thing over. Check for any fine print. Blah, blah, fucking bullshit.

I don't. I just sign on the first line I see without reading a damn word. The only thing I hear—the only thing I can fucking focus on—is the promise of a grand.

"So, when do I meet him?"

Lucius takes the contract and folds it up without doing any of the shit I feel like someone in his position should: make sure that this is what I *really* want. That I know exactly what I'm getting into. Instead, he tucks it between the pages of his notebook.

"Now," he says, rising to his feet. "Follow me, Ms. Marconi."

Follow me. He sounds like the bailiffs in the court when they lead my so-called mother away in handcuffs after one of her frequent convictions. That final.

A creeping sensation crawls down my spine when I stand and follow Lucius out to a black car near the curb. The figure I saw lurking outside the door is gone, but a glance at the driver's seat of the car reveals him behind the wheel.

"Ms. Marconi?" Lucius opens the door to the back seat, waiting for me to climb inside.

I do. No thinking. No regrets. To make sure, my nails dig into my wrist. Hard. Harder. Deeper. I don't stop until the pain cuts through the chaos in my mind. It's clear for five precious seconds, and I savor every last fucking one. Because once Lucius climbs in beside me and the car glides into traffic, I can't smother the fear anymore, and pinching doesn't help one damn bit.

I'm so stupid. I'm a goddamn idiot. Or, like Benny said, *I'm desperate.*

I let a list of everything I need money for by next week run through my mind. *Money. Money. Money.* The chant almost drowns everything else out. Almost.

"Ms. Marconi?"

The car's stopped. I glance over and find Lucius standing on the curb, his hand extended toward me.

"Have you changed your mind?"

I shake my head and scramble out after him. We're in front of a hotel. Or maybe a high-rise—all the rich-people places look the fucking same. This one's pretty big, gleaming in the overcast daylight. The name formed out of silver letters over the entrance reads *The Vermillion Building*.

A doorman is standing out front, watching me. The moment we make eye contact, he quickly turns away.

"Ms. Marconi?" Lucius comes up beside me and nods toward the building's entrance. "I'll take you to meet him now."

"Okay." I run my hands down the front of my sweater. It feels colder out than it did earlier. I can't stop shivering. Though, maybe it's all the hostility thrown my way by the rich bitches who sneer at me as they skip from their posh high rise.

This man, whoever he is, lives large. He'd have to if he's willing to cough up a few hundred dollars per centimeter of injury…

Don't go there. I shake the thought off and pour all of my effort into trailing Lucius across a big-ass lobby decorated in shades of black and silver. The luxury doesn't faze me too much; I've had a few rich clients before, men so cheap and horny that they'd toss a few hundred bucks at a hooker on my end of town.

They were all assholes who never tipped well—and they definitely wouldn't shell out a grand for signing a goddamn piece of paper.

"This way." Lucius enters an elevator with ebony walls, shifting over to leave me enough room.

It's a long way up. This client must live on the top floor. I can only watch the numbers above the closed doors illuminate one by one, marking our ascent. 30...31...40.

As the doors finally open, Lucius steps out into a long hallway with only one exit: a closed door at the very end. Once we reach it, he swipes a keycard into the fancy-looking console attached to the wall beside it and it opens.

"Come in," Lucius says.

I don't know how long I stare before I finally force myself to step forward. This guy must keep the AC blasting, even in the middle of winter. Goosebumps rise over my arms as I let myself take in the sleek entryway. The walls are black. The floors are gray marble. Everything sparkles.

Like a knife.

An odd noise disrupts the flawless impression: pounding. Violent. Brutal.

My heart is in my throat even before I follow Lucius toward that noise, down a short hallway and into a room that looks like it was ripped out of those creepy-ass horror movies Mikie likes to watch. Knives hang from the wall. Hammers. All sorts of tools, some of them rusted from use. The floors are gray with dust, and in the center of the space is a metal pedestal that has a block of what looks like stone on top of it.

Two men are standing before it. While one attempts to beat the hell out of the stone with a sharp metal stick, the other speaks. He's the shorter of the two, wearing a black leather jacket and scruffy jeans. "We lost the shipment," he says, his voice shaking. "Got ambushed by those fucking chink bastards. But all we have to do is—"

"We?" The taller man laughs, shrugging. In an almost casual motion, the stick of metal in his hand leaves the hunk of marble and strikes the other man in the head with its next blow. Groaning, the shorter guy falls to his knees, clutching the back of his skull while blood spurts, coating his fingers and speckling the floor.

"Maxim," Lucius says softly, taking a step forward.

The bigger man turns, still swinging the bar of metal through the air. He's built like a bodybuilder: all muscle, very little fat. He's handsome too—or at least some women might call him that when there isn't brain matter on his chin. I wouldn't, even then. His dark eyes reveal nothing but shadow, nearly hidden by the blond hair framing a stern face that looks like it was carved directly from that block of stone behind him.

"You found a new one so soon?" His voice is deep. Gruff. I think I catch the hint of an accent, though I'm not sure.

Lucius nods while Maxim sets the metal bar on the pedestal and wipes his hands on the front of an already dusty pair of black pants.

"Is this her?" Maxim looks me over once and jerks his chin toward a stool beside a window without waiting for an answer. "Sit." The man on the floor whimpers, and Maxim sighs, turning to Lucius. "Can you clean up this mess?"

"Right away, sir." Without a care given for his expensive suit, Lucius marches over and hauls the bleeding man to his feet by the collar of his jacket. "I'll be in touch, Ms. Marconi," he tells me before leaving the room, the dazed— but alive—man in tow.

A minute later, I hear the main door open and close.

"I told you to sit."

I flinch; with no one else around, that order was meant for me. I swallow hard and approach the stool, turning around so that I face him directly.

Maxim returns his attention to his hunk of stone despite the pool of blood at his feet. His fingers flex, picking up the metal tool again—a chisel, I realize. Then he goes to fucking town. The muscles in his arm coil and pop as he rams the blunt end against the stone block with one hand and grabs a hammer on the table with the other. He strikes hard and the resulting thud echoes throughout the room.

Again. Faster. Harder.

Bang.

Bang!

BANG!

He's lost to the brutality. It feels like hours that I watch him pummel life into the stone until a figure begins to take shape: a woman, tall and slender, her arms reaching toward the ceiling.

She's flawless—until his next blow lands so hard that it sends a crack shooting through her perfectly crafted abdomen. Without warning, he throws the chisel and the hammer aside and they both go flying. The hammer strikes the wall and the chisel decapitates a potted plant in a nearby corner.

With a sigh, Maxim wipes his hands on the edge of his gray tee shirt and turns to face me again. "Did Lucius explain it to you?"

I force myself to nod. "Yeah…"

"*Yes*," he corrects, his eyes narrowing. "How so?"

"I-I um—"

"Do not stammer." He lopes away from the pedestal and approaches a table placed along a wall at the other end of the room. There's a water bottle on top of it, and he snatches for it before ripping the lid off. "Speak in complete sentences," he tells me. He definitely has an accent. Something European. Russian? "Did he show you the contract?"

"Y-yes. I mean, yes, he did."

Maxim nods. "And you read it? You agree to the terms?" He takes another sip of water, throwing his head back so far that I can't see his eyes.

My heart skips a beat while he's not watching. "Yes."

"And you agree to *all* of them?" His gaze cuts through me as he lowers his head again and wipes his mouth with the back of his hand.

I nod twice this time, but my stupid fingers twitch as if betraying the lie. I lace them together and dig my nails into the webs between the ones on my left hand. The pain bites deep—but not deep enough.

"Come here." He sets the water bottle aside and waves his hand, each finger flexing at the joint.

I stand and cross over to him. About a foot away, I stop—not consciously. It's the way his expression changes that makes my heels dig into the floor.

"Turn around."

I do. Hot fingers trace the back of my neck in return, sliding beneath the collar of my sweater to follow the line of my spine underneath. I jerk on the tips of my toes. I can't help it. Each of his nails brushes my skin. Caresses. *Pinches.* The pain shoots through me like the shock I got when I played with the electrical sockets as a kid. Hot and punishing.

"You agree to the terms?" As he speaks, another hand runs along the back of my head before gripping my ponytail. He tugs the elastic loose and stray pieces of hair get caught in each yank.

"Y-yes—" A sharper tug on my scalp turns the word into a gasp. My eyes water at the burning sting. I can't stop myself from reaching up, trying to brush the pain away.

"Don't." He spits the word out, grinding it into my skin. My hand falls. My body sways. Then he tugs harder, forcing me to step back into him. Against me, he feels like a brick wall, built unlike any other man I've ever been with. Solid.

"I will make this time quick," he tells me. "Afterward, we will decide whether or not to continue." His accent hardens, revealing what he really means. *I will decide.* "Do you understand, *kotyonok*?" Two of his fingers twist a piece of my hair, drawing on my scalp as I register that strange word. A nickname? "No. I think you don't," Maxim says before I can complete my train of thought.

All of a sudden, I'm let go. Without his support, I stagger forward and nearly trip over my own feet.

"Leave," he commands behind me. "Lucius will take you home. You can keep the money, but I will not have you waste my time."

He marches toward the pedestal, moving with so much tension that it sounds like a goddamn thunderstorm just broke out in the middle of the room. I can only stare as he fishes the chisel from the potted plant, spraying dirt through the air in an arc. Like blood.

I don't know how long I stand here. It feels like seconds. I'm trying to move—I *am.* Just as my toes twitch a fraction of an inch, he whirls around. When his eyes find mine, I don't see anything else. Just them: black. Dark. Deep. The moment my breathing hitches, it's like a switch being flipped. He shakes his head and the shadows disappear as he beckons me closer with a crooked finger. When I don't react, the finger becomes his entire hand, his voice like a roll of thunder.

"Come."

I rush over to him, my heart pounding, my hands trembling. Once again, something makes me stop just beyond his reach.

"You didn't read the contract, *kotyonok,*" he tells me, his voice catching on the edge of an unstable sound I only have one word for: a growl. He takes a step toward me.

I jump. Frowning, he takes two more. My nerves kick into overdrive and I stagger back three as sweat runs down the back of my neck. I'll never be able to return this damn sweater now. As if knowing that, he grabs me by the wrist before I can go any farther. His fingers bite down over the edge of the sleeve. I hear a ripping sound.

"Look at me."

I can't disobey. Maybe because I never stopped looking. His eyes glow again and I swear I can see myself in them: a dumb little bitch too scared to run.

"I will give you five minutes," he tells me. One of his hands comes to cup my chin and my lungs heave to breathe him in. He smells like musk. Like anger. Like sweat. The rough pad of his thumb grazes my cheek, sliding to the corner of my mouth. He presses, dragging my lower lip down as his eyes stare dead into mine. "Five minutes to change your mind. That is long enough for most."

He turns away again, letting me go, and it's like for those five minutes I don't fucking exist. I just stand. Stare. Maxim goes at the stone block again, chiseling out the woman's shape. Despite her flaws, he beats her body into form, carving at the line of her hips, her eyes, her hair.

Thwack!

I swear that sparks fly with every blow.

Abruptly, he sets the hammer down again. "You've made your choice."

I don't even see his hand move before his fingers snag my collar, dragging me closer. Step by step. When I'm close enough, he moves so that I stagger against the table rather than into his chest.

"On your knees, *kotyonok*." His voice sounds normal again, still deep but less bitter. His fingers rake through my hair once before gathering it roughly into a ponytail. "Now."

He turns away again, letting me go while the command hangs in the air, a terrifying challenge.

This is the part where I earn that little signing bonus.

CHAPTER FOUR

A thousand dollars is all I need. I tell myself that as I drop to my knees, bracing my hands on either side of me. My nails scrape the marble, slightly bending away from their beds. From the corner of my eye, I spot a swath of dark red. I'm only inches from that puddle of blood.

Disgust can't even fully set in before I feel him behind me, his massive palm running over the top of my head. "Turn around."

He's staring down at me, still holding the chisel, when I finally do. And I know the truth, here and now: No amount of money in the world is worth this.

Black eyes follow the line of my gaze and he smiles. "Not tonight, *kotyonok*," he tells me, setting the weapon down again. "No toys. Tonight will be quick." The smile fades as he cups my jaw and tilts my head back while manipulating the clasp of his jeans. "Open wide. At least pretend that you have what it takes before you run."

Run. His thumb pries my mouth open before the thought finishes. He sighs at the sight, flexing his hips to help loosen his jeans. He's wearing black boxers underneath, but even they don't disguise the shape of him. Big. Too big.

"Don't," he warns, the tip of his nail scraping my cheek before I even realize that my mouth is starting to close.

My lips freeze, half open, drool drying on my tongue. With none of the fanfare I'm used to, he peels his boxers down. His cock springs free.

My lips flutter together. Apart. Together. He's hard already. Thick veins circle the shaft, flexing in time with his pulse. It's not the length of him that makes me gulp—it's his sheer size. There is no way in hell I can take him.

"I told you to *open*."

I don't catch the look that crosses his face until it's too late. His hand leaves my chin and moves to my throat, squeezing. I open my mouth so wide that I hear my jaw pop, but the pressure doesn't loosen. It gets tighter as he shifts in closer, jerking my head back. My brain goes away to that cold, quiet place where I can just ignore my body. My nails cut into my palms and I *feel* again. The pain is like a fence.

But it breaks the moment his hand slides around to the back of my neck and takes control over how much I can turn my head. I smell him: musk, raw, animal. His shirt covers most of his abdomen—I can only make out the definition of his hips. They seem carved into his skin. I remember the weapon resting inches away from my head and come up with another word. *Chiseled.*

"We will make this quick," he promises, his voice gritty.

I'm not trying to feel, not trying to see—but I can't miss the moment his hips jerk forward as he pries my jaws apart and then slams in. My teeth keep him out on the first thrust—my mouth just isn't wide enough. He has to force it open, using his fingers while yanking me forward.

That's all I know before my throat closes up. It's ripped open. My gag reflex goes haywire; I'm choking as he thrusts again, rocking on his heels, his mouth clenched in determination. The next second, he's just a blur. My lungs are exploding.

He's too big. Too deep. Too rough.

I can't breathe!

I try to push away, my hands clawing at his hips.

"Let me in," he commands as his cock slides over my tongue for a jagged second. The moment I try to suck in air, he slams back in, almost as if savoring the exact second I start to panic.

Everything goes black. White. My only coherent thought is to breathe in through my nose. *Breathe. Breathe. Breathe!* But it's impossible considering that my stomach is trying to crawl out of my throat. Something blocks its way hard, fast, ramming it back down.

"There." His fingers move through my hair, manipulating my head back farther. "Take *all* of it…like this."

My vision clears; I see his face: cold eyes and a blank expression. Black spots cover him up; they're everywhere. One. Ten. Fifty.

Then, all at once, he lets me go. I'm on my hands and knees. Air floods in down my ruined throat, and I'm running on pure instinct. *Breathe!* Even taking in oxygen hurts so damn much. Almost as bad as what comes up.

My wet fingers trace my mouth when I'm done gagging. They come away warm. Slippery. A coppery taste lingers over my tongue. But he didn't come. I know that, even before he grabs at my hair again, yanking me upright. The world spins and then I'm staring down at dust and wood. The table?

"Here."

Something is shoved into my hand. Something small, firm and cold. My fingers scramble to identify it as a sharp pain bites into my thumb.

"Look at it," Maxim commands, though he raises my hand himself when I'm too slow. "Feel it."

My eyes blink, fighting to adjust—but once they do, I only want to squeeze them shut. I'm holding a knife, one of those spring-loaded ones made of silver with a black leather handle. He makes sure I see the blade. That I notice my blood already painting the edge of it.

Then he forces me to guide it down to my inner thigh. I'm too damn stunned to pull away, and with a tiny bit of pressure, the blade slices through my skin: a burning, fiery line that extends down, down, down.

"A taste," he says while pulling the knife out of my grip. "Should you stay after this."

The wound burns, spanning the length of my thigh, all the way down to my knee. It was a warning—one I don't even get the chance to heed before his weight settles over me. One of his hands palms the back of my neck while the other slides around my hip and undoes the fastenings of my jeans. He pulls them down halfway and doesn't even bother with my panties. He just yanks the panel over with the pad of his thumb.

Make no noise—that's my one rule. No fake moaning. No whimpers. People always interpret them the wrong way. Usually, it's not hard to stay quiet, considering that most of my clients are fat fucks who get winded from fishing my money out of their goddamn wallets. At worst, I'd have to bite my tongue to hold a hiss of disgust back.

A finger. That's all he uses the first time, but it feels like so much more. Chisel, hammer. He tests me with one touch and then drives it home the next. Deep. Too deep.

My knees knock together, my body jerking against the surface of the table, held in place by him. *A finger.* I tell myself that over and over. It's just his finger that's sliding in, stretching me apart, tearing me open. *Another.*

"Relax," he warns as his palm flexes, pinning my skull flat against the table.

His hand withdraws as he muscles in closer, his hips against my bare ass. A crinkling sound cuts the air. Foil. It must take him only a second to get the condom out because, the next, he's in my stomach. He feels *that* deep, and my world narrows down to one purpose: keep *breathing*.

But it's impossible when my throat is on fire. Burning. Searing. Maybe it's out of sympathy for my pussy. How is it possible to feel *this* damn full? This sore.

This goddamn *open*.

When he moves, I see stars. I cry out, but the sound seems to egg him on. He grinds himself into me so hard the table rocks with every thrust, squealing at the joints.

I know pain: all of those "accidental" cuts. I know what it's like when a john gets too rough or tries to gain backdoor access. This is something else. It takes me far past silence. I'm just a body, a hole, used up.

I'm not sure at which point I realize he isn't even all the way inside me. He doesn't fit. Not even by half. Not right away. The resistance doesn't seem to surprise him. He just keeps ramming until my body has no choice but to relent and let him in, inch…by inch…

As he promised, he makes it quick.

One last battering thrust and he groans, his shudders racking through his body and into mine. I feel each jolt even with the condom, and then he slides out. In the hazy moments after, he says something else. Something raspy and gruff smothered into my hair that I barely comprehend.

"Good enough."

I can't respond. I just breathe. Loudly. Erratic. My body is one aching, used strip of flesh, but I just stay here, leaning against the table. Still shaking.

I try counting to ten, but it doesn't work. So I settle for counting to a thousand and picturing green.

I DON'T WAKE UP. I just come to, but I can't stand. I know that much. My stomach is cramping. My legs feel like mush, but I suffer through it all and blink up at the ceiling.

It's semi-dark, but there's just enough gray daylight to let me know that it's after dawn. The little shits have school. Mikie might try to skip without me there, if Daisy didn't burn the damn house down trying to make breakfast.

Rent's still due.

We need groceries. Laundry has to be done. If we don't get some goddamn bug spray, I might have more mouths to feed once the roaches demand a seat at the table.

I have too much damn shit to worry about to lie here on the floor. *Get up.* I flex my toes and flinch. They hurt too. So does my fucking head.

But I've been through worse. That's what I tell myself as I crawl onto my stomach and try to breathe. In and out. Out and in. Out. Out. Out.

I make one stupid noise when I try to stand up. Then I cut the pain off. He left my pants on. I slowly drag them back up and redo the clasp. My sweater feels too loose around the collar. I reach up and feel why: It's ripped.

So much for my job at Penney's.

The first few steps are the hardest. It takes me ten before I can cling to the wall beside the door and follow it out into the main room. The lights are off. The place seems empty. Maxim isn't waiting there when I fumble with the front door and pull it open.

Keep moving. I brace one hand against the wall of the hallway as I head for the elevator, riding it down to the lobby. When the doors open, someone is already standing there.

"Ms. Marconi." Lucius takes one look at me and steps aside, shrugging his suit jacket—a gray one this time—from his shoulders. He drapes it over me the moment I haul myself out of the elevator. I don't even have the strength to argue. He smells like coffee and rich cologne. Somehow on him, the scent isn't as offensive as it was on the Fuckfaces I screwed.

The next ten minutes pass in a blur as he steers me into that infamous black car, and it feels like I simply blink and find myself seated across from him in another café.

"Your payment," he says, reaching into a briefcase on the table in front of him. He fishes out a stack of bills while the waitress lurking around the edges of the room pretends not to stare. Once again, we're the only people inside, and I can make out the shadow of a man near the door, silently keeping watch. "One thousand, in full. If you would like to discuss continuing the contract, then we can—"

"No." I have to press my hands flat against the table to keep them from fucking shaking. "I've got to go home. I've got stuff to do."

"Of course." He nods and sets the money on the table between us. "As with any finalization of a contract, you have twenty-four hours to reconsider."

"So I can go?" I'm already reaching for the money. Grabbing it. Squeezing it. Whatever happened, it was worth it.

It was.

"Yes." Lucius nods again, and I jump to my feet.

Without a jacket, I don't have any way of hiding the money. I fold it up as much as I can and try to shove it into my pocket. The added fullness just makes the front of my pants feel tighter, which draws a groan from my lips before I can bite it back.

"I can see you to your home," Lucius suggests.

I should just leave and take my chances. But getting stabbed would be a rather ironic way to end the past twenty-four hours after having my brains fucked out.

"Okay."

I make him drop me off a block down from my place, and I don't miss the way he eyes the piece-of-shit houses. It's nothing like the posh high-rise he's used to.

"Have a nice day, Ms. Marconi," he says as I scramble out onto the curb.

I don't say anything back. Maybe I'm just too damn tired. My knees knock together with every step I take. A million deep, heavy breaths don't seem to fill my lungs up enough. I'm panting when I stagger up the front stoop and shove the door open.

It's still too early for the kids to be home from school. That means the person rummaging through my kitchen is either a burglar or a shitty-ass mother.

Frankly, I'd take the burglar.

"Frankie-girl!" Melanie stands in front of the sink, holding a frying pan in one hand and a dishcloth in the other. Someone must have let her in, considering that I changed the locks after the last time she'd blown through. Maybe they did it last night while I was lying unconscious on some stranger's creepy workshop floor. That's how Melanie rolls. She sneaks back into our lives when least expected, the biggest goddamn roach in this place.

"What the fuck are you doing here?"

"Honestly, Francesca." She sighs and starts to dry the pan with the rag. "Should you be talking to me like that?"

Her hair's red today. Her clothes look stolen: a pink, frilly shirt and jeans. Though, hell, it's not like I can judge. When your mommy runs off with your rent money, a twenty-dollar sweater from Penney's is the last fucking thing on the list of priorities.

"You're right," I tell her. "I shouldn't be talking to you at all. But you know who I *should* call right now? Your parole officer." I head for the end table, where Daisy keeps the TracFones that still have minutes left on them. I wrench open a drawer and grab the first one I see.

"Sweetie." Melanie sets the pan down and holds her hands out. "I'm not here to hurt you. I just wanted to talk. I've missed ya."

She's wearing makeup: blue eye shadow and fancy liner. I can't even afford ChapStick. Whatever mascara still clings to my lashes, I stole from a drug store two months ago.

She missed me.

I never wanted to see her.

"Just tell me what the hell you want."

"Baby…" She shakes her head and runs a hand full of fake nails through her equally fake hair. "Look. I just wanted to see you. All y'all. I've missed you guys. And…I'm getting married!" Her voice rises like she's fucking excited. Like she thinks I'll be too.

"How did you even get in here?" The kids are gone, but the house looks cleaner than usual. Too clean. Melanie was always a polite thief.

Fuck.

I head for the fridge and throw it open. The beer is missing from the veggies bag. So is all of the saved rent money. My stomach gets that awful sinking feeling, but I swallow it down. That's the funny thing about Melanie. I can't accuse her outright. Maybe Daisy did the smart thing and hid the stash somewhere else?

"I came around last night," Melanie says in one of her smug fucking tones. "You weren't home. Seems like you had a fun night."

I glance over and find her looking down her nose at me. I'm leaning against the fridge more than I should be, biting my lip so hard that I taste blood. My hair is a mess clinging to my scalp. My throat still hurts. I sound like Meryl after she comes back from a smoke break. My sweater is torn to shit.

But, even like this, I feel more responsible than she ever fucking did.

"Yeah, I did." I slam the fridge door shut. "That's what supporting six kids by yourself is, Melanie. Good fucking fun. Not that you would know anything about that."

"Is this what you're going to do whenever you see me from now on?" She crosses her arms over her chest and sighs. "Try to throw me on a guilt trip?"

Ah, but that's the butt of the joke. No one could ever make Melanie Ryder give a damn about someone other than herself.

"Just get the fuck out." I head for the table, swiping at the stacks of old junk mail piled on top of it.

"Ainsley had a bad dream last night," Melanie tells me while I stoop to snatch up the old flyers. "It's lucky that someone was here to comfort her—"

"Don't you fucking do that." The pile of newspapers slips through my grip and lands on the floor.

That's another thing about Melanie. She is a whore. A bitch. A skank. Just like me.

The only difference? I scraped up every ounce of what I had and used it to pack money into a bag of frozen peas every month just to get by. Not Melanie. She was perfectly fine with being a worthless, stupid slut.

"Don't you act like you coming around here for five minutes makes you some kind of fucking mother." I point to the door. Then I jerk my chin at the knife drawer—I know she knows what's in it. The moment the kids left, the bitch probably tore the entire place apart looking for more money. "Now get the fuck out."

"I just wanted to tell you the good news in person," she says, wringing her hands together.

At first, I assume she means her fourth straight marriage. But no. Her eyes are far too fucking shifty for that. I glance at the fridge again. If this stupid bitch so much as touched a dime of my money...

"My new guy, Burt. He's got his own business, baby. Well, he's starting one, anyway."

Oh, fuck. My lungs start to tighten up. I get that sick feeling again. My taste buds are too raw to taste much of anything, but I can still sense the puke rising at the back of my throat. Money. Money. Money. A parade of bills marches through my head. I dig the nail of my thumb into the finger beside it. Harder. Harder.

"All he needs is just a few bucks. Maybe a couple hundred, and by the end of the week, baby, we'll have it turned into a thousand."

"You took the money." I don't even have to see her face. I just know. The same way I know that Daisy was the one to give it to her. "You took *our* money."

"For us, baby," she insists. "Why don't you believe that?"

For us. That was the last thing about Melanie Ryder: She could sell the moon to an astronaut, as one of her last patsies used to say. She could make any idea seem like a good one. She dished out hope like heroin and got her suckers hooked. Daisy was always the weak link, but so was

I until I turned sixteen and saw the true face of my so-called-mother.

"Get the fuck out." I'm too damn tired to scream. Or shout. I need to sleep. I need to shower. I need to investigate why the inside of my legs feel sticky. Warm.

"Baby, I know you don't believe me now, but in a few days, I'll be back and you can bet that—"

"Get out!" The kitchen blurs into one colorless blob, but I still manage to feel my way to the knife drawer and pull it open. I grab one at random and point it in her general direction. "Get out. And if you come near me or one of the kids again, I swear to god I will fucking kill you."

"You're tired, Frankie," Melanie says. "I know you don't mean that."

Either way, the bitch starts walking toward the front door. She already has it open when I get the urge to torture myself just a little further. For old time's sake and all.

"How much?"

"Hmm, baby?" Melanie pauses, her head tilted back to reveal the bone structure everyone swears up and down we share. I used to be proud of that, when people called us twins. In some ways, she still is my other half, I guess: everything I never want to be.

"How much money did you con out of Daisy?"

"Baby, I wasn't lying. I—"

"Enough!" I wave the knife to shut her up. "How. Much?"

She sighs. "Two fifty."

I can tell from the way she says it that she wanted more. That she thought I might have it. That she was desperate enough to stick around and beg me for it.

"Frankie, this really is the chance of a lifetime," she says, giving it one last shot.

My vision clears enough for me to make out the streaks of black stuff around her eyes. The smudges to her lipstick. The slightly uncombed quality of her hair. She worked hard to put on a good show, but some shit you just can't hide.

I don't even waste my breath on giving her another fuck off. I just turn around and flip the faucet of the sink on, drowning out the rest of whatever she says. My knife is still in my hand and my thumb keeps catching the edge of it. Over and over.

I don't know how long I have to ignore her before the door finally slams shut. I sink to my knees, using the counter for balance. My forehead is against the counter, the knife still slicing at my fingers until the pain swallows everything else. Then I reach into my pocket with my good hand and draw the money out.

The lower half of my jaw starts to throb as I fan the bills out beside me. There's so much of it. So little of it. Even with the rent covered, I'll still be in the hole. There are more bills to pay. Winter coats. Food. All of that stuff I never gave a damn about consuming when I was a snot-nosed kid clinging to Melanie's skirts—but even back then, she had never been just a mom. A cheese sandwich made with stale bread or an expired Pop-Tart was never what she was supposed to provide as my mother. Those were always extra payments from a loan I'll never fucking pay off. One I never asked to take out in the first place.

It feels like I sit here for days, bleeding over a thousand dollars. When I finally glance over at the spare cell phone lying beside me, I see that it's only been a minute. It doesn't take much of my pride to dial the number, in the end. It's answered on the second ring.

"Name," a gruff voice demands.

A part of me wants to hang up, but my thumb won't strike the right button. "It's Frankie—Francesca Marconi," I rasp once I remember how to speak.

"Oh." A heavy sigh blows from the speaker. "Ms. Marconi. How can I help you?"

"I changed my mind." While I talk, I pick up a loose fifty and hold it up to the light. The dead man printed on it sneers back at me, the prick. "I want to talk about extending the contract, or whatever."

"Excellent," Lucius says. He doesn't bother to ask any questions, and a part of me wonders why. Though, apparently, he made a habit out of fishing for women so hungry for a few bucks that they'd do anything to see the green. "You can meet me at this address in an hour." He rattles off a street I don't recognize. I have to use up what little bit of battery life the cell phone has left to connect to an unsecured Wi-Fi hotspot and search for it on the internet.

For some reason, I don't take the money when I finally stagger out of the house. I leave it there, a thousand dollars covered in blood. If Melanie comes back while I'm gone, she can fucking have it all.

CHAPTER FIVE

L ucius picked another café. I guess he has a thing for coffee. Though, when I finally reach the place, I don't find the car out front or his little friend lurking beside the door. The moment I step inside, I realize why.

Another man dominates the center of the room. Dominates —that's the only way to put it. His massive body seems out of place seated on a wooden chair before a round table draped in a fancy white cloth. In sharp contrast, he's wearing black from head to toe. The color makes his blond hair glow almost. Like his eyes. They flicker in my direction the moment I creep toward the hostess podium, where a smiling waitress is standing to greet me.

"This way," she says without bothering to ask my name. She instinctively knows which table to stop beside, her eyes expectantly focused on Maxim, who sends her away with a wave of his hand.

To me, he just nods at the chair across from him. "Sit, *kotyonok*."

My knees bend on command, plopping me down onto a burgundy cushion. The table is already set. The silverware is legit silver, laid out in a line.

But there is only one place setting: his.

"I thought I should meet with you myself," Maxim says. "So that there can be no mistake as to what I expect from you."

His eyes flash, demanding a response.

"O-okay—"

"You should know that this isn't about companionship," he tells me. "In fact, this isn't even about sex."

One of his hands reaches across the table, the thumb of it coming to brush my lower lip. It's bitten: a wound I only remember as his touch stirs up the pain. My eyes start to blink, watering. He presses down harder.

When he finally draws his hand away, the thumb is red with blood. He stares at the drop for a second and then rubs it carefully into the tablecloth.

"I only want to hurt you," he tells me as his stare reconnects with mine. "However I want. Whenever I want. In any way that I can. Do you understand what I mean by that?"

"H-hurt me?" My voice is a fucking rasp as my belly clenches up at the reminder of the damage he's already dished out.

He folds his hands, watching me for what feels like hours as the café bustles with traffic around us. I swear our waitress has passed us at least five times, serving as many tables, before he speaks again.

"Come here." He pushes back from the table but remains seated. When I stand, he nods at his lap. "Sit."

I nervously dart my gaze around the rest of the café.

"Don't." The warning trickles from him, so softly that only I can hear it. "Sit."

It hurts to straddle him. With his size, it's like attempting to do a split. Pinpricks of pain shoot behind my eyelids the farther I spread my legs, so I focus on sucking in air, one breath after the other. The moment I'm on top of him, he easily shifts his weight, sliding his chair closer to the table. Too close. The rim of it digs into my lower back, but Maxim doesn't stop. I look down and find him flicking his fingers toward the ceiling.

"Up, *kotyonok*."

It isn't until he attempts to push into the table completely that I understand what he means. *Up.* I have to brace both hands on the table behind me and haul myself up before his weight traps me between it and his chest. The tines of a fork dig into my thigh as all of the silverware clings together when I scoot backward. My face is on fire, but no one seems to notice the scene unfolding.

"Look at me." His hand captures my chin to make me. "These people?" He shrugs one shoulder toward the rest of the café. "They mean nothing. If you are to be with me, that is the first thing you will need to learn. Their reactions, their judgment mean nothing."

He slides his other hand beneath my ass, lifting me from the table's surface altogether. I can only watch. I can only breathe. In and out. My sore pussy throbs as if it already knows just what he's planning.

"Strip." He tells me, even as his fingers leave my jaw and go directly to the front of my jeans before I can do it myself. With one yank, he undoes the zipper—undressing me on a table inside a public place.

I can't process it. I just find myself staring at a balding old man at the table directly across from us. He's steadily sipping his soup without a care in the world or a glance in my direction.

"Look at me."

Pain sears between my legs. I look down and find Maxim's hand there, rubbing against my open fly. A warning.

"Only me, *kotyonok*." His fingers rub again, while the ones beneath me hook within one of the belt loops of my jeans.

One hard yank nearly drags me off the table and onto his lap again. I know without him even having to say it not to move an inch, so I brace my weight back against my palms, arching my hips in the process.

Another tug later and my pants are down my thighs. He inhales when he sees what lurks underneath. I can't look, so I stare up at the ceiling as my jeans are pulled the rest of the way off and tossed aside. He doesn't bother with the same method for my panties.

A metallic clink proceeds the icy scrape tickling my inner thigh a second later, centered in a single point that grazes a path over to my hip. I can hear people laughing. Talking. No one gasps but me when the tip of the knife slides beneath the waistband of my panties. I feel a hard jerk and then the fabric is slowly peeled away by his hands. They're rough. Like sandpaper. Cold. Warm. I can't fucking explain just what he feels like. Maybe it's because pain mingles with every deliberate touch. His nails lead the charge, sharper than the knife.

"Look at me, *kotyonok*."

His voice turns my body into a slave. I see what he's done. What's he's doing. While I watch, he slices through the other side of the thong. Then he gathers up the black fabric and pitches it onto the floor.

I can't help the sound that tears out of me when I look between my legs. Two purple bruises in the shape of handprints make twin marks on my inner thighs. Just beyond my pussy is a slight scarlet smear.

"You have a delicate little cunt. I hurt you. *Without intending to.*" The pad of his thumb drifts down, running between my legs, coming away red. He doesn't look pleased about that. His eyes darken to the shade of his shirt as he raises his fingers to my mouth, pressing his thumb against my bottom lip.

I know what he wants. It's sick, but I fucking know. My tongue drifts out, flicking the bloody smears away, and I swallow hard without tasting.

Chuckling, Maxim lowers his hand—and rams it between my legs. His thumb circles my entrance. Once. Again. Harder. When he raises it again, his eyes contain a dare.

"Taste, *kotyonok*."

I lick my lips first, tasting bitter, dry flesh. I try to focus on that flavor as I lean forward, sticking my tongue out on cue. I'm about an inch away from his hand when I realize what he wants.

When my tongue finally touches him, it's like licking a frozen pole in the middle of winter. The icy, numbing jolt feels the same. Disgust makes me gag. *Just swallow.* All I have to do is swallow and I won't taste.

But he's watching me, waiting as my taste buds slowly register the substance they've picked up. Salt. Musk. Me. Drool floods my mouth, urging me to spit.

"Swallow," Maxim commands.

I do, and somehow, it all goes down without a fuss.

"Good." He pushes back from the table just enough so that he can take me in without having to crane his neck. His eyes flicker up and down the length of me before settling between my legs. His nostrils flare, inhaling my scent as my flesh is bared to him.

It takes everything I have in me not to slam my thighs together. *Focus on him.* I don't take my eyes off his face, trying to decipher any hint of what he might be thinking. Insanity most likely. He has to be insane. And, any minute, the manager of this place will storm over and order us out.

I tell myself that. I comfort myself with what a part of me knows is just a lie.

"Why do you want this?" Maxim wonders. His fingers fan out along his jaw, smearing blood onto his gold stubble. "You're young. You can find other clients. You don't seem familiar with sadism."

Sadism. My brain blanks at how dangerous he makes that word sound. The scary part? I don't even know what it means—I don't want to.

"I asked you a question." His eyes flash, and he sits straighter.

"I need the money," I blurt out.

Rather than seem insulted, he nods in response, still rubbing his chin. When his hand shoots out in an arch, I flinch, thinking I missed something, but a waitress appears at his shoulder seconds later.

Her eyes skim over me, her pretty smile perfectly in place. "How may I serve you, Mr. Koslov?"

Maxim waves his hand toward the table, and the woman nods before taking off.

"Did you really read the contract?" he wonders after she's gone. His eyes flick up to mine and narrow a dangerous fraction of an inch. "Be honest with me."

"Yes?" It's the Melanie in me that wants me to lie—but the man intimidates even my fucking genetics. "No."

"You didn't," Maxim says, deciding for himself which answer of the two is correct. "I suggest you educate yourself, *kotyonok*." He bends forward, rummaging through something at his feet. A bag? He withdraws a folder from whatever it is. "Read."

He tosses the stack between my legs.

It's black, containing a pile of pages that flutter as I flip it open and smear blood over them. It's the same list Lucius showed me, but this time, I inhale every fucking word. It's more than just a catalog of injuries and their corresponding prices.

So much more.

To start with, my eyes pick up where they left off: *In the event of accidental death, the designated relatives of the aforementioned party will receive a lump sum amount of $500,000.*

I wheeze, sucking in air. The room spins for a second, but I keep reading.

Clause 4: The aforementioned party will remain with the undersigned for a duration of specified time, not to exceed forty hours per week.

Clause 5: The aforementioned party will submit fully to all terms stated by the undersigned. To void the contract at any time, the aforementioned party must invoke the use of the designated "safe word," nullifying the contract and forfeiting the entirety of the remaining payment.

I tear my eyes away from the page and find Maxim watching me.

"I'd have to stay with you?"

"Read silently," he warns. "When you finish, we will discuss it all."

My throat jerks to swallow as I keep reading. It's all I can fucking do.

When I finally finish, my palms are slick. I can't seem to breathe in deeply enough. The light in the room is blinding. At the same time, it's too dark. Maxim's face is covered in shadow. I can only make out his smile: pure-white teeth in a beautiful, lethal row.

"I'm finished." I set the folder aside, letting it slip through my fingers and onto the edge of the table. It slides off, but Maxim doesn't reach for it and something warns me not to even try.

His eyes cut over my shoulder, just as the waitress appears beside me. On one of her hands is a steaming plate of food: steak, potatoes, and roasted vegetables. In the other is a mug of dark liquid. Coffee, I guess.

Maxim nods toward the table, and I start to climb down.

"No." His hand grabs my thigh, pinning me in place while the waitress sets his plate down right between my legs.

The hot rim sears whatever bits of my thighs come into contact with it. I fling my legs apart as far as I can, only to graze the mug of steaming coffee with the left one as the waitress sets it down too.

"Thank you," Maxim says, sending her off.

He turns his attention to his food, sizing up every item on his plate before reaching for a fork. I'm partially sitting on the one his fingers settle over, but he doesn't prompt me to move my thigh. He clenches the handle instead and pulls. Sharp, harsh pain bites so deep that I can taste it. My eyes flutter shut.

"Open, *kotyonok.*"

My vision snaps back into focus as he stabs at a roasted carrot and raises it close to my chin, allowing the smell to tickle my nose. A frown tugs at his mouth before I realize what he meant. *Open.*

I pry my lips apart far enough for him to slip the piece of carrot between them. *Shit.* It's too hot. I have to choke it down, my eyes watering.

"Good," Maxim growls, and I instinctively know what action satisfied him: not my obedience, but the pain.

He reaches for a steak knife and I shift my weight to lift my right thigh slightly in case he grabs it the same way he did the fork. His fingers close over the handle of the sharpest one. He pulls and then flips the blade at the last minute so that the edge bites into my skin regardless. Not hard enough to draw blood, just enough to sting.

"I didn't say you could move," he warns before cutting into his steak. Pink liquid pours out from the first cut. It's cooked rarer than most people I know would dare to eat. Without batting an eyelash, Maxim slices off a piece and spears it with the fork. "Open."

I obey. As the minutes pass, he winds up feeding me more of his food than himself. I quickly pick up on the method to his madness: He takes his time, giving me every morsel that wafts the most steam. After each bite, he watches me chew and I wait for his silent cue to swallow. He nods afterward. I breathe.

"Good, *kotyonok*," he tells me before taking a bite of steak for himself. "Very good."

My heart skips a beat, riding a merry-go-round of pain and fear. I think it's over. He doesn't seem interested in the final slice of steak and lets it linger on the edge of his plate while he samples the veggies. It's the very last thing left when he finally stabs it with the fork and raises it.

He sighs, his eyes between my legs. My skin is on fire, but I don't dare look away. I just wait.

Slowly, he lowers the steak. Too low. I can't fight the noise that breaks from my throat when he drags the meat along my inner thigh.

"I wish I could taste you myself." He sounds curious. Hungry. He wishes he could taste me, but I know why he can't.

I'm bleeding. I could be dirty. Lucius mentioned something about a blood test I have yet to take.

"Soon," Maxim says, shattering any coherent thought into a million pieces. "As for now, open, *kotyonok*."

I obey, turning my brain off as he places the blood-stained meat on my tongue. I don't think about it. Not the taste. Not the flavor. I simply swallow, but a sharp pinch on my hip stops the food from going down.

"Not yet."

I have no choice but to let the food sit there, at the back of my throat. His eyes stare into mine, pinning me in place. Daring me to make a move without his say so. It feels like hours before he lowers the fork and nods.

I choke the meat down.

He smiles—or at least his lips lift higher than their usual stern line. It's the most terrifying thing I've ever seen.

"And *now*—" He sits back in his chair, tilting his head up to meet mine. "You may now ask your questions."

The folder is still on the floor. I glance at it and Maxim smiles again.

"Start with the one I know you can't stop thinking about."

I have to suck in a breath to get the words out. "I gotta—"

"Sentences." My punishment is a pinch on my hip, sharp and demanding.

"I mean, I would have to stay with you?"

He's right. That damn clause keeps circling my brain. Only the look in his eyes keeps me from dwelling on it. That dangerous promise. *I only want to hurt you.*

"Yes," he says while my heart shrivels up. "Three nights a week for the first week. To acclimate. Five nights after that."

"But I have kids."

His face doesn't change, and I can't tell if he thinks it's a lie or not. Slowly, his gaze returns to my pussy.

Oh. "T-they're not—"

"You may have a few days to make arrangements," Maxim says over me. "If you need additional funds, contact Lucius."

"But I—"

His eyes flash in warning. "Anything else, *kotyonok*?"

"Kotee…" I give up trying to parrot the term. "What does that mean—"

"Next question."

My brain changes tactics automatically. "T-the safe word?"

According to the contract, it was the only way out of this agreement. One word that could end it all. A kill switch.

"Yes?"

"What is it?"

He brushes his jaw with the tip of his thumb. "The women typically decide that for themselves."

The women. More than one. More than me. Desperate enough—pathetic enough—to do anything for cash.

"What do they usually pick?"

He cocks his head and seems to think for a minute. "The usual tropes. Red light. Stop now. Enough please. However, I suggest you select something you would never typically say. Once you utter the safe word, our contract is null and void. You only need to say it once."

Pick something that I would never say? Melanie herself, showing up once again out of the blue to fuck up everything, made one choice pretty fucking tempting.

"What will it be?" His tone demands an answer.

"Happy."

That creepy almost-smile shapes his mouth again. He sits forward, his hair framing his face. "It is typically a phrase. Something you would never say."

"Then *I'm* happy. I am happy."

I can't tell what he thinks of it. He just nods. "As you wish, *kotyonok*."

"So…" I lick my lips, flexing my fingers against the table. "M-may I ask another question?"

"Ask away."

"When would I start?" My voice catches, sticking the words at the back of my throat. It feels like asking about my execution date. "And get paid?"

Maxim flexes his arms at both wrists, straining the muscle coiled beneath his shirt. "You can contact Lucius within forty-eight hours once you've made your arrangements," he says. "As for payment."

He lunges forward and I flinch, but his hands reach between my outstretched legs, toward his feet. He snatches something else from what's there: a briefcase I see when I crane my neck. Whatever he lifts from it is black. Thick. An envelope.

He slides it onto the sliver of space in front of his plate. "Take this in advance. A taste."

He stands, flicking the edge of his collar between a forefinger and thumb. "Wait ten minutes before you leave," he tells me. "Don't move. I don't even think you should blink—not for as long as you can stand it. You leave so much as a second too early?" His thumb grazes my chin again, still red with my blood. "You will be punished when I see you again. Do you understand?"

I nod and he turns away from me. I watch him go, and he draws attention with every step he takes. It's only after he leaves that the other diners finally seem to notice me. Sitting here, half naked. Shameless. Motionless.

In the end, I don't wait ten minutes before leaving.

I wait fifteen.

CHAPTER SIX

I always used to fantasize about what I'd do if I won the lottery or something and had enough cash to kiss my jobs goodbye. I'd stroll into Penney's and bitch-slap fucking Meryl before telling her that she could fuck off forever. At the diner, I'd buy a round of pie for everyone and make it rain dollar bills over old Mr. and Mrs. Johansen, the owners.

But it's funny. With more money than God tucked into my pocket, it seems like all I can do is just scuttle from one place to the next and fill out the necessary paperwork without doing much else. When I'm asked for the reason *why* I'm quitting, I shrug and mutter, "Something came up."

To be more specific, Maxim Koslov came up—presumably while cutting me. Hurting me.

"I only want to hurt you, kotyonok."

Once I'm completely unemployed, I take the bus out to the

nearest mall. Without even touching the envelope, I buy Daisy a coat for her goddamn trip. Mikie gets a game system. Ainsley gets a doll. The twins get some toy set that looks violent and loud. At the register, I pull out the stack of Maxim's money and withdraw the first few bills while the cashier watches me in confusion. It's more than enough to cover it all.

Then I keep moving. I buy a new cell phone and put minutes on it. I also buy myself a new pair of shoes. Nothing fancy. Just something black. To hide dirt. Scuff marks. Blood…

After that, I head home, my arms bruised and sore as the weight of the bags bites into my skin. The kids aren't home when I stagger through the front door. The money is still there, lying in a row by the sink. I pick up each bill one by one and shove them into the veggie bag at the back of the fridge.

Then I haul myself up the stairs, climb into the tub, and run the faucet, lying here while the water slowly fills it. I've made it too hot though. Sweat drips down the back of my neck, my skin burning and turning an angry pink. By accident, I did it. Accident.

But at least I can think clearly for five damn minutes, and as always, only one thing matters: money.

And, after today, I only have one route to getting more.

I'll have to leave Mikie in charge, considering that Daisy just fucked up her last chance. I can't risk Melanie coming back and taking even more than she already has. I can't.

That's the only damn thing I'm sure of when I leave the tub and get dressed in someone's jeans and someone else's tank top. I snatch the black envelope from my other pants and shove it into the pocket of a pink sweatshirt I grabbed off Daisy's bed.

When I leave the house again, I head straight for downtown and don't stop until I reach the rental office. I pay three months in advance—that's how much the money in the envelope will cover. There's still enough left over for the gas and electric.

I used to think it would be fun having this kind of cash. In reality, I just feel numb. My body remembers what it had to do to earn it. What I had to suffer.

It's not worth it.

No, it *is* worth it.

It's worth it.

I tell myself that over and over until I'm back inside the house and the sounds of shouting drown the thoughts out.

"I SAID GIVE IT BACK!"

"Shut up." I don't even have to yell—not that I could. It's only as my voice rings out over Ainsley's that I realize just how fucking awful I sound.

"Are you sick, Frankie?" Daisy wonders while I slam the front door behind me. "You sound awful."

Her concern is easy to shrug off once I make out the chaos unfolding in the living room. They found the stuff. A graveyard of cardboard and plastic bags litters the floor. Ainsley got to my suitcase and stands in the middle of it, still wearing her muddy, tattered shoes.

"Frankie!" She observes me, her hands on her hips, lips pursed. "You want to hear what happened today? Bobby R. sat with Amy at recess and gave her his cookies! Then you know what he did?" Her eyes widen. "*Then* he poked her in the forehead and ran off with his friends. Amy says it's because he likes her. He *likes* her, so he hits her? Ugh boys are so weird. I told her she should punch him back—"

"Shut up," Eric calls from across the room. "No one cares! Hey Frankie, look at what I got." He brandishes one of his new toys.

Seeing them like this makes it all sink in. Maxim gave me two days to "make arrangements." I should take that time to find a way out. Steal his money. Ride off into the sunset. What memories does this piece-of-shit house hold that I couldn't find somewhere else? After all, Melanie taught me that nothing in this world is worth tethering yourself to. Not even your own damn kids.

"I have to go away for a few days," I say.

"Why?" They all try to speak at once.

"Can I come?"

"Where?"

"I don't want to go to fucking school—"

"Mikie's in charge," I say and they all shut up again.

Daisy watches me, her eyes wide with fear. Or maybe it's guilt.

Mikie steps forward, blocking her from view, and I shove every last dime I have into his hands. "If anything happens, call me." I give him my new number, and then the questions start all up again.

Though they aren't questions, really...

"Did Mom get that for you, too?"

"Did you see what she got me?"

"I can't believe the bitch actually came back."

Breathe. I squeeze my eyes shut and suck in air. In. Out. In. My hands clasp together, the nails of each finger digging into whatever skin they can reach. Pulling. Raking.

"Frankie?"

"I've got to leave..." I stumble toward the suitcase and snatch it by the handle with Ainsley still inside. She falls out and starts to cry. Daisy's the one to comfort her while I race up the stairs.

They're watching me. Whispering. Talking about me.

But that's not the fun part. *Melanie.* They think Melanie would really give a shit about them long enough to drop off a dollar, let alone hundreds worth of shit. That Melanie would sell her body and soul for rent.

That Melanie actually gave a fuck.

I'm not angry. Not even as I break into the one corner where Daisy still keeps her shit. It's at the very back of the room she shares with Ainsley in a cardboard box marked *Mom*. I dump it all onto the floor and find myself laughing out loud. Ainsley's shoes have holes in them. Daisy went without a winter coat all of last year, and so did I because the two youngest grew out of theirs too fast and needed new ones.

But, of course, even when she's not fucking here, Melanie has the nicest shit in the house. I think some of it is even designer. Shirts. Pants. Stuff she never came back for. She could always con some horny fuckface into buying her more, after all. A fancy handbag was her price tag.

Would she let a guy like Maxim do whatever the fuck he wanted to her? Maybe. But not for me, or any of the others. She'd probably up her rate and do it for *two* fancy handbags.

"Frankie?"

I flinch and find Daisy creeping near the doorway. The floor creaks so badly that I should have heard her. I can't think. My thumb pecks at my forefinger. Hard. Harder. Harder.

"Frankie…I… Mom came back, and I gave her—"

"I have to go." I snatch up the rest of Melanie's shit and shove it all into the suitcase. Daisy's still talking when I push past her and take the stairs two at a time. I should say goodbye or something. Kiss them all goodnight. Probably.

But I don't. I just push the door open and shove the suitcase out onto the stoop. "If anyone skips school, I will hunt you down and kick your ass." With that, I slam the door behind me.

Now, I can think. Three months with Maxim would give me enough money to survive for a year. I can't comprehend that. I can't dwell on it. I just latch onto the reality: a year of not worrying. Not hiding. Not fucking scraping and crawling to get by.

It sounds too damn good to be true.

It probably is.

I WALK ten blocks before I finally fish his business card from my pocket and dial the number Lucius gave me. I don't expect him to answer, but he does on the first ring. The only words to leave his mouth are, "If you have made your decision, Ms. Marconi, please supply the address where we might meet."

I give him the next block I reach, and not even ten minutes later, a fancy black car pulls up to the curb in front of me. The weirdo driver climbs out and circles around to take my suitcase and toss it into the trunk. Lucius is already waiting for me in the back seat.

"Good evening," he says. His hands are folded on his lap. He's not wearing a suit tonight, but dark pants, a gray coat, a sweater and a matching scarf wrapped neatly around his throat. "Mr. Koslov most likely won't be expecting you so soon. I can book a hotel room for you, in the meantime."

I don't know how to tell him that I already spent all the money he gave me. Instead, I dig the nails of one hand into the back of the other and wait while he pulls a cell phone from his pocket. He barely touches it before it starts to buzz.

"Lucius," he says, bringing the phone to his ear. His eyes cut over to me. "Yes, sir. Right away, sir." He hangs up and tucks the phone back into his pocket, a frown tugging at his mouth. "He said to bring you to him now."

Lucius doesn't explain how the hell Maxim could have known where I was. I don't have the balls to ask. Roughly ten minutes later, the driver pulls up before the black high-rise and there isn't time for fucking questions anyway.

"I will take you up." Lucius steps out onto the curb and extends his hand for mine.

Everything passes by in a blur. One minute, I'm outside, staring up at a building I could never dream to live in. The next, I'm dragging a brand-new suitcase into the entryway of a penthouse suite.

Maxim isn't here waiting, and I don't hear any sound coming from the room with the stone and tools.

"It is customary that I give the women a small tour of the layout," Lucius explains while adjusting the ends of his scarf. "This room is the main receiving area for guests."

He starts down a hallway that leads into what looks like a living room—the disgustingly rich variety. There isn't much furniture, but what little there is looks like it's made of real black leather accented with red silk pillows. The glass end tables might be crystal. Exotic plants sit in the corners within huge marble pots.

Classy.

"Over here is the dining room." He points a short distance down the hall.

It's bigger than the living room, dominated by a long, ebony table and polished chairs. By the time he shows me to a kitchen and a study, I have a general gist of the color scheme and style Maxim prefers. Dark colors: blacks, reds, grays. There are no family photos hung on the walls or personal touches like the decapitated Barbies or Kool-Aid stains in my house.

Just quiet, clean perfection.

"And this will be your room," Lucius explains as he opens one of the doors at the very end of the hall.

I can only stare as I follow him inside it. My room.

I've never had one. Not in all of those years living out of trailers with Melanie. She had already been working on her fourth kid when we moved into the house, and she took one of the only two bedrooms for herself.

My new room is large. There's a bed in the center of it, draped in a black canopy. Beneath it, the sheets are white and the marble flooring of the rest of the house becomes ivory carpeting. In the corner of the room is one of those fancy vanities with a mirror framed in white. Two French doors on the opposite end open up to the closet, I guess.

"There is a schedule," Lucius says while I brace my suitcase against the wall, "for how Maxim prefers his days to run. Since he doesn't seem to be here, you may dress for dinner and wait for him."

"D-dress?"

Lucius nods toward the closet. "The clothing is organized into three sections," he says. "Day clothing is in the first section. Then evening wear. Last is night clothing. If you can't find anything in your size, just make do with what you can and I'll send for the tailor in the morning."

He turns to leave, and I watch him go, too uneasy to voice the questions crawling up my throat. There are rooms he never showed me. I think it was on purpose. Maxim's rooms.

I wind up creeping back into mine and closing the door. Inside the closet, I find it divided up just like Lucius said. It's like three mini wardrobes shoved into one. In the first section, the clothing is lighter: pinks, whites, grays. Everything looks like a dress, made of lace. In the next one, the clothes are all black: longer dresses and a few crisp blouses and skirts. The last one just has flimsy nightgowns.

Rather than pick something for dinner, I grab a clean sweater out of my suitcase and a different pair of jeans. I sit on the bed for a while before I start pacing the middle of the room.

My room.

I can almost see the other women who've lived in it before me. Just imprints. Shadows. Someone who wore a medium. Another who wore an extra small. Someone who preferred heels. Another who liked flats.

It's like a hotel for the desperate and pathetic. I find myself staring at the bed next, wondering how many people have slept in it. Fucked on it.

Without deciding on a number, I wander out into the hallway, retracing the path Lucius took. My footsteps echo —it's that damn quiet in here. It's that damn large. My house could fit in the living room alone with plenty of room left over for Maxim to entertain.

It's nice, even on my second trip through, but I keep going until I reach the entryway, and then I continue past it until I'm surrounded by rows of sharp tools.

He finished the statue of the woman. She stares down at me, her arms reaching toward the ceiling, her hips flexed like she's dancing. A few details are missing, like the curls in her hair or the lines of her stomach, but it already seems perfect. Even with the jagged crack slicing through it all.

I think it takes minutes before I gather up the nerve to step closer to it. It would be taller than me even if it weren't on the pedestal. The dusky glow streaming in from the windows casts a bluish sheen over the stone. She almost looks alive. And if she were, I can imagine what she'd say: *What the fuck are you doing?*

"You were not given permission to enter this room, *kotyonok*."

I shiver at the sound of his voice: equal parts rage and something that could be amusement. I hear him laugh, but the step he takes toward me sounds heavy. Deliberate.

"Come here."

I turn around. He's near the doorway, leaning against it, his arms crossed over his chest. He's wearing the same clothing he wore at the café: the black shirt and pants. Here, with very little lighting, the shadow makes his eyes seem darker. His body looms over mine, even taller than I remember.

"I must break you in." It's a promise as his hand cups my chin, tilting my head back to meet his gaze directly. His eyes narrow, scanning my face. "Did Lucius give you the tour?" he wonders before pulling away.

"Y-yes," I choke out, digging my nails into my wrist. Sharp. Deep. "Yes, he did."

Maxim's eyes narrow further. "Then I assume that nothing in the wardrobe was in your size?"

Shit. I swallow hard, trying to keep the truth from showing. Learning from Melanie, I've turned lying into an art form. "I didn't think so—"

"Come." He turns on his heel and leads me to the room designated as mine.

I watch him approach the closet and throw both doors open. His fingers skim the clothing in the evening section and he pulls out a dress. Then another. Several more.

"Strip," he tells me without turning around.

My teeth sink into my bottom lip as my hands start for the clasp of my pants.

"The sweater first," Maxim says, and I change tack.

It's cold in the room. I'm shaking as I wind the fabric of my shirt up and over my head. Something tells me to take my bra off before he can even issue the command himself. Then I wait...

After another minute of searching through the clothes, he looks at me over his shoulder. His eyes perform a lazy sweep down my naked torso. He nods. "Continue."

This time, he watches as I work on the stubborn zipper of my jeans. It takes me five tries to get the damn thing undone. Maxim starts toward me on the fourth yank and it springs open on the next try.

I slowly peel them down, not really knowing what he wants. A tease? No. His jaw is clenched, so I yank them down and kick them off my ankles. Once naked, I stand with my arms at my sides.

"Beautiful," he grits out as his gaze settles between my legs. My inner thighs throb; he's staring at the bruises. "Come."

I start forward on cue, and once again, I know instinctively when to stop: just beyond his reach.

"Turn around, *kotyonok.*"

I do, feeling warm air fan the back of my neck seconds later.

"Raise your arms."

The moment I comply, something soft and flimsy grazes them. A dress. It's black, lacy, and loose-fitting. The V-shaped neckline plunges between my breasts—one of the few things I didn't inherit from Melanie was her cleavage.

"You are thin," he says near my ear. It doesn't sound like a compliment. "I will have Lucius find you things that are more suitable."

"Thank you," I croak out. I don't know what else to say. It's not a gift. Something tells me that my personal style won't matter a damn bit in what outfits I wear. He has a wardrobe already picked out; I'm no better than Ainsley's Barbie dolls.

"Do not thank me," Maxim subs as if to drill that point home. His hand encircles my neck from behind, his thick fingers resting over my windpipe. "Never thank me."

"O-okay—"

"And now," he says over me, his fingers tightening their grip just enough to make it harder to speak. "Are you ready for your punishment?"

My blood runs cold. He's flipped a switch again and another man has taken his place. One who speaks in grunts and grumbles rather than a suave tone. A man who digs his nails into my skin so hard that I flinch before he shoves me toward the bed. I lose my balance halfway and wind up on my knees. The carpet cushions the blow. At the same time, it turns pain into fire as momentum drags me forward.

"What did I do?" I can't help the question. Not even the prissy, bitchy, whiny tone to it.

My guess is wandering his home without permission.

"You disobeyed me, didn't you?"

His footsteps form a foreboding melody: light and soft. Steady. He's taking his time, as if savoring the way I jump with every vibration running through the floor.

"Earlier today, in the café. Do you know how?"

It's the world's most dangerous version of a pop quiz. I always failed those in school, which is one of the many reasons why I dropped out. "I…"

"Think." A tiny bit of skin on my shoulder is pinched. Hard.

"You t-told me to wait?"

"Yes," he says. "And for how long?"

"T-ten minutes—"

"And how long did you wait, *kotyonok*?"

I swallow hard as the answer sticks in my throat. "Fifteen."

"Fifteen," he says. His fingers run through my hair again, smoothing the back of it flat. "Five minutes too late. When I give you a command, I expect you to obey." He rakes his fingers against my scalp and turns them into a fist. "Do you understand?"

My eyes start burning, blinking back moisture. "Yes! I understand."

"Good." His hand withdraws. "Your first punishment will be simple. Get on the bed."

My pussy starts to ache. It's still sore. His voice in my ear reminds me of his cock. Thick. Big. Too damn much.

"Now." He doesn't touch me, even as the slight way he raises his voice hits me like a slap.

I jerk forward on my hands and knees and crawl onto the bed. The comforter is soft beneath me. Softer than anything I've ever felt. In a sick way, it's the polar opposite of the pain I feel on my ass a second later. Sharp. Piercing.

I gasp out, craning my neck back to see the source. Something shiny glints through the air, held in Maxim's fist. It's small. Silver.

The knife.

"On your stomach." His thumb traces the blade, smearing something red all over the surface. "That was number one."

Number two hits my left shoulder above the collar of my dress. It's deep enough to bleed. Deep enough to sting.

I go limp, throwing my arms out beside me, my gaze on the wall.

He takes his time with number three: a long, curved cut along my hip and blood dribbles down after each brutal slice. My heart pounds. Stops. Starts up again. Surges. Stammers. Dies.

"I don't hear you keeping count." His voice is thunder again. I feel it rather than hear it, ripping through my spine.

"F-four," I rasp as the blade bites in again, on my other hip this time. He is more daring than I ever would be, slicing in without a care.

"What's next, *kotyonok*?" His voice sounds deeper. Jagged. "What next?"

I suck in air the moment I feel the start of the next cut. The tip of the knife sinks in.

Oh god.

My bottom lip trembles when he starts to saw. In and out. Over. Over.

"*Kotyonok*—"

"F-five." I can't stop my eyes from welling up as warmth drips down my arm.

"I'm going to fuck you now," Maxim tells me, running his fingers through my hair, tugging them loose whenever they get caught in the tangles. "I will fuck you hard. If you get so much as a drop of blood on the sheets..." His fingers cup my hips, yanking my ass higher until I'm on my knees, face down. "You will be punished. Do you understand?"

I nod into the mattress while his fingers trace a path down the back of my neck, my spine, the curve of my ass. He travels all the way down to my pussy, grazing his nail along my rim. I hear the zipper to his jeans come undone. I feel the bed shift beneath his weight. His hands fan out over my hips, positioning me toward him before I can crawl away.

"You're bleeding," he reminds me. *Don't disobey.*

The cut on my arm is leaking the most. I twist it, feeling the blood run down toward the crook of my elbow instead. The one on my hip is at a tricky angle. I have to tilt my hips slightly to keep the blood from dripping off. I can feel every tiny, warm bead bubbling up, streaking my skin.

And then the bed jerks forward and I only feel Maxim. Inside me. On top of me. I bite down onto the comforter, choking myself with a mouthful of fabric. I won't scream. Won't cry.

But he's so damn big. My body doesn't know what to do with his size. It clamps down tight. Whenever he moves, I feel it in my stomach. My skull. He's pulsing inside me. Pushing through me. Hot. Heavy. Solid.

Fuck.

He pulls out slowly and my body attempts to follow, my ass arching toward his hips to slow the friction and lessen the pain. I have to rise onto my elbows, letting the blanket fall from my mouth in a trail of drool. *The blood.* I twist my arm even more. My heart beats faster. The blood flows harder.

"You are tight, *kotyonok*," he tells me, gritting the words out against my skull. "But not out of fear."

How he knows as much? I can't focus enough to care. Again, he doesn't sound happy about it. Just annoyed. Irritated. I'm too tight. He has to ram his way back in.

Holy fuck. His weight throws me forward. The top of my head smacks off something hard, and I have to choose between being silent or tracking five different streams of blood.

Something gives and I cry out. And then he moves again and I learn an entirely new way to scream: in hoarse whispers and squeaks.

"Not a single drop," Maxim warns somewhere during his fourth thrust.

I squeeze my eyes shut and stop resisting. I let him fuck me and tune into every inch of my skin. I feel it all. The parts where it's gaping and open. Where it's slick with warmth. The pain is a constant buzz running through my veins. Boiling over in places. Ice cool in others.

I have to move: flexing my thigh or clenching my arm to keep the blood from flowing. But sometimes tensing up so that I feel every ridge of the body slamming into mine. It's white-hot agony. One taste of it and my thoughts go crystal fucking clear.

Then numb again.

Clear.

Numb.

Clear, clear, fucking clear. There's one position where I feel him the most. Where he slams into me so hard that I just see white each time. I taste his violence in my throat. In my blood.

And then I don't feel anything...

And I feel everything.

Oh God.

My muscles clench up. Tighten. Clamp down over his cock in ways I don't tell them to. I don't want them to. I gag on my own screams. It's too much. Too raw. Too hard.

The only way to save myself is to throw myself against him until I don't feel anything. No pain. No fear. Just clarity washing over me like a goddamn storm, ripping me open and tearing me apart.

I need it.

I crave it.

I'd sell my fucking soul to make it last.

But it doesn't.

I crash back to Earth and find an animal fucking me mercilessly hard, growling words into my skin with every thrust. They sound angry.

"You bitch." The world shatters into pieces when he pulls out of me and flips me over. I land on my back, blinking up at a devil crouched beneath a canopy of shadow. His eyes flash, his jaw clenched. "Do you think you can get inside my head, huh?" He grabs me by the throat and drags me closer, nudging my thighs apart with his knee. His fingers tighten, lifting my head just far enough so that I have a view of him entering me. The way he slams in. The mess he makes.

Fuck. My eyes roll back into my head—it hurts that much. It's consuming. Swallowing.

It feels.

It feels…

It *feels.*

I lose my voice. I lose my fucking mind. He fucks my brains out. Fucks me in a way that any other john could ever dream.

I'm cold. I'm numb. And then I'm on fire—like the bastard doused me in gasoline and lit a match. My legs burn up. My hips. My cunt. My soul.

I'm dying. Rigor mortis sets in fast: I stiffen, every muscle clenched so tightly that I can't breathe. Maxim is the only part of me that's still alive. Still moving. Still fucking.

Striking the same deep, distant part of me over and over and *over*.

Obliterating it.

I taste blood. I'm drenched in it, rocking back and forth, side to side, until I can't breathe.

And as my vision goes black, a single thought sneaks into my fading mind. For the first time in my fucking life, I feel nothing.

Maybe this is freedom.

CHAPTER SEVEN

He's gone. I know that even before I wake up. Maxim is gone.

And I failed. I got more than just blood on the sheets. Me. Sweat. Drool. I smell it all lingering on the air beneath a masculine musk. While he may not be in the room, he's not far. My body senses it, reacting to the cues my other senses can't pick up.

My heart is already racing even before I hear the footsteps. Heavy. Unsteady. I drag myself upright the moment he appears in the doorway, staring down at me with ice-cold eyes.

"I changed my mind," he tells me, sounding almost human once again. His pants are back up, but blood is splattered on the hem of his shirt. A few lethal drops, still dark. Still wet. "Get out. Now." He jerks his head toward the hall.

I try to move and everything goes *black*. My teeth clamp over my bottom lip, trapping any noise I want to make. Words break through anyway. "W-what did I do?"

The pain isn't strong enough anymore. I can't think. Fear claws through my brain. Money. Money. MONEY. I bet that bitch came back and Daisy probably handed her the rest of the cash. Mikie was probably letting them all run fucking wild. Ainsley and Eric probably killed each other.

There are so many fucking *probably*s.

I shift my weight toward the end of the bed and the pain comes back. Like a bitch-slap. I can think for a split-second: *Run.* He grabs me before I can even move an inch. His fingers clench my right shoulder, tugging the arm nearly out of the damn socket.

I slide from the bed. Feel air. Hit the floor, all still held by him. Dragged by him.

"Get out."

I'm moving too fast. Burning carpet. Ice-cold marble. It's a shock when I finally land at his feet, the leather of his boots nudging my hip.

"Get out," he repeats, digging the toe of his boot into my thigh.

It hurts too much to stand. But I'm too terrified not to move.

I find a way to my knees as a compromise. My stomach keeps nudging the back of my throat. The room is spinning.

My lips part and something warm trickles down my chin. Throw up? *Oh.* I glance down as the liquid in question drips down onto my thigh. Blood.

"What is it?" he demands. It's like I'm hearing him while my head's under water. He sounds loud, but not loud enough. "Money? Is that it? Or were you sent to me? To tempt me, is that it?"

I can barely follow what the fuck he's saying, but for the first damn time in my life, I don't want to lie. "Money," I say, the letters running together into one sloppy sound. "I need the money."

"Hmph." Maxim draws himself up to his full height. Some of the darkness in his eyes clouds over. He's thinking. I try not to look away, but my head's too heavy. He has to tilt my chin with the pad of his thumb. "Do you want to stay?"

My throat ignites as I swallow. *No.* "Y-yes," I tell him. "I need the money."

He frowns, stepping back enough that I can make out the door to the suite behind him. "Give me your hands." His own go to his waist, tugging something free from the belt loops. A strip of leather. Dark. Thick. "Your hands."

They shake as I raise them from the floor as high as I can. They barely go above my chest. Maxim has to bend in order to wrap the end of his belt around them and tug, tying them together.

"Stand up," he tells me next, watching as I crawl to the wall and lean against it to find enough leverage to haul myself upright. Inch by goddamn inch. Sweat breaks out over my forehead, gluing my hair to it and basting my skin. "Look at me." I follow the direction of the cool fingers that nudge my jaw. "Up, up. Good."

Black eyes watch me without a shred of empathy. Mercy.

"Do you want to stay?" he asks me again.

I just nod. I don't know why. It's the pain—it sucks my common sense away. It drowns my fear.

"Then stay here, just like this. All night. Until I come for you." He pets me just once, his fingers lingering in my hair. "You move so much as an inch and when I'm through, you won't be able to walk for days." His thumb caresses my cheek, the nail grazing the skin. "Do you understand?"

It hurts to suck in enough air to reply. "Y-yes."

"Fine." His thumb traces my mouth before he pulls away. With one hand, he yanks the door to the suite open—just enough so that anyone walking by would catch a glimpse of me. Just enough for me to run. "Goodnight."

He returns down the hall, heading deeper into the maze of rooms. Minutes later, I hear a door open and shut.

At least ten minutes of silence pass before I realize he's serious. Stay here, standing, all night. Just because he said so.

I leave, he'll let me go. I think it's what he really wants me to do anyway.

But I stay.

The kids are probably sleeping. Melanie probably crawled her way back into the house. Money. Money. Money. It makes the world go 'round. It makes my world stop spinning.

I stay here, like this, for *money*.

Not because of the pain. Not because of the fact that, even with my knees knocking together and my body weak with abuse and exhaustion, I can think. I can feel. *Everything*.

I submit to him for the money.

Nothing else.

HE WAKES up at the crack of dawn. I hear him moving; slow and lazy footsteps drifting through a maze of rooms. He's taking his time.

I desperately try to stay conscious even as my eyelids become too heavy to lift. I don't know how the hell I'm still standing, but I cling to whatever senses I have left until he finally approaches.

"You're here." He almost sounds surprised as he rounds the end of the hallway.

Warm fingers brush my chin, lifting it the moment he comes close enough. I can't make out his face clearly—just those eyes: dark slits where a normal human's would be. He watches me struggle to obey his previous commands. My entire existence is a *struggle*, fighting to stay fucking upright.

I suck in air as he lets me go and my toes start to slide against the marble.

"Go get some rest." He loosens the belt before finally turning away, heading toward the room with the statue.

I hit the floor on my knees, choking on the air that floods in. Was I holding my breath all night? Or only for those tortured few seconds of his touch? I can't tell, and my body is already shutting down. My eyes are closed when his voice reaches me from the sculpture room—a warning.

"In your room. On the bed."

I tense up. He can't really mean to fuck. Not this early. Not again.

"Get some rest," he adds, as if reading my mind. "Though I suggest you move quickly, if you wish to sleep for long."

I don't even try to stand up. I crawl. On my hands and knees at first, and then just with my fingers, dragging myself down the hallway. It feels like I never move. Hours have to pass. I'm dripping with sweat.

I'm still in the fucking entryway.

Move, damn it. I give in to the pain, pushing through it, suffering every fiery jolt of it. I don't stop until my fingers strike wood. I have to rise onto my knees to get the door open, and I use the last bit of strength I have left to close it behind me.

My mind goes blank after that.

I DON'T JUST WAKE up. I'm resurrected—that's what it fucking feels like. Like that scene in Frankenstein: I'm electrocuted into existence by the cold reality that someone is in my room, standing over me, breathing their poison into my skin.

"Wake up," Maxim calls almost gently. "You've slept long enough."

Slept? It feels like I've had my eyes closed for only a few seconds before I'm peeling them open again. I can see him standing in front of me, his polished boots reflecting my appearance. Pale and broken.

He moved me onto the bed, I realize when the mattress shifts underneath me. I'm on top of the comforter, but it no longer feels as soft as it did before. It's crusty now.

"Wash yourself," Maxim tells me, running his fingers through my hair. "Lucius will arrive shortly. I will be gone for most of the day." He withdraws his hand and seems to float over to the door; my eyes blink too fast, turning the motion into a series of broken images, like a beautiful, terrifying slideshow. "When I return, I expect to find you properly dressed for the evening. Do you understand?"

"Yes..." My lungs heave to suck in enough air. "I understand."

In the twisted silence after he leaves, I try to remember how to make my goddamn body move. I flex my toes. My ankles. When I try to roll onto my side, I overshoot, falling off the bed altogether.

A bathroom is attached to my room. I find it by accident when I crawl to the first door I see and pull it open. There's a tub and a separate shower stall. Marble counters line one wall, and the floor is a cool, gray tile like the kind in the entryway.

I leave red over it with every inch I drag myself forward.

Hours. I spend most of them in the shower, trying to wash the blood away without studying the injuries left behind. I can feel them anyway. Every pinch, bruise, cut, and ache.

I find a towel and manage to pull myself upright, using the counter for balance. The bitch I find looking back at me in the mirror isn't worth the effort it would take to examine her. So I just run the faucet and swallow mouthfuls of cold water to wash the taste of blood from it. Afterward, I tear my fingers through my wet hair and dry myself. Once the towel is too red, I drop it.

When I open the door to the bedroom, a stranger is waiting for me, his arms crossed over his chest.

"It's all right, Ms. Marconi," Lucius says, stepping out from the opposite end of my room before I can panic. "This is Mr. Bartley, the tailor."

As if on cue, the man opens a case at his feet. Rather than clothes, it has a bunch of fabrics inside of it. Silks. Satins. Lace.

Lucius watches while Bartley drags a tape measure around my hips, his eyes narrowed.

"We should start simple for now," Lucius suggests.

"Of course." Mr. Bartley nods and then packs up his case once he's taken my measurements. "I will send up a few items Mr. Koslov should approve of," he says before heading for the doorway.

"Thank you," Lucius calls after him. "Please send the doctor in."

He turns his attention to me and gestures to the bed. The bloody sheets are missing, replaced by a new comforter. White. Pristine. It's like slapping on a Band-Aid: You can't see the mess underneath, but you can still sense it.

"Have a seat, Ms. Marconi," Lucius urges. "It should be a quick examination."

The doctor is an old man with balding, black hair. He pokes and prods at me with a stethoscope and then draws blood— several tubes of it. Lucius steps forward to take them and then leaves the room, while the doctor grabs a sheet of paper from his briefcase and rattles off a million questions.

"How old are you?" he asks.

"Nineteen."

"Have you ever had children?"

"No."

"Any illnesses that you know of?"

"No."

"Use of any illicit drugs?"

"No."

I'm sure he's going to start asking questions about my fucking family history any minute, but he folds up the page after scribbling a final line down and shoves it into his briefcase. Just then, Lucius returns with several garment bags slung over his arm.

"These should last you until the custom work is finished," he says, setting them down beside me. He unzips the top one, revealing a plain, black dress with a lacy neckline. "Wear this tonight," he says, but I almost feel like he's warning me. *Please. Or else.*

"Okay."

"Until then, you may wear the clothing you brought." He gestures to my suitcase, which is still where I left it. He grabs it for me before I can attempt to stand on my own and fishes out a pair of sweatpants and an oversized tee shirt. Smart man.

He turns around while I get dressed and doesn't hesitate to offer his arm for support when I attempt to pull my pants up. I can tell he's not being nice for the hell of it. It almost seems routine to him, and once again, I have to wonder...

Just how many other *women* were there?

"You have a few hours before the evening meal," Lucius says once I sit back down, fully dressed. It's not hard to grasp the implication: *before Maxim comes back.* "I suggest that you get acquainted with the layout of the suite."

He pauses, as if waiting for me to say something. Ask something.

I finally manage to croak out, "Um, didn't you already give me a tour?"

He nods. "Yes. The rooms I showed you are the ones you are permitted in without Maxim's permission, barring the carving room, of course."

I flinch, remembering my punishment for exploring that particular area alone.

"I suggest you learn every inch of them," Lucius adds. "Know your boundaries. I will return sometime tomorrow."

He looks me over once, trailing his gaze along my damp hair and the bruises the sleeves of the shirt don't hide on my arms.

"Good day, Ms. Marconi."

When he leaves, I force myself to stand. Move. Walk. I take Lucius' advice and explore every inch of the suite that isn't behind a closed door. I learn my boundaries. This house must be a temporary one—someplace apart from where he actually lives. It smells different than it should. Too clean. Too *empty*, much like Maxim himself: perfectly fucked-up flawless.

Maybe that's what Lucius wanted me to realize: the level of control it would take for someone to live like this. With rooms organized by color scheme, in a home without an ounce of dust in sight. The devil is in the details, after all, and Maxim Koslov seems to take perfection to the extreme.

Only now am I starting to wonder why he would fish prostitutes from the street for sex.

"I only want to hurt you."

Rather than think on it too much, I keep searching. Keep moving. I wind up traveling the same three rooms over and over, memorizing the placement of every expensive piece of furniture. They all seem unworn and unused. Just decoration. I swear some even have the price tags still on them.

I run my fingers over the leather couch in the living room. It's too firm, having never been broken in. The pillows feel stiff.

The dress, however…

It's not new. Not really. I head back into the room just to be sure, running my fingers over the fabric. Someone wore it before I did. Maybe once. Maybe twice. Not long enough to really make an impression or truly call it hers, but enough times for her scent to sink into every thread.

After my stint at Penney's, I know a damn thing or two about borrowed clothing.

Biting my lip, I head toward the closet and go through the clothes again. I sense the same thing from every single fucking item. They've all been worn before, some more than others. By different women. Different ages. Sizes. I register at least twenty different body types before I force myself to step away and turn my focus to the bed.

It's the only thing in this damn place that doesn't feel used. No matter how many women he's paraded through this house, the bed—go figure—isn't as broken in as the closet. Not as many women have bled on it or slammed their foreheads on the headboard.

I wonder why. Though it's not like it's that big of a mystery. How many ran away after the first night? How many dumbass bitches came back for a second?

I try to wash my thoughts down the sink of the bathroom, scrubbing at my teeth with my toothbrush that tastes more like Ainsley than anything else: days' old sugar and cookie bits. I drag a brush through my hair without looking at myself. I dig my nails into whatever part of me they can reach whenever the panic manages to break through and threatens to ruin everything.

Money.

That's all that matters.

It's what makes the world go 'round.

I *need* this fucking money.

When I finally pull the dress on, it fits me a little better than the last one. It's clean as well, but I can still feel the traces of the woman who wore it last. She was taller than I am by an inch, with bigger boobs and longer hair to frame the scalloped neckline.

I bet she didn't sweat as much as I am now. She didn't bite her lip so hard that she bled and dripped blood into the delicate fabric. I know for a fact that Maxim never tore it off her.

He's home. I sense his arrival, even from this deep inside the suite. I hear the lock of the front door click followed by the thud as it slams shut. In the resounding silence, his voice rings out, cold and demanding.

"Come here."

I take two steps before I realize I'm barefoot.

"Now."

Fuck it. I risk meeting him wearing the dress and nothing else. I can't tell if he's annoyed by the fact when I finally find him pacing the length of the living room.

"Come." He jerks his chin and leads me into the kitchen. There, he directs me to stand in a corner while he drops a paper bag onto the counter and pulls out everything inside it. There's a hunk of fresh meat like the kind bought directly from a butcher, along with onions, celery, greens, and bread.

He seasons the meat and puts it into the oven with potatoes before starting on a fresh salad with the greens. The bread he slices carefully with a blade taken from a butcher's block at one end of the counter.

When he finally strolls out of the kitchen, I don't know whether to stay or follow. So I stay, driving my nails into their respective palms. Over. Over. Over.

"*Kotyonok.*"

I spring away from the wall and find him in the dining room. He opens the drawer of an ebony sideboard, revealing a stack of ivory plates and a box of silverware.

"Set the table," he tells me before leaving the room again, probably to return to the kitchen.

My hands shake as I grab two plates from the cupboard. I set one at the head of the table and the other close by. I find fancy-looking wine goblets and add those as well. A fork. A knife. A spoon.

But I can't tell which size is needed—or what goes where. Shit. I never had to worry about it before. In my real world, setting the table meant throwing a paper plate down and grabbing the least filthy piece of silverware from the pile already in the sink.

I keep fiddling with my placement, moving each different fork and spoon around. I don't stop until I hear him finally come in. He chuckles when he sees my progress and drags his thumb along the edge of one of the goblets. Almost in slow motion, the rest of his fingers fan out, knocking it off the table so hard that it shatters on the floor. He swipes at the place setting just as easily, leaving only one plate behind. *His.*

"Remember, *kotyonok*," he tells me without bothering to explain what he means out loud.

He leaves the room again, and I drop to my knees, picking up the broken glass with my bare fingers. But I'm too clumsy. I grab the pieces too hard and cut myself. On my palm. My wrist.

I bleed.

My blood paints the shards of the broken plate as I pile the rest of the glass onto the biggest piece—but I don't dare leave to find a trash can to throw it away. So I wait, still on my knees.

When he finally returns, he's holding the steaming roaster with the cooked meat and veggies inside. He places it at one end of the table and returns with the bread and the bottle of wine. Without making himself a plate, he sits at the head of the table, reaching for his goblet with one hand. He spies me as I lurch to my feet and nods toward his plate. *Serve me.*

I grab the wine first and circle around to his corner. I tip the bottle and pour until his eyes flash, warning me to stop. Then I lift his plate and take it to the roaster. I don't know how much meat to serve, but I don't dare ask, either. So I cut my losses and slice off two pieces, trying to make them as neat as possible. It's only when I start to transfer them onto the plate that I realize my hands are still bloody. Still bleeding.

"It's all right, *kotyonok*," he calls from his end of the table. It's like he's inside my head, feeding off my fear.

I serve him a single potato and a few slices of onion. I drag the knife through the bread next and lift the cut piece without touching it with my fingers. When I set the plate down in front of him, Maxim eyes it carefully.

Finally, he nods. "Sit."

I start for the chair, but the way he shakes his head stops me dead in my tracks.

His eyes cut down to the floor. "Sit."

I drop to my knees beside his chair, feeling his fingers come to brush the top of my head.

Another chuckle rumbles from his chest, deeper this time. "Not here…" He seizes chunks of my hair, pulling me upright.

Through streaming eyes, I see him nod again. To the table.

I scramble to haul myself onto the edge of it, wincing as my body starts to throb. The pain isn't deep enough to help me think. I'm thoughtless as I watch him sigh and casually reach for his dinner fork.

"You need training," he says while palming a knife with his other hand. He stabs the end of it into his meat and starts to cut. Once he's sliced off a piece, he spears it onto the fork and brings it to his mouth. Those dark eyes cut up to mine, reducing me to slivers in the same damn way. Before I can react, he grabs my hand, smoothing out each finger to expose my ruined palm. His attention is given to every cut, every scar—both old and new. Carefully, his thumb traces a bleeding wound as his eyes drift up to mine again. "Do you know what you did to offend me last night?"

The way he says *offend*. My blood turns to ice. My toes curl. I can't breathe. Can't think. God, I need to think.

"I never want to offend you—"

"Do you know what you did?" His voice dips to that dangerous level. He's barely human now, seconds from becoming a monster again.

"No," I breathe. I breathe and breathe and breathe, but air never seems to fill my lungs.

"Oh?" He raises the meat to his mouth and takes a bite. "You orgasmed," he tells me after swallowing.

Self-preservation kicks in. My answer is automatic. "N-no I didn't."

"You *did*. The only woman ever to in these circumstances." He slices off another piece of meat and wipes the blade along my bare thigh. It's hot. I suck air in through my teeth at the burning sting. "Pleasure is one thing not addressed in the contract. In fact, it takes true depravity or true *skill* to do so while in agony. So can you tell me, *kotyonok*? What got you off?"

I don't know what to say. I don't even know whether or not to lie. Why?

I don't orgasm. Ever. That's what the fuckers who pay me for sex do. That's what Melanie does whenever she screws someone over. It's apparently what Maxim does while fucking me half to death—and it's something he thinks requires *skill* in my case.

The only defense I have is the truth. "I don't do that."

The knife lands against the edge of the plate, spraying steak juice over the table's pristine surface as Maxim laughs so hard that his head falls back. His eyes find me again a second later, but the longer he stares, the angrier he seems.

"Do not play games with me." His hand finds the knife again, allowing the tip to brush my thigh. Once. Twice. "What was it, hmm?" The blade teases the flesh above my knee. Beads of blood bubble up and drip down. Drop by precious drop. "The money? You can admit that. Maybe you think you can swindle more out of me than you've earned? Or something else?" He digs the blade in so hard that I jump and choke on a strangled cry. "Do you have something planned? Some game? Some trick? Some secret to get you off even while being used like a whore?"

"No!" Liquid spills from my eyes, hotter than blood. "I don't know—"

"It seems that you need a demonstration." With a sigh, he tosses the knife aside. His hand lands over my waist before I can react, pinning my back flat against the table. "Lie still," he warns.

His touch is like the IV they stuck in Melanie the last time she OD'd, dripping fear into my veins as he takes my thighs in either hand and drags me toward him. The hem of the dress rides up. My hip knocks his plate to the side, dangerously close to the edge of the table. My right elbow brushes the tip of the knife. His fork is in between my legs.

So is his mouth. Hot breath splashes against the inside of my thighs—the only warning before his tongue flicks out to graze my pussy. I can't even come up with a coherent way to describe it, just broken, random words. Wet. Hot. Strong. God, his tongue is *strong*. He batters me open with it, and I whine at the pain. Too much. Too rough.

I've heard about this. Never experienced it for myself. Never wanted to. Putting my mouth on strangers' cocks was bad enough. I never wanted any of their mouths on me.

Trapped beneath Maxim now, I know that my original fears were fucking legit. The things he does. The way he moves. Nibbling. Sucking. *Biting*—really biting down there. So hard that I see white. I can't feel. Can't think.

I just exist. As gross as it is, the slang for this act seems to fit now more than ever: He's eating me out. Piece by fucking piece. He growls at the taste of me, his nails piercing my skin, his teeth grazing my flesh.

It's awful.

It's incredible.

It's disgusting.

It's fucking insane.

"S-stop," I choke out even though I know that the plea means nothing. I can't refuse him. Can't say no.

Surrender leaves me paralyzed as my brain swirls with every lazy flick of his tongue. There is only one way out. What was it? Three words. *Happy? I'm…*

A wave of pain hits me all at once like a punch to the chest and my thoughts shatter. *Pain,* because it knocks me under. It sets me free. I can think. I can feel. I can scream. Really scream.

I'm flying.

I'm falling.

I'm drowning.

I'm crashing back down to Earth.

He doesn't catch me; he just watches me burn.

"*That* is an orgasm," he says while I blink up at the ceiling and listen to air wheeze in and out of my throat. "Do you remember now?"

I shake my head. That wasn't an orgasm. Not fireworks, or sparks, or the toe-curling, mouthwatering pleasure described in those fucking stupid-ass romance novels Melanie used to read—the ones Daisy does now, hiding them under her bed.

That was pain. That was death.

"Your cum." Maxim drags a thumb between my legs and holds it up for me to see through blurred, unfocused eyes. It's glistening. Wet. With blood. With something else. After a moment, he brings it to his mouth. "Sweet," he declares after his first taste. It's not a compliment.

Several more seconds pass as he stares, waiting for me to confess something. Come clean. Admit it: *I orgasmed.*

But I can't. I need to think. My fingers flex, rubbing against the open wounds on my hands, but my thoughts never clear.

I'm not sure exactly when it happens—but his face changes. Maybe it's after the tears already welling in my eyes fall faster. Or when my entire body tenses up in the face of his slow-building reaction. I've been hit before. Beaten. Slapped. None of those blows packed the punch of his rage.

I jump as he pushes back from the table without warning, rising to his feet. "Go to your room," he tells me, turning to the nearest window displaying a shadowy view of the city. "Lie on the bed. Wait for me."

I haul myself upright and nearly fall off the table in my rush to reach the door. I don't stop running—but I'm going in the wrong direction. My unsteady footsteps don't take me out of the suite like they should.

I'm in my room.

On the bed.

I'm waiting. He told me to lie down, so I do, counting the seconds that pass, trying to breathe. I can think at least. Fear acts like pain, swirling through my veins, making every breath feel white hot. Suffocating.

I can't move an inch. Not even as I hear him pacing in the other room. Fast. Faster. A violent crash echoes off the walls as if something was knocked over. Then another, followed by the chime of breaking glass. Again. More.

It's like a twisted fucking soundtrack is playing as he starts in my direction, bringing a wave of chaos all the way up to my door. A thud ricochets off something close by, resonating through the walls. I feel the vibration race up the bed, joining with the massive slam the door makes as it flies open.

Maxim took the knife from the dinner table.

The edge sparkles as he approaches the bed, step by step. "I know who you are," he says, his voice an unstable rasp. "So I suggest you come clean."

CHAPTER EIGHT

"Francesca Marconi," Maxim bites out as if reading off a piece of paper. "Age nineteen. A poor goddamn whore from Horn Hill. Her price is sixteen thousand." He chuckles to himself, and I have to crane my neck back to see his face: a twisted mask of rage. "Maybe it's the money that gets you off," he tells me, nudging my outstretched leg with his knee. "So cheap. So pathetic that you have to sell yourself to any man willing to pay for it. Or so you want me to believe." He drags his thumb along the knife. "Is that it?"

I nod, more tears spilling down my cheeks. "Yes. I-I need the money—"

"So you keep saying." He frowns, tapping the knife's edge against the mattress, inches away from either thigh. "But I'm not entirely convinced."

The blade drifts higher and my hand flies out to block the tip, but I don't dare sit up. I just breathe. In and out. Out. In. "P-please!"

"You have children. *Siblings*." His eyes flicker back up to mine and the look twisting his mouth could almost be called a smile. "Did you think I wouldn't look into that? Did you think I would truly believe that this tight fucking cunt"—he gestures with the blade—"produced children?"

I can't breathe. My thoughts get harder and harder to grasp. No. God, no.

"There are six of them," he says, adjusting the blade so that the edge of it ghosts my hip, drifting down. Around. Up again. "Michael—"

"P-please." A retaliatory cut to my thigh can't shut me up. I don't even feel the pain. Just fear, all-consuming. "Please!"

"So then *tell* me."

Tell him what? I don't even know. I'm so fucking stupid. I left them alone. I left a sixteen-year-old in charge.

"Who sent you to me? Maybe I should ask Daisy-Rae?" Maxim wonders. "Or Oliver, Raymond, and Eric."

The knife dips into the flesh of my belly, slicing easily through the fabric of the dress, but the pain doesn't wake me up. It kills me.

"Perhaps, Ainsley?"

He digs the knife in deeper. His eyes never leave mine and I realize it now that this man…

He's a monster.

He could have killed them.

They could already be dead.

I couldn't even protect them.

"S-stop. P-please—"

"You move so much as a goddamn inch." His hands go to his fly, ripping it open, freeing his cock. "And I'll kill them. *All* of them, one by one in front of you. I will make you watch. Do you understand?"

My body shuts down as he takes a condom from his pocket and pulls it on. Fear pins me in place and I let it. He could cut me, burn me, do whatever the fuck he wants to me.

But not to them.

"You have five seconds to tell me the truth. Who do you work for? Who planted you, hmm? They have to be powerful, because you are fucking *convincing*." He waits, and my eyes go to his knife. One. Two. Three. Four. He sighs, tossing the blade onto the floor. "Fine. Spread your legs."

I have no choice but to obey. My legs drag themselves apart —just enough for him to force his way in between. I cry out when he enters me. It's not like before. My body resists. It hurts, it *hurts*. And, for the first time, the pain doesn't take me away. It doesn't clear my head. It breaks me. Thrust after thrust.

This isn't hooking. No amount of money is worth this. It doesn't sink in until I hear him groan, his hands positioning my hips so that he can pin me flat with his weight, filling me up, ripping me open—getting off on the pain he causes. I can't hold it back. I scream. I cry.

The same way I cried for Melanie. The same fucking way I cried the first time I peeled my pants down for fifty fucking dollars. The tears that only cutting myself can hold back, along with that sickening thought I can never seem to escape: *I failed. I failed. I failed.*

All at once, the world shifts as the unbearable pressure inside me relents.

"Look at me." Warm fingers grip my chin. "Look at me!"

I have no choice. He hovers over me, still wearing his shirt, his eyes piercing through my skull. That anger is gone. All I find is…

I don't fucking know.

"Look at me," he growls before I can even start to turn away. His hand cups my chin so hard that my teeth clip together. The motion tilts my head from the bed, forcing me to meet his gaze. For what feels like hours, his eyes search mine, hunting for something—but finding nothing. Slowly, his mouth falls out of a snarl and back into a cold, emotionless line. "I will never, *never* hurt your family. Do you understand?"

Tears drip down my chin. I'm still crying. All this time. I thought it was background noise—maybe he left on a television somewhere that was playing a horror movie where the dumb bitch being murdered just couldn't fucking stop whimpering.

"Look at me." He tightens his grip and shakes, making my body jolt over the mattress. "Do you understand? You never have to fear that from me. Do you understand?"

He's lying. I can't believe him. I shake my head, stammering, "Don't, don't, don't, don't—"

He stands up. His hand goes for the knife and he throws it onto the bed. When I lunge for it, he watches me, his eyes cold, his arms at his sides. He doesn't move when I curl my fingers around the handle.

I point it at him, and he turns for the door.

"Come."

I don't want to. I *have* to; my body makes me, obeying the warning tone in his voice. I step off the bed and hit the floor, blinded by more goddamn tears. Fear and pain—my brain doesn't know which drug to give in to.

Strong hands curl beneath my shoulders, ignoring the way I'm flailing around with the knife. When he hauls me upright, the blade falls. I'm in his arms a second later, being carried through the rest of the suite and out into the hall.

"Trust me." He brings me down a stairwell and out into a dark, enclosed space. A parking garage?

The sounds I make echo off the walls of it. Choking. Gasping. Gagging. Screaming. Strangled sounds.

The next second, Maxim approaches a black car and shoves me into the back seat. As the car begins to move, I'm thrown forward by the momentum, smacking my head off the front seat so hard that I taste blood. My vision blinks in and out. I see lights. Colors. A million different sounds flood my ears: sirens, shouts, laughter.

"Look at me." Maxim stands over me, his body leaning in through the open door.

The car stopped moving. It's dark wherever we are. After two days in his suite, I almost don't recognize the shitty street corner I find myself on when he hauls me out of the car and makes me stand beside him.

My house gleams in all of its fucked-up glory. The lights are on. Even from here, I can hear Ainsley screaming—but before the fear can bite deep, I make out what she's saying. Curse words. Apparently, Eric got to her stupid-ass dolls again.

"I cannot say the same for you, but I will never hurt *them*," Maxim tells me, his voice trickling into my ear, louder than anything else. "Do you understand? Say it."

I can't trust. However, with this man standing so close to the only shit I've ever worked for, I can't afford not to.

He drags me closer to him as my legs shake and my knees knock together. His arm goes around my shoulders, pinning me to his side—not for support.

"I…" My voice is a rasp. He has to lean closer just to hear me, his lips like ice on the side of my throat.

"Say it."

"I believe you. You won't hurt them."

"And?"

I inhale a ragged breath. "Only me."

Satisfied, he turns back to the car, and I climb woodenly inside, fastening my seat belt this time.

The tears still fall as he pulls away and returns to the high-rise. From fear or pain?

I can't tell.

He doesn't carry me this time. I'm left to limp up the stairs behind him, and he's already in the suite when I finally catch up.

"Get some rest," he tells me, his eyes between my legs, tracking the blood dripping down them. He closes the door behind me, watching as I cling to the wall in order to pass him. "I know now," he says as I start down the hall.

I look back and find him rubbing his jaw with the pad of his thumb. "I know now what gets you off. Masochism." He frowns like it's a dirty word.

One that I don't know the meaning of.

Sighing, he tells me, "It's the pain you enjoy."

He turns away before I can tell if that annoys him or not.

Honestly, I'm not even sure which answer I'd want to find anyway.

A KNOCK on the door wakes me before the sky has turned gray around the edges. I haul myself upright, clinging to the nearest support for balance: the bathroom door. Once I'm on my feet, I blink, slowly bringing the rest of the room into focus. The bed is across from me, the blankets rumpled but still mostly intact.

I didn't sleep on it.

I didn't sleep at all.

In a daze, I head for the closet and find the clothing Lucius gave me hanging inside it. I pull on a dress at random, too exhausted to examine it. Day? Evening? It's white, I think, with a lacy collar. Once I peel the black dress off my body, I fold it and leave it on the floor, unsure of where else to put it.

When I stagger into the bathroom, I look at myself in the mirror this time. Really look.

What a pathetic bitch.

She watches me with bloodshot eyes, her hair a mess, her bottom lip bloody and swollen. She's so damn pale. Her pretty fucking dress can't hide the bruises on her arms. Or the cuts. The blood.

But the injuries aren't the worst part by far. Her greedy fingers seek them out, rubbing the open sores, chasing every bit of clarity like an addict with a high. Pathetic.

I turn away from her and attempt to wipe myself clean. When I drag a washcloth between my legs, I can't silence a gasp. A groan. A scream. *He broke me.* It's not even an understatement: I feel like a goddamn virgin again. A virgin who took a sledgehammer first.

Biting any noise back, I wash myself the best I can, and the rag comes away bloody. I set it down and rinse my hands in the sink. I don't know why, but I sit on the edge of the bed afterward, waiting, rather than leave the room on my own. His footsteps return not long after, stalking a lazy path to my door. He tests the handle first, almost as if he expects to find it locked.

"*Kotyonok?*" The door opens without resistance and Maxim steps in.

My entire body reacts to his presence; I sit straighter, my gaze honed in on every inch of his bulky frame. He's wearing gray today, slacks with a long-sleeved shirt. His eyes drift over in my direction, but rather than command me to change, he jerks his head toward the end of the hall.

"Come."

I trail him into the kitchen, where he makes breakfast, the same way he did dinner, pulling the ingredients from another brown paper bag. Eggs. Bacon. Herbs. He works silently for a few minutes before seeming to remember I'm here. When he looks back at me, he's still holding a frying pan.

"Set the table, *kotyonok*."

He cleaned the dining room, or someone else did for him. It's pristine again, every piece of glass swept from the floor. There's even a new plate to replace the broken one, and I set it in front of Maxim's chair, placing a fork and spoon on either side.

My fingers twitch in and out of fists as I stand in the corner and wait. Almost an hour later, he re-enters the dining room to place a pan of eggs and a tray of bacon onto the far end of the table. The moment he directs his gaze at me, I jump forward, ready to pile the food onto his plate.

When he beckons me to sit, it isn't on the table this time. He nods to the chair beside him and draws it closer once I obey, his hand gripping the sliver of cushion right between my legs.

"Today is your last day with me," he tells me before starting in on his eggs. He stabs a chunk with his fork and raises it toward me. "Open."

I pry my jaw apart to accept the food he shoves onto my tongue. My stomach growls: I'm hungry. I'm starving. The food goes down before I can even taste it. Silently, he offers me more. A piece of bacon. A bite of biscuit. All of it eaten directly from his hand.

"Have you had enough?" he asks when he finally sets his fork down.

When I nod, his eyes flash darker.

"Do not lie." He lifts the plate and holds it out to me. "Get more."

My fingers shake as I add another pile of eggs and a few more strips of bacon to the plate. This time, he feeds me all of it, commanding me to open on cue and demanding with his eyes for me to swallow. Obeying him is like rewiring the nerves in my body so that they no longer take their cues from my brain. Only from him.

He stands when I choke down the last bite and gathers the dishes himself. The next few seconds pass while I watch him wash the plate in the sink and then carefully dry each utensil before putting them away. He wipes his hands after he's done and directs his gaze toward my feet.

"Go put on some shoes."

I scramble toward the bedroom, sensing him on my heels. The moment I open the closet, he's behind me, observing which shoes my hands brush over. He makes a low sound in his throat when I thumb a pair of gray flats, so my fingers jump to a pair of black heels instead. Nothing—a sign I take as silent permission. I rush to pull them on, surprised when he lowers his hand to help me back to my feet.

"I will not fuck you tonight," he announces as the nail of his thumb lightly brushes my palm. "So you can stop clenching your thighs together whenever I look at you."

My cheeks heat up as if the observation were a slap. I look down. He's right: My knees are kissing, my legs shaking. I didn't even realize I was doing it.

"I'm sorry—"

"Sorry?" His mouth takes on a different shape than the stern line I'm used to: a slant. The next second, he drops down on one knee.

Fear rockets through my veins as both of his hands go to the skirt of my dress, winding it up to my waist, revealing the pink cotton underwear I stole from Melanie.

"Hold," he commands, and my fingers race to keep the wad of fabric in place.

I can only stare while he reaches into his pocket and pulls his knife out. The blade hisses as it springs free, stabbing at the air.

"Don't move," Maxim warns as he brings the edge of it against my inner thigh, right below my entrance.

A whine trickles out of me as the blade edge kisses my flesh, slicing a single line no longer than a fingernail. I still feel it bleeding, drop by drop.

"*Now* you have something to apologize for," he tells me as he tucks the blade into his pocket and stands. "Or you will if you get so much as a drop of blood on that dress." He lets the threat hang there while motioning for me to lower the skirt. Then he jerks his chin. "Come."

I follow him back into the hall, squeezing my thighs together with every step. The skirt of the dress swishes out, away from my legs—but he cut me too deep. Blood drips down.

"This way, *kotyonok.*" His voice leads me into the sculpture room. The one of the woman is gone, replaced by another block of stone: a darker-colored gray this time. After grabbing a smaller chisel and a hammer from the selection on the wall, Maxim sets to work, hammering the shit out of it while I watch.

Within minutes, I can see why he wanted me to wear shoes. Bits of stone and dust go flying, coating the floor. I back myself into a corner, just watching him. I scan the rest of his body before my brain can register what a bad decision it is to take my attention off the weapons in his hand. His shirt ripples beneath the repetitive motion of chiseling. It starts to bunch up around his waist, revealing a sliver of something that isn't skin: black fabric. An undershirt? Maybe.

But, when he lunges into another blow, the cotton shirt shifts. I can make out the ridge of something along his abdomen, like the top of one of those girdle belts Melanie uses when she likes to pretend she didn't pop out seven children. Going off the muscle shaping the rest of his body, I don't think he's hiding a beer gut.

I drift my gaze back to his hands and let myself become hypnotized by the way he hacks away at the hunk of stone. With anger. With rage. For hours and hours and hours.

In the process, he makes something beautiful: a face, delicately roughed out in the middle of the shapeless chunk. Just like that, he's beaten life out of nothing with only strips of metal and his goddamn fists.

Am I impressed?

Horrified?

I don't know as he finally turns to face me, wiping his hands on a rag snatched from the table along the wall.

"Come here." He reaches out when I'm close enough, kissing my cheek with the pad of each finger. The bite of a probing nail erases any gentleness from the gesture. My heart starts to race, even before he nods toward the wall. "Turn around."

I do, feeling his eyes scan the back of my skirt, hunting for blood. I'm holding my breath.

"Lucius gave me the results of your testing last night," he says. "You are clean."

That should be a good thing. Especially considering what he did with his mouth last night. But, once again, I get the feeling that he isn't happy. Just irritated. Confused. I'm beginning to realize that a puzzled Maxim is a very dangerous thing.

He clenches his jaw and seems to chew over the words he wants to say. "Most women in your position are not."

I flinch at the thought of it: him fucking and sucking a million different women, infected with god knows what.

He laughs as if seeing the thought cross my brain the moment I think it. "I know what precautions to take. A man with my tastes cannot be choosy." The laughter dies off. "But you are young," he adds, frowning. "You are clean. There are other men who could pay regularly for sex should you know where to look. You haven't."

He pauses as if waiting for an answer, but I don't know which one to give.

Maybe that I've been there, done that. No amount of money is worth my pride—or so I used to tell myself.

"I've had women prettier than you come to me before," he says. "With tighter cunts than yours. Women who suck cock better than you could dream." He drags his thumb across my cheek in a gentle caress. "I've fucked them harder than I have you. I enjoyed them more. None of them lasted the week." He takes a step forward, urging my head back so that I meet his gaze directly. "You will not last the week. Get on your knees."

I sink without breaking eye contact, obeying the command he doesn't issue out loud. *Look at me.* One of his hands fists itself in my hair, holding my head in place, while the other tackles the clasp of his pants.

My heart slams against my rib cage as I crouch in a layer of dust while he pulls out his cock, already hardening, and aims it toward my mouth like a bullseye. I open. He rams in, deepthroating me without warning this time.

I choke. I gag. I breathe in through my nose and suffer through it. He groans with every inch he claims—but I'm too sore. Too raw. He can't fit himself in all the way, only getting half of his length in my mouth at one time. He finishes anyway, grunting out.

It's only when I feel the first spurt of cum hit the back of my throat that I realize he didn't bother with the condom this time. My throat clenches up on instinct, trying to spit him—*it*—out.

His hand comes from nowhere, the fingers pinching my nose shut, his voice a husky, hollow rasp. "Swallow it." He thrusts again. Another hot burst floods my mouth, threatening to spill from my lips if I don't take it down. "All of it. You lose a drop and you will be *punished*."

The tone of his voice chills me to the core. So I gulp, gagging with him still in my mouth, fighting to swallow everything he gives me. All of it. His fingers tighten with every attempt, his breaths fanning my forehead. "That's it. Fuck, take it."

He thrusts so hard that I see black, and my throat woodenly jerks to accept the final load he has to give. He doesn't make me savor the taste at least, but I know better than to let myself throw up when he finally wrenches himself out.

I hit the floor on all fours, breathing in. *In. In. In.* My stomach lurches, pissed off and full. It's something I've never done. Ever. Something dribbles down my chin and I swipe at it in a panic. Drool.

"That was just a taste," Maxim says above me. "The next time I fuck you, you will clean me of every drop."

My body jumps at the mention of fucking. I can't move. I just watch his shadow flicker on the wall as he steps over me and heads for the door.

"I want you gone after midnight, if I don't return before then." He cocks his head for one last glance at me. His eyes settle over my hips and narrow. "In fact, I *will* return," he adds, "to administer your punishment."

I follow his gaze to the front of my dress and feel my heart sink to the pit of my stomach. A tiny pinprick of red has seeped through the fabric, but I don't move, even after he leaves. I just lie here, counting my heartbeat. Too fast. Too slow. Faster.

The room's dark by the time I finally decide to run. Escape. I go back to the bedroom first, even though I don't plan on taking the suitcase. I just stare at it, Melanie's shit in a place she would love. Would it bother her, having her brains fucked out every night?

Probably not. It wasn't like she had much left anyway.

I back myself into the hallway, closing the door behind me, and take a step toward the entryway. My only way out. Freedom.

But something makes me turn, and I follow the hallway deeper into the suite, taking the path Maxim's footsteps do whenever he storms away after leaving me half conscious and bloodied on the bed. They lead me to a closed door at the very end of the hallway. My fingers shake as they grip the knob and twist it open.

I see black. Everything, from the walls to the floors, is the same shade. So is the massive bed placed against one wall. The pillows, the sheets. The lamp shades. The wardrobe in the corner. The doors leading off to either the closet or the bathroom.

All of it is black, with no ounce of color other than the silvery glow of the light bulbs.

I thought my room was creepy with its closet of borrowed clothing. But it, at least, seemed lived in, even if for only days at a time by numerous people.

This room is a crypt. It has that heavy, stale air the show floors in furniture stores do: completely untouched. Unlived in. My house has more signs of Melanie than this room does of Maxim. The man isn't just fucking insane. He's a goddamn ghost.

I can't reach the front door fast enough. My fingers pry at the handle, wrenching it open. Then slamming it shut.

Stay.

Go.

Run.

My head aches as it tries to process several different options at once. He knows where I live. He already threatened my family once. The fear that has grown since the moment he first ordered me down to my knees spills over. It rides a single thought I don't want to face: *He'll kill me.*

And I need the money. Money. Money. Money.

Rent is a black hole I am only now beginning to climb out of. One month here could give me enough money to scrape my way out of debt for good—or long enough to breathe. Think. Do something other than fuck, cheat, and steal to get by. This money could give me *hope.*

Most of his women lasted only a week, but I need a month. One fucking month.

You need to leave, a part of me urges. But it seems to know the same thing I do.

I can't, and he finds me there an hour before his deadline, still standing in front of the door.

CHAPTER NINE

"You've made up your mind," he says coldly, his gaze sweeping me over from head to toe. "If you continue to ignore my generosity"—he steps over the threshold, leaving the door open behind him as his hand cups the side of my face—"I will no longer extend it. Leave."

He gestures to the open door with a wave of his hand and even steps aside to let me pass.

I don't move. "I need the money." It hurts to say it, worse than any thrust he could ever inflict on my throat or my pussy. Knowing how pathetic I am hurts. It's the only kind of pain I'd rather suppress than feel.

"Fair enough." He reaches back to close the door behind him and steps in farther, cutting into my personal space. He smells funny: like spice. Like food. He must have eaten somewhere else.

My stomach grumbles.

He laughs. "Hungry, are you?" His hand leaves my chin, goes to my throat. "My seed wasn't enough to satisfy that greedy little mouth?" He cradles my windpipe, still brushing my jaw with the pad of his thumb. "Let me discover for myself just how greedy the rest of your body can be."

He steers me back. Back into the living room, shoving me onto a firm surface. The couch. I tense while he nudges my legs apart with his knee before his hands claw at the front of the dress.

He rips it up. Off. I wait, panting and half-naked, while his eyes trace out a small path up and down the length of me. Down my throat. Between my breasts. Over my stomach.

"Lie back for me," he commands.

His body is stone against mine, crushing me against the leather. His lips trace the line of my throat and then part slowly enough for me to feel his teeth nip at my flesh before they sink in.

"You're fucking sweet," he grits out once he releases his first bite. Again, he doesn't sound happy. Just angry. Just hungry.

He bites me again. Harder, this time. On my shoulder. My collar. Lower…

I breathe out sharply when his breath fans my left breast. His fingers come up, cupping it. Squeezing while his thumb brushes the nipple.

The things I feel…

It's all pain. My throat goes dry. Each touch ripples through me like a pulse, jolting all the way down to my pussy. Stronger. Faster. More.

"You enjoy that?" Maxim wonders as he seizes my nipple between his thumb and his forefinger and pinches again. "My desperate little *kotyonok*?"

He does it again. Harder. Punishingly.

My next inhale turns into a gasp.

"You do." He hovers over me, his tongue swiping. Licking. Another bite.

Oh god.

My fingers grip the couch, fighting for enough leverage.

He licks again before sucking a nipple between his teeth. Then he bites down.

My head flies back, striking the rim of the headrest. My pussy is on fire.

And he does it again. So hard that I can taste the pain. I see it. Feel it: It's like steel, thick, immovable. The surface doesn't have an ounce of give, even as my fingers twitch against it. His chest? If so, the theory of him having a beer gut goes *bye-bye*: He is solid muscle. At least until I feel something softer underneath, stretched too taut to be skin. Elastic?

"*Don't.*"

His tone alone warns me to make my hands fall—but not fast enough. My punishment is a bite so deep that it breaks the flesh. I can't even suck in enough air to scream. I just writhe, choking on agony, trapped at his mercy.

"Your blood is sweet too," he muses, capturing a bead with his tongue. "Sweet and greedy like the rest of you."

He watches it continue to fall, seeping around my nipple. Several tiny, weeping ridges circle it—the imprint of his teeth.

I'm on pins and needles when he starts on the right. He's rougher with his tongue, grinding my nipple into a sensitive, burning point. My body jerks every time he touches it. Looks at it.

I can't even stand to feel him *breathe.*

I nearly thank God out loud when he finally draws back, but his hands go tightly to my hips, sinking beneath the waistband of my panties. I shiver as he tugs them down, eyeing the ravaged flesh of my pussy underneath.

His eyes cut up to mine, narrowed, glowing. "You're fucking *weeping* for me, *kotyonok.*" He raises his hand so that I can see his glistening fingers.

With blood, I tell myself when my eyes don't bother to focus. *Nothing else.*

Nothing else.

A ragged shudder racks my body, ripping the thought away. His fingers are back, running along my inner thigh, grazing my pussy, slipping inside. He groans. I gasp, struggling to *look* as he growls the command. But I can't. My head is too heavy; he's moving too slowly.

"You like this?"

I don't. I can't think. I—

"You *like* this."

A nail grazes the sorest part of me and the reaction resonates like an electric shock. Muscles I didn't even know I have cramp up and tense. My nerve endings explode. And there's clarity. Brief. Harsh. It's like a whisper of calm through the chaos of my mind.

I see him clearly for a split second. I smell him. Taste him, his breaths fanning the skin of my throat. A muscle in his jaw twitches. What feels like a thumb brushes me open, making way for a longer, thinner finger.

I say something. Something broken and forbidden that earns me a sharp pinch on my hip. The pain is almost worth it as the fire building in my blood gets a drip of gasoline to feed it.

"More?" Maxim wonders, his voice harsh, shattering against my skin like broken glass.

I didn't ask for it. I know I didn't. I couldn't have.

He gives it to me anyway. His thumb rams in to join the first finger. Thick. Full. But not full enough.

LANA SKY

"I would tear you apart with my cock tonight," Maxim says as a watery, broken sound trickles out of my throat. He growls in response, swirling the pad of one of the searching fingers along my inner walls, making them shake. "So delicate you are."

The pain is still there. Still screaming through my system. He's right. He'd break me. Rip me apart. Tear me open.

"And yet the thought of it"—another searing thrust and brutal caress—"seems to make you even wetter."

He laughs. It's too loud. Insane. Each booming chuckle ricochets off the inside of my skull. I try to shake my head. I don't want it. I'm not...

His fingers spread and I go silent. Limp. My body starts to rock with the force of each rough, bruising thrust. He won't use his cock, but he'll fuck me just as violently with his fingers. And somehow I feel more. Too much. He's pinching, twisting, touching, taking, tasting.

Fuck.

I see lightning as the pain hits me all at once. It's so sharp, it drowns me. Desolates me. This is all I am. All I know. Fucking and being fucked. Right into oblivion.

But it doesn't last. He pulls the fire away just when I'm about to tip over the edge. Lose it all. When I finally blink my vision back, he isn't laughing. A frown shapes his mouth as if it'd been chiseled there, beaten in with every sound I made.

"I've given you enough for tonight," he tells me, sliding his fingers free, ripping away my only lifeline to sanity.

My thoughts cloud over. Can't think. I'm forbidden to move—but my hand jumps anyway, the fingers grasping at the air.

"You want more?" His voice... I've never heard it so thick. It's like he's breaking every word off of stone—hammering humanity out of the monster he really is. "Say it, then. You want more." He snaps his fingers, shining, bloody. "Beg."

I don't want more. I shake my head, biting my lower lip.

He steps back, starts to turn.

I whimper. It's the only sound I can make. Not words. I can't say it.

"Do you want it?" He steps forward, bracing one knee on the cushions of the couch beside me. His fingers come to circle my throat, tilting my head back so that I'm forced to stare into those swirling black holes he has for eyes. "How badly do you want to come?" His fingers sweep down, catching a swollen, bitten nipple between them. "Do you need it?"

Fire licks through my veins, but it's nowhere near strong enough. Harsh enough. I *need* more.

"Y-yes."

When he bears down, I can't hide the scream that rips from my throat. It's too soft. Too damn close to a moan.

"Then fucking ask for it—"

"P-please."

His eyes disappear, narrowed into slits. The next second, he's on his knees, his hands on my hips, dragging me forward. His mouth catches me.

And my body does the screaming for me. It explodes. Ignites. Blows up.

Kaboom! It's a scramble to reassemble myself in the chaos. Nothing in the world compares to his tongue. It's soft. Strong. Licking. Sucking. Breaking. Breaking. Breaking.

This time, I don't get just a taste of clarity. I get a full fucking dose. My thoughts go so clear that, for the first time in my life, I don't feel anything. No fear. No pressure. No stress.

Just *nothing.*

The relief is almost enough to soften the blow when I come crashing back down, face-to-face with Maxim. His lips are wet, his eyes glowing. I can't move, even as his tongue flits out to graze my cheek.

"What I wouldn't give to fuck you right now." His tone is a warning. A threat. "To teach you just what a mistake you've made. To make your body regret every ounce of pleasure you stole from me."

He grinds his hips into me and I feel his erection, straining and heavy. Fear eats away at the pain. At the same time, it fans the flames higher.

"But not tonight." He runs his wet fingers through my hair and then pulls away, rising to his feet. "Tonight, I will have mercy on you."

He sounds too soft—way too gentle. I'm almost fooled until the moment he reaches into his pocket and draws a knife out. I swallow hard at the realization that it's a different shape from the one he normally carries. A leather sheath covers a blade that stretches nearly the entire length of his palm. The handle is thicker, almost as if it'd been carved to fit his grip alone. Casually, he tosses it into the air and catches it by the covered tip. The handle gleams, a dark polished wood. My eyes have trouble focusing on it, even as he crouches on one knee and drags it along my inner thigh.

Mercy? That fucking word taunts me as the cool tip of the handle grazes up and down my flesh, inching closer and closer to my pussy with every stroke. Just like that, my head clears. I'm on the razor-sharp edge of clarity. Literally.

"I would cause damage if I took you with my cock," Maxim says in a husky rasp, almost as if to remind himself of that fact while the front of his pants bulges and strains. "But, if I let you rest completely, *kotyonok*, it would be nearly impossible for you to take all of me again."

I inhale raggedly as the knife handle grazes my outer lips.

"It's happened before. I need to make sure that you remain…stretched."

Tears burn behind my eyes. I blink them back. They sting even worse. I can't help it. My knees twitch, aching to slam together and never let him in. As if he can read my mind, one of his hands palms my right thigh.

"I suggest you don't resist," he warns as the wooden edge bats the rim of me once. Twice.

Air leaves my lungs as it slams in without warning, stretching me apart in ways his fingers could only dream. He doesn't hold back, thrusting so deep my vision fades. The fullness is second only to his cock. I can't do anything other than gasp for air, my fingers flailing for leverage. My nails grip the leather couch, digging in, tearing.

"Let it in," he growls as he thrusts again. Harder. Slower.

I don't have any choice but to relent. Muscle and flesh are battered and stretched into submission. Rather than push the handle out, they tug, pulling it deeper, allowing the invasion.

The gruff sound Maxim makes at the back of his throat betrays his satisfaction with every awful inch. "That's it."

I'm so damn sore. So raw. I barely hear him. It takes all of my energy just to breathe. My chest heaves, almost as if mimicking every inch of me he claims with the knife handle. In and out.

I think the violation is the worst of it. Being fucked with a knife—it can't get any more humiliating than this. But he proves me wrong when the callused, heavy pad of his thumb drifts up to the flesh above the knife. Teasing. Rubbing. One brush and every fucking muscle in my body tenses. The knife feels bigger, impossibly huge inside me. My skin feels hotter. *Fuck.*

"Look at you. Even this gets you off," Maxim remarks, his voice low and gravelly. Angry.

A part of me tries to react to it and muster up a shred of fear. But my nerves are mush. The motions of the knife churn my insides into a hot, boiling ball of sensation. I can't focus on anything else, just this. His thumb is too fast. Too slow. I'm floating. The angry, gravelly sound that revs up in his chest when I arch my hips sets everything off. Like a match.

But right before it hits the nearby puddle of gasoline, he douses everything in a fire extinguisher.

"No." The handle twists, its curved edge pressing against my inner walls, driving a howl from my lips. "Remember this lesson, *kotyonok*." He withdraws the handle, leaving me gaping and open. But the hazy warmth in my stomach turns to dread when I hear a dangerously soft hiss. My eyes flutter down and I find him sliding the sheath off, revealing the blade. "You come only when I say you can," he tells me. "Do you understand?"

I nod. I don't think I'll ever fucking stop. Not until he puts that knife away.

"Do not move."

He lowers the blade between my legs. Icy kisses of pain graze the swollen lips of my pussy. Teasing. Prodding. I wish

I could say that it feels worse than the handle. I wish. I wish.

"I don't think you are ready for this just yet," Maxim admits before he pulls the knife edge away. His eyes flash a heart-stopping shade of black. "Yet."

I try not to let myself dwell on the promise in his tone as he stands, re-sheathing the blade. Weak with relief, I just collapse into a puddle against the cushions, watching Maxim's features become a blur.

"Our time is up," he tells me before retreating down the hallway. "You can go."

I want nothing more than to do just that. Leave.

But despite how hard I try, I can't summon the strength to even lift my head.

CHAPTER TEN

I'm ripped from oblivion by the howls of someone ranting about their decapitated baby.

"You killed her!" the thin, high-pitched voice accuses. "I'm going to have Frankie beat your ass when she comes back—"

"She probably won't come back," a boy counters. "Maybe she's glad to be away from *your* fucking ugly face—"

"Hey! Knock it off!"

The trickle of authority sounds out of place in a voice not quite deep enough to have come from a grown man. I blink my eyes open as I hear the staircase tremble a second later. A shadow flickers along the wall. Tall. One of the older kids. They reach the bottom step before they find me. Going off the scent of stale corn chips, I think I'm on the couch. Ainsley always left crumbs between the cushions.

"Shit!" I startle at the voice and my vision returns in bits and pieces as Mikie comes closer, a backpack slung over his arm. "Frankie? You scared the shit out of me! Hey, you okay?"

"Fine." I turn my face toward the musty cushions, curling the rest of my body into a ball. I'm not wearing the dress. I know that even before I look down and find that someone dressed me in my sweatpants and one of Melanie's tee shirts. The word *juicy* is written in pink glitter across my chest. Considering how much effort it takes to suck in air, I doubt I was the one who did this. Which brings up another interesting question: I can't remember how I got home. Or how I even left Maxim's suite.

"Where the hell did you even go anyway?" Mikie asks.

I force myself to turn in order to watch him cross over to the front door. My suitcase is beside it. Even from the distance between it and the couch, I can still make out the thick, black envelope sticking out from the front pocket.

"What's this?"

"Don't touch it!" I croak, flinging my hand out as if to physically shove him back.

"Damn, Frankie." Mikie lowers his hand and backs away. "Okay, okay I won't. By the way, I tried calling you when you were gone."

I flinch. The phone. I left it in my bag. By accident. Maybe…

I'm lying. Deep down, a part of me knows the truth I don't want to face: I wasn't given permission to use one. So I didn't.

Guilt hurts worse than whatever my body feels.

"I'm sorry," I force myself to blurt out. "I was…busy."

"You sound like shit." He opens the fridge and grabs a bottle from the very back, holding it up to the light. "I replaced your stash," he says before dropping the bottle onto the sliver of cushion beside me. "Here."

I'm too tired to ask or care how he got the booze or how he knew about my stash—let alone what happened to the bottles already there. I lift the bottle and let him rip the cap off for me, but I'm so fucking tired that he has to lower the rim of the bottle to my mouth before I can even take a sip. I manage to gulp down three times before he pulls it away and sets it on the floor.

In the cool, gray light wafting in from the window, he looks more like Melanie than ever—the only one of us who really does. He has her eyes, which are known to shift from blue to green. Her chin. Her laugh. Her dimpled smile. He doesn't wear it as much as she does though. Not now, at least.

"Frankie…you're bleeding," he whispers as the staircase trembles again beneath several different footsteps.

Shit. I cut my eyes over to the busted armchair in the corner of the room. There's a blanket draped over it, the remains of someone's toy fort. Mikie races over to grab it and barely has me covered by the time the rest of the kids make it downstairs.

"Shut the fuck up," he hisses when Ainsley cries out my name. "She's sleeping. Everyone get your shit and let's go."

He sounds so stern. So damn mature. And no one argues as they march across the living room, fishing backpacks and homework from under chairs and on top of tables. The front door opens, the screen door slamming against the outer siding like usual.

One by one, the kids stream out. The only argument is put up by Ainsley, but Mikie silences her with a hissed, "You can talk to her after school." When the very last kid has jumped off the porch, he says to me through the open doorway, "I'll try to stall them after school. Long enough for you to put makeup on or something. I don't want Ains seeing your face like that…"

I reach up, feeling along my lower lip. It's sore. Pulsating. Swollen. When I peel my eyes open again, Mikie is gone and a Teenage Mutant Ninja Turtle blanket is covering the worst of me. My toes stick out from under it though, crusted in dried blood.

It takes me hours to crawl upstairs and into the bathroom. I shower. I scream. I drag a brush through my hair and even steal Daisy's makeup from under the sink to do what I can to minimize the dark circles under my eyes.

My bitten, cracked lips are a hopeless cause though, so I come up with a lie. I tripped and bit myself there. Once.

Twice. Oh, and I fell onto glass and cut my hands. And my back. I smoked too many cigarettes and burned my throat. I'm limping because…

The lie loses water after that.

It's not like I have the time to put it into practice anyway. Somewhere between searching Daisy and Ainsley's room for spare clothing, I wind up on a bed. So I sleep. For hours. Ages. I'm barely conscious when they come home, screaming and shouting and racing up the stairs. Someone shakes me. Tries to talk.

But I still can't move.

I can't speak.

I just exist, trapped within a cocoon of pain.

I wish I could say that it is an awful way to feel—more than enough of a reason to never go back to Maxim Koslov. But the truth is…I've never felt more at peace.

Never.

FEAR IS A FUNNY FUCKING THING. Three days without him is like someone spending the same amount of time wide awake. It's fine at first—hypothetically speaking. You regain the energy your nightmares sucked out of you. You might even feel hopeful—maybe you won't have them anymore. Maybe this is the start of something different.

A brand-new day.

A brand-new reality.

But as the hours wear on, each second steals a little more of your sanity away. The worries you can't escape gnaw at your psyche like buzzing flies, growing louder and louder. Eating you up.

Money. Money. Money. Moneymoneymoneymoney.

You sing yourself that tired old lullaby, but the sleep doesn't come. Your eyes stay open, seeing every goddamn thing with no shadows to block it out. You can only find snatches of peace again when you doze off, pinching yourself, cutting yourself. Slicing your inner thighs open for one taste of clarity.

But it never lasts no matter how desperately you chase it like an addict begging for a high. You even begin to crave it. The silence. The freedom. The fear. Suffering through a nightmare starts to look better and better in contrast to the thought of having to go another hour painfully aware.

Then finally, you nod off and the nightmare takes over, flickering around the edges of your conscience. It swallows you up before you even realize you've fallen asleep.

And you begin to understand that the only thing more terrifying than the monster you find lurking within it is the fact that…

You've missed it all along.

Because the fear feels more familiar than anything else.

A BLACK CAR comes for me on the third day at the ass crack of dawn, right after the kids have left for school. I have a frying pan in my hand, in the middle of scraping burnt eggs out of it from Daisy's attempt to cook breakfast.

The moment I happen to glance out the window, it falls out of my hand, landing over my left foot, and I can't even cry out. I just move. It's like my body's on autopilot. I grab the suitcase waiting by the front door and snatch up the envelope sticking out of it for the first time. It's heavy. I wind up shoving most of the cash into my stash with a note for Mikie to use it while I'm gone.

Before I head out, I make sure to slip the cell phone into my pocket, and I already have the front door open by the time Lucius mounts the top step leading to the porch.

"Ms. Marconi," he says with a nod. "Mr. Koslov is ready for you, should you choose to return." He pauses as if he's waiting for something, not actually climbing the last step to reach me.

He expects me to say no.

But I say, "Yes." My hands shake as I drag the suitcase behind me, close the door, and lock it.

Lucius only stops to take my suitcase from me and pack it into the trunk before ushering me into the back seat.

The driver takes off. My heart starts to beat again and the sleepy feeling that clouded my thoughts for three damn days eases up.

I *wake* up.

It's a rude, violent return to awareness.

The first coherent thought to cross my brain is, *What am I doing?*

Far too soon, Maxim's high-rise appears on the horizon before I can figure out an answer to that question. I'll go with the safe option: *money.* That's right. I'm here for the money. Nothing else. No one else. The money. Money, money, money, money.

"Ms. Marconi?"

The car's stopped. Lucius is standing out on the curb, holding the door open for me. I swallow hard and follow him out before he can voice the question lingering in his eyes: *Are you sure?*

"You'll meet him alone today," he explains instead after retrieving my suitcase from the trunk and gingerly placing the handle in my grip. "His request."

Something about that wording makes me flinch. It takes me a second to regain control of my body, but I'm still numb when I start forward, toward the main doors of the building. Somehow, I manage to pass through them without turning back. I reach the elevator the same way and ride it up. It comes to a stop way too soon, leaving me no choice but to cautiously approach the lone entrance at the end of the hallway.

My fingers curl into a fist, but I don't even have to knock. I'm just inches away when it flies open to reveal the monster lurking behind it, his hair hanging loose to frame his face, his eyes darker than I remember.

"It's *you*. Lucius didn't say…" His mouth twists into that dangerous frown of confusion as he beckons me closer with a wave of his hand. "Strip."

The fact that there is no one else around somehow makes the command seem more degrading. My heart starts to pound, hammering against my rib cage. To stall, I lean my suitcase against the wall and unbutton my jacket first, which I borrowed from Daisy. Before I have to wonder what to do with it, Maxim holds his hand out.

His fingers clench the fabric, bringing one of the sleeves to his nose. "This doesn't belong to you," he declares after a sharp inhale. Then he tosses it away, somewhere inside the suite. His eyes seize on my shirt next. It's Melanie's, tight and low-cut the way she likes. On me, it's shapeless, and it doesn't take much effort to slip it off, over my head.

Dark eyes track my every movement, and I shiver. Go fucking figure. Almost a year of fucking strangers should have hammered into my own psyche that I'm no delicate, innocent little flower. *He* does this to me, breaking every single wall I've built up simply by impatiently flexing his fingers. My teeth start to skewer my lower lip as I hand the shirt over, and he sniffs that item as well. Frowns. Tosses it.

"The rest," he commands.

I strip down to nothing while he observes every piece of me. My pants next. My bra. My sneakers. Finally panties.

Those he inhales more than once, grinding the fabric between his fingers, growling at whatever he senses. Whatever he tastes. "These belong to you," he tells me before balling them into a fist and shoving them into his pocket. "Come."

He steps aside and I follow him into the suite, shivering as he closes the door behind me.

The layout hasn't changed. It's just as dark. Just as cold. Just as perfectly clean as ever. Though on second thought, the couch is off-center by a hair. There's a dent in the middle, so slight that no one would ever notice it. But I do.

"You're shaking." Warm fingers graze the length of my spine before fanning out along my collarbone. "Having your regrets already?"

I want to say yes. Regret. I *need* to feel that. It would be better than this. This ache. This itch I don't know how to scratch.

One of my thumbs inches toward a cut on my wrist and rubs until the skin burns. The brief sting does nothing to clear my head, and Maxim frowns when I don't answer.

"Are you that desperate to earn more money for yourself, *kotyonok*?" He cups my chin, forcing me to meet his gaze.

I nod. It's the only thing I can do.

In response, he flashes that dangerous half-smile. "How much are you worth?"

We both already know the answer. After all, he said it himself.

"Sixteen thousand." I have to drag the words out. It sounds like such a pathetic number when said out loud. Even Melanie would have a higher price tag. "Sixteen—"

"Enough." His thumb presses down over my mouth, sealing my lips shut. "I will not fuck you tonight," he tells me, easily switching topics as his eyes drift down my naked torso. "Not while you smell like—" He leans in and sniffs— a dangerous omen. I'm left paralyzed as his features quickly twist into that terrifying trifecta: narrowed eyes, crooked frown, and slightly clenched jaw. "*This.*"

It's a sin in his world: smelling like burned eggs, and toast, and tears, and crayon wax, along with Ainsley's vomit from two nights ago when she ate too much pizza and threw up. Like life. Like reality. Free from him.

"I need to wash you," he adds. It's a lethal promise. A threat. One that tightens around my throat like a noose as he turns and heads down the hallway, commanding with his posture alone that I follow. He doesn't lead me to the bathroom attached to my room, but into another I know instinctively to be *his.*

It's bigger. The floors are granite, the walls polished wood. A massive bathtub is sunken into the center of the floor—the kind of thing Daisy would kill for, lined in black marble and adorned by silver fixtures that sparkle like knives.

"Get in." He jerks his chin toward a series of steps built into the sides of the tub.

I reach the middle of it by the time he switches the water on and it pours in like a waterfall from a single faucet.

"Sit," he snaps.

I do, tucking my calves beneath me so that I'm on my knees, facing his direction. A heartbeat later, warm water laps at my hips. Too warm. Scalding.

Maxim just watches as steam bubbles up and my skin turns red. It's like I'm boiling alive, and it's not even the temperature of the water that's doing it. It's the look in his eyes. For a rare, brief moment, the man is an open book: He didn't want me to come back. At the same time, he never really thought I would.

I guess he expected to train a new toy tonight, and that forces him to compile a new lesson for me on the fly. His thumb drifts up to stroke his chin as he thinks. After a second, he frowns—a bad fucking sign. Whatever he's come up with could probably be summed up in one word: *punishing.*

Once the water reaches my stomach, he shuts it off and approaches my end of the tub, seemingly satisfied. Relief creeps into my muscles as he removes his boots and tosses them aside. His socks go next. Finally, he rolls each pant leg up to reveal the toned calves underneath and then enters the tub, sloshing water with every step.

"Give me your hands."

My throat contracts with a frantic swallow. His voice... It's too deep. Too soft. My brain has no input as my body reacts solely on instinct. I wrench my hands into the air, extending my arms toward him.

Slowly, his fingers entwine within his belt loops, working the strip of leather loose. I'm unprepared for just how roughly he wraps the length of it around my wrists. It's like he wants me to feel every variation in the leather—every groove in the surface. My sick mind skips ahead, wondering which end would hurt more if he ever decided to use it like a whip.

The sad part? Something tells me he one day will.

"Keep them like that." Grunting, he pulls the ends so tight that I lose sensation in the tips of my fingers as the leather bites in. But the physical pain doesn't even come close to whatever I feel as I watch him cut a lazy path through the water to snatch a rag from a marble countertop.

When he returns, he snaps the length of it into the air to command my attention. Once. Twice. While I watch, he wets the end of it in the water and drags it along the tops of my shoulders, bathing me of everything that isn't him.

"I'm disappointed," he tells me once he sees the scabbed-over marks his teeth left on my breasts. The fingers of his other hand trace one of them, pressing down on the skin hard enough to make it bleed. "You heal too quickly."

If only that were true. My skin feels nothing but raw as the rag travels to the worst of the injuries. Rubbing. Twisting. Ripping them open again until the draining water turns pink. Red. I'm already gagging on smothered cries when he lowers the rag, swiping my hip in scarlet, painting me with my own blood. Marking me as his.

Finally, the cloth slips from his fingers and splashes somewhere beside me. I almost think it's over. That I'm clean enough to satisfy him. But he's still frowning as he scans my torso.

"Open." He curls his thumb against my lower lip, using it to pry both apart when I don't obey fast enough.

One-handed, he undoes the clasp of his pants and slowly peels his boxers down like a magician in one of those TV shows building up to his final and most mind-fucking trick. Watching me like this—bleeding, bound—has made him harder than I've ever seen him. Or maybe it's the fear he's breathing in from my skin. The knowledge that I know, deep down, coming here, back to him, was wrong.

"I'll make this quick," he tells me, cradling my jaw in one of his massive hands.

I'm not sure why he warns me, though I brace myself anyway, and he doesn't hold back, seeking out the tightness of my throat on the first thrust.

Four days of rest and silence weren't enough to prepare me to take him. My throat closes up, my gag reflex going haywire with every forced inch of me he claims. His eyes glow brighter at the resistance, his touch harsher. Brutal fingers rake through my hair and gather chunks of it to control every bit of him I'm allowed to take—and how much I have to swallow.

All of it.

Too much. My nose starts to burn. He's in too far. Too long. I can't breathe, so I choke, feeling warm, salty wetness trickle from my nostrils before he finally tugs himself away, grunting with the effort.

"I told you not to lose a single drop," he warns.

There's no use in trying to explain. My body has become his tool. His *weapon,* betraying me just to get a rise out of him.

A literal rise. I don't know how it's even possible. Maybe he was never really finished after all. He's still hard, straining, erect. He doesn't take his eyes off me, even as both of his hands grip the base of his shaft. He tugs. Strokes. My face heats up as I turn away, staring down at the reddish water instead.

"No," he growls. So I have no choice but to look up. Stare. Watch.

He handles himself roughly—almost as roughly as he handles me. He grinds his fingers along the underside before making long, brutal strokes with his fist. I jump as my pussy clenches in sympathy. Sympathy…

"This excites you. Watching me?" He makes it sound like a question, but there is no right answer.

Once again, I've confused him. I shake my head, and he frowns as his fingers slow their assault.

"Stand up."

It takes me five tries to without slipping on the bottom of the tub. Once I'm on my feet, Maxim approaches slowly, still stroking his cock.

"Is that so?" His free hand reaches between my legs, tracing the outer rim of me along the damp, dripping skin. *That's* the only reason why I'm wet down there—the water.

As if to prove me wrong, he curls a finger, stepping in closer, teasing my entrance with it. He's almost gentle at first, grazing the skin in a featherlight sweep. I don't even expect the moment he rams the entire digit in too deep. Too easily. God, I can feel his nails contrasting with the thicker shape of his knuckles. The sound he grits out into my ear as he feels me quiver beneath his touch? It's inhuman.

The next second, my trembling knees are forced to support my weight alone as he steps back. I lose my balance and land sideways at the edge of the tub. My nose is in water, sucking in a lungful. I can't even move before my hair is used like a leash: first to push me down, then to yank me upright and shove my body against the steps.

My vision clears and I find him hovering above me. The look in his eye issues the command he doesn't say out loud. My legs spring apart as he palms his cock and grinds the tip through my pussy, rubbing me open.

"Wait." I gasp at the air, struggling to form words. "I thought—"

One brutal thrust sends water sloshing around us. Warmth sears through my pussy, but nowhere near as deep as it should. I glance down and see why: he only managed to fit a fraction of himself inside me.

"You don't think," he tells me, lifting my hips from the water so he can ram in another inch, so hard that I see stars and shadow. White. Black. Yellow fucking fireworks. "You never think. Not while you are with me—"

Another thrust and my eyes roll back. I swear I can see the inside of my skull, my brains being whisked to mush.

"*I* think. You listen. You obey. You feel."

Feel...

I wish he would just fuck me—I could survive that. I could keep my brain intact the way I have with any other man. Any other john. I knew how to save myself, just as long as I *couldn't* feel.

But he's on a mission to destroy me. Sex is a tool to him; he controls every touch, the same way he beats sculptures out of stone. The only difference is how he speaks with every battering thrust, growling the words in a language I don't understand. Sentences. Phrases. God, they sound like promises. Brutal, lethal promises. And then he switches to English.

"…string you up. Make you regret. So tight," he grits out in a throaty rasp. "Fuck, so fucking greedy. *Too* tight." His thumb catches the top of me, rubbing, pinching.

Fuck. Sparks shoot through my body. My knees bend, inching closer to his waist, hugging him, sensing the ripples of every muscle as he drives himself in. In. In. Deep. Deeper. I can't breathe. My body turns into a vise, wrapped around him, tightening.

"You're coming," Maxim hisses before biting my neck in punishment, drawing a noise from me I can't classify. "Without permission."

Thwack! The flat of his hand flies out to strike my hip so hard that sparks dance before my eyes. I'm going to bruise, and the added pain hijacks whatever reaction had started inside me. I grit my teeth against a scream. It's too tense. Too hot.

"You will come when I say you can." He wrenches himself out and flips me over, forcing me up onto my hands and knees.

In this position, he goes even *deeper*. Harder. The friction doesn't just burn—it sets me on fucking fire. I inhale the flames, mindless and numb as my body explodes around me.

But he never lets me fall over the edge. Just when my thoughts start to clear, another slap stings my hip. My ass. A nip on my shoulder. A pinch. A deeper bite. He anticipates every hit of clarity my body seems to be chasing and slaps it away, further out of reach.

I'm on the edge. I can't possibly feel any more swollen and greedy. But he pulls out right when my inner muscles start to spasm and drags me by my hair over to the sink.

"Look at yourself." He's strong enough to cup my hips and lift me right off the floor, spreading my legs so that I can see our reflection in the mirror. His straining cock weeps from the tip, dusky and swollen. The pink flesh it aims for doesn't look anywhere near wide enough to take all of him though. He's too damn big. "Watch." He jerks his hips and sinks inside me anyway. Up this close, I can see his muscles cord as he works his way in, battering through any resistance. "Watch your face change," he growls into my shoulder as I bite a cry back. "Those fucking greedy eyes."

I look away, staring at the floor when I feel another slap on my hip.

"*Look.*"

The woman he's fucking is a goddamn whore. Her brown eyes are glazed over. Her mouth is open, releasing tiny gasps as her body jerks back and forth. She's too pale. Too needy. Too desperate. When I look into her eyes, she's not thinking about money.

When he's in to the hilt, my arms go limp, and without the support, my cheek hits the counter. I lie here, letting him ride me. Use me. Fuck the living shit out of me. Too much. Not enough. I'm shaking, my mouth watering, my toes curling.

Maxim is all I know. Inside me. Around me. Huge, relentless, and powerful.

"Beg for it, *kotyonok*," he commands before I even know what it is my body seeks. It craves it. Needs it. If he doesn't —if I don't—I'll go insane.

My inner muscles clench down, gripping him so hard that I feel every pulsing ridge of his length, every strained and throbbing vein. All of it slammed up inside me.

All mine.

"Fuck, not yet." He punishes me with his full weight, bearing down, ramming in before I can savor a full dose of clarity. "Beg."

"Please—"

His hips swivel, and this new pain takes me higher than the fucking ceiling. Higher than any hit of heroin or cocaine. So damn high I won't ever come back down.

Ruthless, Maxim sinks his nails into my hips, extending the pain, making me float. "I need to hear you say it."

Hearing him *need* anything from me—it shatters my mind. My soul. I'm pieces of a person falling at his feet, and he shoves them back together however he sees fit. Any control

I had fucking disintegrates. A stranger takes over my throat.

"Please, please, please—"

"Please what?" He pets me, running his hand along my hair. The gentleness contrasts with his next bruising thrust. I'm a rag doll at his mercy, cherished and abused all at once. "Speak to me. Beg. *Umolyat.*"

"Let me come."

He bellows out more words I don't understand while using his thumb to reach between us. Flicking. Rubbing.

Shit.

My back bows, arching my hips into him, riding him, every last thrust. I can't speak. Can't moan. Can't move. I suffer his invasion. I let him break me into pieces. When he comes, the pressure spills over as he yells out, biting into my shoulder. I scream. Sob. Whimper.

And then all sound dies off as he jerks inside me, spilling everything he has left to give. So much. Never enough.

I'm numb when he pulls out, leaving a warm, thick trail down my inner thigh. Only now does it strike me that he didn't wear a condom.

"*This* is how it will be from now on, *kotyonok*," he tells me, his voice gruff as he uses his grip on my hair as leverage to pull himself upright. "I am clean."

I'm not brave enough to even question that.

Other fears cloud my thoughts, washing away the oblivion he fucked me into. Like the fact that I'm not even sure if I'm up to date on birth control—the one selfish thing I always tried to save money for. "I'm not—"

"I had you injected with a serum on your last night here," he says. He looks at me expectantly, and I have to assume he means some kind of contraception. "It is effective in only a few days. You will not get pregnant. That is the one thing you never have to worry about me inflicting upon you."

He steps away from me, his cock somehow still semi-hard, and I don't know what shocks me more. The raw *pain* in his voice? Or the fact that he had me injected with a hormone-altering drug without my permission? *Or* the fact that he came inside me and I'm not disgusted. I don't *feel* disgusting.

Just exhausted. Sore. Empty.

"Don't break on me now."

I feel his breath on my neck, his fingers gliding through my hair. He grabs a lock of it and tugs my head until I face him from over my shoulder.

"You aren't finished yet." He nods to his cock, which is still glistening.

Oh. I suck in air to find the strength to sink to my knees, twisting around.

He palms his cock with one hand, angling the tip of it toward my mouth. "Clean me off. Every last drop."

I part my lips, creeping closer on my hands and knees. Watching me, he narrows his eyes, his breaths coming faster. Harder. I don't swallow him whole this time. I lick. Every drop. Every bitter, strange, musky flavor that coats him.

He lets me work quickly without having to savor—for now. His posture doesn't relax until my tongue captures the very last drop. By then, he's already erect again, dripping precum from the swollen head.

"That's enough." He runs his fingers through my hair, pushing me away from him as his fingers curl around his shaft, stroking it again.

I just stare as a tortured groan builds up in his chest. His knuckles turn white and his cock jerks, spraying cum into the air. On me. I know better than to flinch away. I just sit here on my knees and take every last spurt, letting him paint me with them. Mark me.

He growls when the final drop splatters my chin, satisfied, and adjusts his pants, redoing the clasp. "*Now,* you are clean," he tells me, snapping his fingers for me to stand.

When I do, he removes the belt and leads me to the door of my bedroom. The moment he opens it, I know that something has changed. The bed is still there beneath the black canopy, the white sheets neatly made. But attached to each post of the bed frame itself are four black strips of leather secured by delicate silver strings.

Chains.

CHAPTER ELEVEN

M axim approaches the bed and gently thumbs one of the straps open. It looks like a bracelet: a bracelet with a metal clasp.

"Come here."

I have no choice but to step toward him, swaying on my feet. I can't tear my eyes away as he lifts the cuff, allowing me to see every inch: the silver buckles to lock it shut, the silken lining, the sturdy, ebony leather around the outside.

"Lie down."

The mattress creaks beneath my weight, definitely softer than before. The slight change proves more than anything that this bed was rarely used for fucking in the past. One night and our bodies have already made an impression in the padding.

"Lie back."

Impatient, Maxim arranges me himself when I don't move quickly enough. He pushes me down and steers my ankles toward the foot of the bed. When he seizes the wrist closer to him, he secures it into a cuff, snapping it tight. He moves toward the ankle next and binds it too, his jaw clenched in concentration while his seed dries over my skin. When the other ankle is secure, he finally turns his attention to my last remaining limb. I sense his hulking shape from the corner of my eye, watching me writhe as much as the bindings will allow.

He curls his fingers around my free wrist and lifts it. "You so much as think about getting free and you will be punished," he tells me as his thumb brushes the back of my hand. "You will wait for me, until I return. You will think of me. Only me. Do you understand, *kotyonok*?"

"Y-yes." I have to force the word out.

Maxim grunts, unconvinced. His fingers lift my chin, tilting my head back against the soft pillow beneath it. "This is not punishment," he says softly, nodding to my outstretched limbs. "This is a gift. I want you to savor how good it feels to be clean."

I hear him drift down the hallway, his footsteps steady and sure. Hours pass, though I sense him wandering the rooms of the suite: eating, sculpting, doing whatever else it is he does as the hours trickle away deep into the night. My muscles are already cramping from misuse when I finally sense him approach my door again—but he continues past it, toward that room at the very end of the hall.

Left without a distraction, my mind plays a dangerous game; it pictures him inside that lifeless, black room. How he might strip down in the silence and climb into the massive bed alone. Oddly enough, I can't imagine him actually sleeping. Just waiting, lurking beneath the covers.

Fear alone doesn't explain why my stomach bunches into knots at the thought of it. His body vulnerable, his eyes shut, that face set like a statue's.

My loose hand twitches, the fingers flinching against my stomach. He told me to think of him—only him. By the time I lose sensation in my toes, I'm in danger of breaking that one rule.

I have to pee. So badly that my stomach hurts, my legs straining against the cuffs, desperate to clamp together. I know better than to wet the bed. The only way to buy more time is to use my fingers, sliding them down between my legs, rubbing the flesh of my pussy.

Only like this can I remember my task: think of Maxim. Just him. Only him. Nearby. Around me. Inside me. Always.

But the wrong reaction takes over; the air I breathe in becomes laced with gasoline. Every touch is a match, fanning the flames higher. I writhe, trapped and helpless, a slave to the motions of my hand. It's like I can hear him inside my head, commanding me, taunting me.

Only me, kotyonok. Only me...

I gasp as the doorknob to my room twitches—then the door flies open. A monster draped in shadow lurks behind it. His eyes hone in on mine, bathed in the glow of the hallway as he inhales sharply, tasting me on the air.

I drop my hand, but it's too fucking late.

Muscles ripple beneath his skin as he steps forward, his fingers flexing. "I said you could think," he tells me softly. "I never said you could touch what is *mine* without permission."

Fear paralyzes me. I just lie here, staring up at the ceiling beyond his head as he approaches. I don't dare look at him directly. I can't.

"Do you need something from me?"

The question makes me flinch as his nails tease my tender flesh. Need… My pussy clenches.

"I—"

"Spit it out," he scolds, but the anger isn't there. He almost sounds amused.

"I have to use the bathroom."

He nods and turns toward the cuffs on my ankles. I hold my breath as he slowly—*slowly*—undoes the clasps on the right one before deliberately moving over to the next.

"Give me your hand."

I raise my free wrist, but my stomach drops when he lifts the empty cuff. I know better than to argue, even as my bladder threatens to rip its way out of my stomach. He snaps the latch closed, but then his fingers grab the chain, following it all the way to the nearest post of the bed frame. I crane my neck to watch him unhook the loop securing it, using the free length like a leash. He lets it fall and dangle beside me over the edge of the bed. Then he casually strolls around to the other end and does the same to the opposite cuff.

"Up, *kotyonok*."

I can't scramble to the edge of the bed fast enough. I stand on throbbing legs, but I hesitate to move without permission. Permission he doesn't give, not even when I sense him beside me, his breath heavy on my neck.

"Put your arms behind your back."

I obey, wincing as they throb at the awkward angle. Cold metal brushes my hip as he gathers up the dangling chains, linking them together before grabbing the loose end. "Come."

He nudges me toward the bathroom and watches me sit on the toilet. Just when I'm about to let my body relax, he shakes his head…and then leaves the room.

I never knew my body could be in this much pain. My eyes sting, filling up with moisture no matter how quickly I blink it back. I curl my toes, kicking them against the floor. My nails claw at my wrists. Control. *Control.* I need to keep it.

But that's impossible. Maxim has all of it.

He doesn't go far, just into the bedroom before the closet. I can see his shadow sway against the wall as he thumbs through clothing and shifts hangers. When he finally returns and nods, I nearly cry with relief.

The desperation to pee is enough to wash away the embarrassment of having him watch. Having him listen. When I'm finally finished, he comes up beside the toilet and gestures for me to stand. I expect him to unhook at least one of my wrists so that I can wipe myself.

Instead, he does it for me, snatching a wad of toilet paper and dragging it between my legs without warning. Once. Twice. There's nothing sexual in his touch, which somehow makes it worse. Once done, he flushes it and washes his hands in the sink.

"Kneel," he tells me, jerking his chin toward the tub.

This one is smaller than the other. There's only enough room for me to sit lengthwise, so I tuck my knees beneath my chin. He runs the water lukewarm this time, letting it get as high as my breasts.

I don't know what to expect when he leaves me here and returns with a rag and a bar of soap. It smells: spicy, flowery. Roses?

I don't ask and he doesn't say a word as he runs the rag over my skin, cleaning every inch of me. My back, my shoulders, my belly, my hands, my face. He even wets my hair, combing it with his fingers before lathering it up with shampoo. As the water drains from the tub, he towels me dry while I sit on the edge of it. Then he dresses me in the clothing I assume he got from the closet.

I can tell, even before he begins to drag a pair of black, lace panties up my legs, that these items aren't like the others. They've never been worn. They don't carry any other smell. Just his. Just mine.

The bra matches the panties—black lace—and I find myself staring down at it as he adjusts the straps. I've never owned a full set of underwear before. Not one cut from the same cloth, tailored to fit only me. It's not really a good feeling to know that I'm the first one to wear these clothes, including the red sleeveless blouse and the black skirt he dresses me in next. It's like being the first convict to sit in a brand-new electric chair.

More people will come after me. Even as the various pieces are tightened to fit my body, it's not out of love or kindness. I won't ever own a single goddamn stitch.

"Stand, *kotyonok*."

When I do, he directs me over to the mirror and somehow finds a brush to tackle my hair with. He's surprisingly gentle —surprisingly good. He tames my damp, wild curls in no time and slicks them back to reveal my bruised, bitten neck. I'm stupid enough to breathe out a sigh of relief when he finally unhooks the cuffs from my wrists and leaves them open on the sink.

It isn't until I follow him out into the living room of the suite and spot the black box resting on the couch that I realize my mistake. It's square, with a red ribbon draped over the top. Maxim opens it for me, displaying a dark leather circle on a scarlet pillow within. A chain of gold dangles from a hook set in the center of what looks like a longer cuff at first.

Make that a collar.

"Raise your chin." He lifts the collar and sets the box aside. He loops the leather around the back of my throat, fastening the clasp without tearing his eyes from mine. "Beautiful." He steps back, fingering the length of golden chain. It nearly reaches my waist, swaying back and forth with every move I make.

"Come." He starts for the entrance of the suite, pulling the door open as I stagger at his heels. When I'm close enough, he snags the length of golden chain to steer me after him. There is no one in the hall beyond his suite to witness or in the private stairwell he takes to the garage.

Once we reach that infamous black car, he ushers me into the passenger's seat this time, fastening the seat belt over my chest. I just stare as he circles around the car and takes the wheel, sitting tall in the driver's seat.

It's overcast and dreary, I see once he pulls out onto the street. Rain falls, splattering the windshield, creating a strange, muted backdrop as the car drifts through the thick of traffic. He never switches the radio on. Never speaks. The silence seems to suit him just fine, so I take his lead and keep quiet.

I try not to wonder where we're going—keyword being *try*. Dread sinks in any way, making my throat contract against the collar as my breathing picks up speed. Wherever he's headed, it's out of the city, over a bridge. I watch the buildings grow progressively smaller and then disappear altogether. In the blink of an eye, we go through a tunnel and enter a world of shadow and trees. Swaths of land pass by, but after maybe twenty minutes, Maxim turns onto a deserted stretch of road, following it deeper into the woods —though, despite all appearances, this place doesn't seem too far off the beaten path. The road is paved, for one, and the farther down it we go, the less untamed the wilderness seems and more beaten into submission.

I don't know what to make of it all until I finally catch sight of a structure at the top of a hill. I must gasp or make some other noise, because I sense Maxim's gaze on the skin of my throat.

"You are impressed, *kotyonok*," he says with the hint of a laugh.

Maybe I am: a building rises from the foliage as if formed from the shadows. Given that, before this, my idea of *classy* consisted of the nicest department store in the mall, I don't have many words to describe it. Just that it's big. Beautiful. Foreboding—the shiver racing through my body insists on that part. Made of black stone, the place resembles a mansion, but I doubt that its true purpose is just as someone's home. Maybe it's the way Maxim is dressed: a sleek black suit and a blood-red tie. I doubt he's on his way to a house call.

So it's not *just* a mansion. With every inch we travel toward it, its silhouette looms bigger, square in appearance when seen from the front. I think it's at least three stories, stretching nearly double that length over the expanse of the hill. If Dracula suddenly developed Maxim's flair for sleek, modern design, he'd probably build this place. Turrets twist at the sky, while huge glass windows reflect the muted backdrop of the forest, adding hints of emerald to the ebony façade.

The entrance, by far, is the most breathtakingly elegant thing I've ever seen. It makes the front of his high-rise look like a shack, no better than mine. Stone columns frame a black door, its edges trimmed in gold. A path made of dark stone leads to it before forking into a massive circular driveway. Maxim stops the car in the center of it, and a man dressed in black comes from nowhere to take his keys and drive it off, presumably to park.

"Come." When Maxim takes the length of my chain, I don't have a choice but to follow him up to the front of the mansion and then inside.

Three adjectives march across my brain to describe what I see: Impressive. Breathtaking. Clean. Make that four, as a shiver dances down my spine and conjures up another term: *Cold.*

The entrance reminds me of him in every way, from the granite floors to the steel-gray walls. The design holds the same layer of icy intimidation. Three silver Xs placed above a curving archway across from the entrance don't provide any clue as to what this place represents. Neither do the two other archways composing the rest of the circular space, each leading off into different directions. Left. Right. Forward. I can't see much of either path: just darkness stretching on.

"This way." Using my chain like a leash, Maxim leads me through the right one and into a room with an open floor plan.

I blink, taking in every inch. A long ebony-topped bar dominates one end, and an L-shaped stage divides the room in half on the other. Crowning the space is a row of floor-to-ceiling windows overlooking what seems to be the valley down below.

The decor reminds me of his suite: black leather with bright drops of blood-red accents. Circular tables cover a corner of the room, though the place seems mostly empty except for a few men milling about, dressed in dark-colored suits meant to blend into the shadows. My mind skips ahead, picturing this place once night falls. It would make for one hell of a club—the kind I certainly wouldn't want to sneak into though.

"Come." With a sigh, Maxim pads over to a table nearest the windows and sits, resting his head back against the top of a leather chair. "Sit, *kotyonok*." He nods to his knee.

I mount him, facing the rest of the room, feeling unseen eyes on me. On him. Just by being here, this man commands the entire space. At the same time, he demands privacy and not one member of our audience is brave enough to break it. He's almost like the sun: You know he's there, though you know better than to look at him directly.

You'll go fucking blind.

"Relax." His thumb curls around the length of my chain before I even register tensing up, drawing me into him so that I feel the contours of his chest against my back. His breath tickles my shoulder, heavy and spiced. "I will not be long. I just have some business to attend to." His tone doesn't have the hard edge I'm used to.

So fuck it. I take a risk and lick my lips until I'm brave enough to spit out a question. "Is...is this where you work?"

"Work?" Another chuckle rumbles from his chest, jolting my body with the aftermath. "*Kotyonok*, this is where I *play*."

As if on cue, someone new enters the room, briefcase in hand. Lucius. He's wearing gray today, a shade that almost blends in perfectly with the floor. When he spots me on Maxim's lap, he nods in greeting. "Sir. Ms. Marconi."

Maxim waves his hand through the air, dismissing the pleasantries. "Do you have the reports?"

As he approaches the table, Lucius flips the briefcase open, pulling the contents out for Maxim's inspection. Folders—a lot of them. "It's as you suspected..." He trails off, his eyes flickering in my direction.

Maxim nods, though I sense it rather than see it. "Go on."

"Someone's tipping off the Xi syndicate to the distribution channels. They're there at our every turn, destroying what little inventory they don't steal. And that's not all." His breaks off again. "Perhaps it's better if—"

"I said you can speak freely, Lucius." The teasing pull on my collar becomes a violent tug. My head flies back, striking Maxim's shoulder. I don't even think he realizes how tightly he's pulling. I wheeze. My eyes sting, forced to blink up at the ceiling from this angle.

"Levoi Malkov demanded an audience with you," Lucius says flatly. "Tonight."

All of a sudden, the pressure on my throat lets up and I nearly slide off Maxim's lap as my lungs flood with oxygen. My hand flies to my neck, which is throbbing.

"That's quite the word to use," Maxim says, rubbing his chin. "*Demanded.*"

I can't name the emotion lurking inside his tone. My nerves spark, my muscles tensing up in warning.

"I know." Lucius sighs again and runs a hand over his bald head. "I've tried to explain that you are busy, but he *insists*—"

"He knows something," Maxim says, clasping his big hands together, leaving me just a sliver of space to remain on his lap. "Three hits on my distribution in three days. That bastard knows something."

Lucius nods. "And you can be sure that your grandfather is aware of every minor hiccup, as well."

Maxim stands. I fall. My knees strike the floor as I scramble for balance. I know better than to move, even before I feel the solid, unmistakable nudge of his boot against my neck.

"Stay down," he tells me, applying just enough pressure to make my hands shake as they struggle to support my weight.

Just when my wrists feel like they're on the verge of giving out, he withdraws his foot, but doesn't move. I can see the shape of him from the corner of my eye: rigid, hard. It's like watching a tornado swirl to life right in front of my goddamn face.

"Where?"

I hear Lucius ruffle through loose papers. "I'm not sure—"

"Make it be here." Maxim storms across the room like a living, breathing bolt of lightning, sending anyone and anything racing out of his path.

Lucius follows him, and seconds later, shouting echoes off the walls—Maxim—followed by softer, stern murmurs. They talk for what feels like hours while I just sit here, kneeling. My kneecaps throb. My toes feel smashed in their heels. I don't know how much longer I can take this before Maxim finally returns.

"Come," he says to me, reclaiming the seat he left behind. He flicks his fingers when I don't move fast enough, and I scramble onto his lap. Lucius is gone, but Maxim takes his time flipping through the stacks of paperwork he brought. His *sweet* time. Hours. My eyelids are drooping by the time he finally nudges me with his elbow, prompting me to stand. "Come."

I follow him across the room, limping as blood returns to my limbs. More people are here now, rushing about like workers, carrying trays, pouring drinks behind the counter. Around the bar is a hallway stretching back into what seems to be another section of the house. Closed doors line most of it from what I can tell. Maxim stops at one of them, pulling it open to reveal a small room with gray walls. A vanity sits at one end, beside a wooden wardrobe. Some sort of dressing room?

To strengthen that suspicion, Maxim leads me over to the vanity and makes me sit on a tiny black stool before the mirror. Then he heads for the closet, fishing out a length of scarlet material; a dress.

Silently, I pull my current outfit off and let him dress me. I expect the new gown to feel borrowed or loose—but it fits. Too well, and that's not all. Unlike the clothing I found in the closet in my room, this dress has never been worn. As with my current outfit, there is no other scent—just mine.

"Look at me," Maxim commands before I can focus too much on the implications of what that means. He runs his fingers through my hair, frowning. Then he unpins the curls altogether, letting them fall down to my shoulders. "You're from Horn Hill," he says, naming the notorious strip of the city. It's not a question—he knows my address.

For whatever reason, he wants me to acknowledge as much out loud.

"Yes."

"A slum," he says, still adjusting my hair. He teases a single lock, twisting it around his finger. "Maybe that explains it."

Again, his pause feels expectant. He's waiting for me to fill in the blanks.

"Explains what?" I croak.

"Don't pretend you don't know." With a calculated focus, he tucks that stray piece of hair behind my ear. "It explains your familiarity with violence. Such as why I beat a man half to death in front of you and yet—even days later—you haven't asked me about it. Or why you ignore what I *know* you can sense about me."

His suspicions conjure up a million examples. Like the day he attacked someone with a chisel for no apparent reason. Or the mystery around his name—such as why Benny seemed relieved that I'd never heard of it—and Lucius' mention of a strict nondisclosure agreement.

I swallow hard but an icy dread continues to crawl up my throat. "D-Do you want me to?"

His jaw clenches. I've said the wrong thing. "I mean—"

"It is smart that you haven't," he says over me. "Almost *too* smart. Anyone else would have run by now. Look."

He guides my gaze up to my reflection in the mirror and it's easy to allow myself to be distracted. I don't recognize the bitch staring back at me now. She looks like a doll—and not the flawless, porcelain kind. She looks like one of Ainsley's after Eric has gotten his hands on them. Roughed up and glassy-eyed, wearing a pretty dress that doesn't match.

"Beautiful," Maxim says gruffly, one of his rare compliments, but his eyes are on my hands, scabbed-over and bruised.

When we reenter the main room, darkness has already consumed the horizon and blood-colored lights cast a disturbing glow over the black marble.

In less than an hour, it's been transformed; *now,* the open space resembles a club more than anything. An exclusive one, tailored to the kind of people who aren't surprised to find a man leading a woman around by a leash. Though, to be fair, Maxim could make any sin seem acceptable: wrath, lust, gluttony. As he strolls the floor with a predatory grace, it feels like he's already mastered them all.

CHAPTER TWELVE

Here, his cold smile looks different outside the confines of his suite—it doesn't waver as much. He could almost pass for at ease. At least to those who aren't close enough to feel just how much tension his grip contains.

Tension that *cracks* with every step I take in his shadow.

In the dim lighting, the other people in the room look like blurs decked out in fancy suits—the type of men and women who wouldn't ever give me a second look outside of this place. Filthy fucking *rich*. And, I realize as my gaze falls over a few women wearing outfits no better than mine, filthy fucking *filthy*.

Maybe Maxim's allure rubs off on me, because their eyes flicker in my direction more than once, as they toss him murmured greetings. Too much. With every inch they claim, Maxim's grip on my chain tightens, drawing me to his side. Close. Closer. I don't even think he realizes he's doing it. Not until a guy dressed in black eyes me up and down, his gaze settling over my chest. He smiles at me, and out of habit, my lips flinch limply in return.

Shit. I know, even before I feel the telltale pressure on my throat, that I made a dangerous mistake.

"Look at the floor, *kotyonok*," Maxim murmurs into my ear. "Now."

I dart my gaze to my feet, eyeing the heels he picked for me, nothing else. No one else. Fear churns through my veins like poison—and something sharper. Something I can't fucking name. I don't want to.

Either way, my punishment comes swiftly; his free hand cups my breast, clawing at the fabric and opening the barely healed wounds. I shudder, hypnotized by the sight of his tanned flesh on blood-colored fabric. Stroking. Claiming. Even if I wanted to slap him away, I wouldn't fucking dare. One by one, darker splotches seep through the silk around his touch. It's almost like my body itself is desperate to please him. Even if I have to bleed to do it.

"Look. Only I can give you *this*." His fingers clench, grinding tender flesh between them, and my gasp is drowned out by the sound he grunts in response. One almost too terrifying to classify: low, guttural. A growl.

"Only me, *kotyonok*," he warns as his thumb tugs on the strap of the dress, letting it fall to reveal my nipple. Right in the middle of the room. In front of everyone. While I watch, Maxim's hand tugs at the other strap and in a slow dance of scarlet fabric the whole thing falls to pool at my feet, leaving me naked except for my black panties.

Vulnerable.

Utterly his.

To drill that point in, he makes me stand here, feeling several pairs of eyes on my bared skin. The sad part? There could be millions, but none would pack the punch his nearness does. His possession runs deeper than anything he could tether to my collar.

It's the money.

"Come." He yanks on my chain and I nearly stagger into him as he takes a seat at a leather booth near the stage, pulling me down beside him. On *top* of him. Pulsing, his erection stabs at my ass, barely restrained by the fabric of his pants or the flimsy lace of my panties.

It's not my body that gets him off though. He's thinking of his punishment. *My* punishment. I picture the knife and my thighs clamp tighter together.

Gradually, soft music plays and Maxim's lap becomes a sensual, devastating cage. I have no choice but to either go insane from the isolation or stare from the bars of it.

Elegantly dressed women and men flicker past our table, preening for Maxim's attention, though I avoid looking at any one person directly. The rest of the club seems like the safest bet, and it's an odd mixture of vulgar elegance. Girls dressed in strips of black leather and lace carry wine on trays, circling through the crowd as the night wears on. Overall, it's not a rowdy shithole like the kind I'm used to. It's quiet. A low, dangerous hum seems to permeate everything beneath the casual murmurs and sparse bits of laughter.

The atmosphere makes me feel like I'm in a giant fucking jack-in-the-box. Any second, the ominous music will wind down and something will explode. Maybe Maxim's cock? His fingers find my open wounds again. Every time I flinch, he grows thicker, harder, prodding my lower back. It's a struggle to focus on the rest of the room: silvery spotlights over a brilliant black stage dominated by a single stool. When a woman prances toward it wearing nothing but two piercings through each of her nipples, no one bats an eyelash.

Not even when a larger man with a matching set of piercings climbs onto the stage after her and grabs her hips, positioning her over the black stool in the center of the spotlight. He palms his cock, veiny and throbbing. Aims it between her legs. Thrusts in deep while she howls out a breathy moan.

It's nearly a full minute before my mind accepts what I'm seeing: sex. Violent sex.

"You're uncomfortable," Maxim remarks, his voice low beneath the pulse of the music and the moans of the performers. He doesn't sound concerned. If anything, I've learned to fear the raspy edge to his voice. "Out of everything I've put you through, *this* unsettles you?"

Slowly, his fingers slide from my breast and blaze a trail to my hip, dipping beneath my panties. Rough and assured, he finds my entrance and circles it once. I only manage to suck in a single breath before he plunges inside. "Or *curious*," he grates into my ear, thrusting what feels like a thumb in and out. "Are you, *kotyonok?* Though I don't have to fuck you in such a way for the world to know that you are *mine*. Do I?"

His free hand gestures to the crowd around us, all of whom ignore our corner of the room. Even as I gasp. The power he holds over people—over me—is an entirely new kind of pain, more potent than the brief hits I'm used to. He proposes humiliation, and my body begs for clarity.

"Not that I would be opposed to it."

My mouth goes dry at the mental image: Maxim fucking me senseless in front of everyone. No amount of money in the world would be worth that.

It wouldn't.

"Give me a reason to," he commands against my throat. "One reason."

I know better than to say anything. So I just watch through blurred vision, tortured by the man beneath me. The two actors don't slow down as more people approach the stage and sip their wine as they climb into booths. If anything, they amp up their actions, their grunts and groans competing with the music. They don't care that people are watching—in fact, the audience seems to turn them on *more*.

Which is fucking disgusting. *Disgusting.*

And I don't think I take my eyes off them once.

Excitement and fear mingle in my blood as Maxim keeps a mocking pace, matching every thrust. Every brutal fuck. Hard. Fast. Rough. My thoughts swim, impossible to decipher, as fire trickles through my veins. *Shit.* My eyes flutter, my breath catching in my throat, as I find myself writhing against his hand.

It's sick. God, I wish they'd move *faster.*

"You're early tonight." The unfamiliar voice counters the ache building in my body.

Just like that, I'm slammed back to Earth, slumping against the table. I blink and find a man standing at one end of the booth, casting a shadow that obscures most of his face. He's tall, I know that much before I turn away to eye the wall of the booth. Dark-brown hair gleams in the glow of the lights, matching the color of his elegant suit.

I feel Maxim shrug, his fingers withdrawing, and I risk his wrath to peek out of the corner of my eye.

"I'm *angry* tonight," he says, his teeth flashing in a beautiful, heart-stopping smile.

The man matches the expression, and even though I can't see his face clearly, I can tell his grin is just as chilling. "I can see that," he says, the hint of an accent giving his words a musical edge. *British?* "I gather your friend is aware of our policy?" He inclines his head to me.

Maxim twists his wet fingers through my chain again, just enough to make it harder for me to breathe. "Of course. What about yours?"

The man glances over his shoulder, toward a woman standing a few feet away. She looks younger than I am, but not by much. She's slender, with blond, curled hair, pale-blue eyes, and full lips. Her beauty doesn't erase the darkness in her eyes, highlighted by the black dress clinging to her frame. I guess she's seen as much evil as I have.

"Yes, she knows, all right." There's an underlying meaning to the man's words when he faces Maxim again. The fingers of his left hand fiddle with something on the middle finger of the right: a gleaming bit of metal. A ring? He turns away before I can make it out clearly. "I'll leave you to your fun. I would say try not to make too much of a mess, but I beat you to it already." With the eerie grace of a predator, the man drifts off, gliding through the crowd while Maxim turns his attention to the stage.

His jaw is clenched, his eyes narrowed. He wasn't bluffing: He *is* angry.

"You know what I am, don't you?" he asks, catching me off guard by the heat in his tone. Instinct warns me not to speak, only listen.

But on the surface, a part of me has to obey and I try to stammer out a reply as a million potential answers flood my mind. Who is he?

Psychopath.

Criminal.

Murderer.

"Don't speak," he warns. "Just nod. Yes? No?"

My head jerks in some semblance of agreement and he looks away, his brows furrowing. "And yet you continue to play this game," he murmurs, though I think he's talking more to himself than to me—a terrifying fucking monologue. "Let me ask you something: can you handle it? You've lasted this long." He barks out a chilling imitation of a laugh. "But I think that's more due to naivety on your part. If you really saw…if you *really* knew, you'd run—"

"Sir?" Lucius appears before us, leading another man to our booth. He's pudgy and balding, with dark, cold eyes that linger on my collar. A gray suit strains over his beer gut. If I squint a little and ignore the price of his shiny boots, he almost looks like one of my regular clients: the typical arrogant Fuckface.

"Levoi," Maxim says, his tone flat. He lets my chain go and jerks his chin to the bar in a silent command. *Go.*

He doesn't have to tell me twice. I scramble to my feet as the other man sits, and I don't stop until I'm at the counter. The bartender looks at me but never offers up a drink. Maybe he knows my age, or maybe there's some unspoken rule about Maxim's toys. Alcohol makes you bleed more, after all.

But I'm too fucking chicken to test that theory. So I wait until a firm hand grazes my lower back, urging me to follow.

My spine tenses as I turn to face the rest of the room. The person who touched me is only a few feet away, his blond hair gleaming in the scarlet glow. Only now, as I come up behind him, do I understand the purpose of the round tables I noticed earlier. Each one sports colorful roulette boards, tended by a man dressed in black. Maxim heads to the table by the window, the man called Levoi in tow. He doesn't command me to sit on his lap this time. I just stand, my arms crossed over my chest, while the two men take up opposite seats and place their bets.

They begin to speak in Russian: a low, terse conversation that seems oddly polite at the same time. Every now and then, Maxim will nod or flash a dangerous half-smile, but the other man almost seems bored. His eyes keep flickering around to the scantily clad waitresses or the newest sex show on the stage. A busty blond and an energetic redhead are at it now, gyrating their bodies to allow the audience to see every angle of their…performance. I don't even notice the creeping sensation along my hip at first. Then the touch becomes firmer—unfamiliar. Maxim's fingers aren't this stubby. I flinch, caught off guard by the flash of yellow as one of the men suddenly lurches over the table.

"*Nyet.*" The tone is a whip, though mostly level. The piercing, dark eyes directed my way don't leave any mistake however. It was a command. "This one is mine," Maxim says, switching to English—a jarring change. "If you want a girl for the night, I am more than willing to supply you with one. *After* we come to an agreement—"

"Agreement." Levoi throws his head back and laughs. The unsteady sound cuts through the music, and suddenly, the current actors on stage fall silent. The whole damn room does. "You think I'm here to compromise, *boy?*" he wonders in an even thicker accent than Maxim's. "You don't understand. Anatoli sent me here himself. Apparently, he thinks that you don't have what it takes to run his operation. He's on his way back to the States. If I were you, I would worry less about your toys." He claws at my side, dragging me closer without warning. I stagger, sprawling onto his lap, my face inches from his crotch. "And more about what will happen to you when your grandfather calls you to heel."

"I will only warn you *one* more time," Maxim says softly. Too softly. Fear coils in my belly, but it has nothing to do with the thick, rough fingers tangling in my hair. "Respect where you are and take your fucking hands off what is *mine.*"

"I see you need to learn your place," Levoi says.

The flat of a palm connects with my ass so hard that I jump. *Thwack!*

"Is that so?" Maxim questions.

Then chaos ensues. Nearby, something crashes onto the floor. The next second, the table goes flying. A cold grip snatches my arm, yanking me upright and shoving me aside before I can make sense of any of it.

And then pounding. Over and over—every bit as brutal and calculated as the hammering of the chisel. It's only when I find my balance and glance down that I see just what masterpiece Maxim is working on now.

Levoi's face is a bloody pulp, his body jerking with every blow as Maxim pummels him with both fists. Blood flies. No one moves. The room starts spinning.

"This way." A steady grip on my arm makes me turn. Lucius is standing beside me, his lips set in a stern line. "Trust me," he says when my eyes flicker toward Maxim's back. "You'll want to come with me, Ms. Marconi."

He drapes his own jacket over me and steers me out of the mansion altogether. A different car than the one Maxim drove is waiting, and that familiar driver is already in the front seat. Once we reach the high-rise, Lucius walks me all the way to the door, letting me inside the suite. He doesn't follow me in.

"What was that?" The question spills out of me as my brain reboots, reconciling the horror I've just witnessed.

Rather than answer me right away, Lucius rubs his chin and glances over his shoulder at the gleaming closed doors of the elevator. It's almost like he's waiting, checking that Maxim really isn't there.

"That was *business*," he says finally, turning to face me again. His voice dips, giving the word a chilling double meaning.

"I suggest you forget about everything you've seen tonight. Everything you've heard. Though…"

"Yes?" My breath catches in my chest. I can't shake the feeling that whatever he's about to say, it's a warning I need to hear.

"I strongly suggest you avoid mentioning anything of what you heard to Maxim as well. Especially his grandfather. Goodnight, Ms. Marconi. Oh, and your clothing arrived the other day," he adds, before heading to the elevator. It's such a jarring change in subject that I just stare at him, blinking twice. "I had it placed inside the closet of your bedroom."

"Th-thank you." After he leaves, I swallow hard, my mind already hesitant to imagine the type of clothing Maxim prefers his women to wear.

Lace and black seem to be recurrent themes, I find once I reach my bedroom and throw the closet doors open. At a glance, it doesn't look much different than it did the other day. The clothes are still organized into three separate sections, each one with a slightly different color scheme. But, when I look closer, I realize one major difference: Every single item of clothing is new. Tailored for one person. One woman.

Even the shoes are all the same size: mine.

I know better than to read more into it than the obvious; every woman probably got her own wardrobe for however long she lasted. I bet Maxim only kept a mixture of different sizes just in case he had to buy a new toy.

Just in case.

I feed myself that lie as I settle on a black, plain dress for dinner and wait while the hours pass by and the shadows creep over the edges of my room. It's nearly midnight when I pull on a lacy, gray night dress and climb into bed.

Without permission.

But, by two a.m., I'm convinced Maxim won't be returning any time soon. So I risk it, and I've barely drifted off to sleep when the first ear-shattering crash echoes throughout the suite.

It came from his room—I can tell that much. I hear another crash. Another. It sounds like someone is throwing something—a lot of *somethings*. Stomping footsteps mingle with the chaos. And shouting. Yelling.

Brutal, violent noise.

I'm out of bed when glass starts to shatter, and I stagger toward the door, opening it just enough to peek out into the hall. I don't smell smoke. Nothing's on fire. But the shouting grows louder.

The chaos beckons me forward, step by step, while my hand trails along the wall for balance. Another crash resonates through the floor the closer I come, and I find the door to his room already open, swinging as if on broken hinges.

Beyond it, the once completely black room is a collage of broken color. Lighter clothing is strewn over the floor. One of the end tables is in shambles, pale wood spilling out from the flawless façade. The closet is open, the racks within broken and twisted.

In the middle of it all stands Maxim. He's breathing heavily, his head lowered, his body shirtless—and it seems to be the most damaged thing of all. Tattoos and scars riddle the taut flesh stretched tight over coiled muscle. Near the ridge of his abdomen is something that almost looks like a wound at first: a circle of pink flesh. I have to blink before I recognize it, only because of a stint of working at a nursing home a year back. One of my patients had colon cancer and had to get a colostomy. He has the same wound-like area on his stomach: a stoma, I think it was called.

"You should have stayed in bed, *kotyonok*."

I'm already turning to run. My fingers brush the doorknob —too damn slow.

"Stay."

I feel the weight of his command like a slap. My heart starts pounding as I have no choice but to step over the threshold of his room. The carpet feels dangerously soft at my feet, and it's disguising the way they tremble.

He makes me come closer to him than I ever have. Close enough to touch. To breathe him in. Rather than command me to stop, he shoves me down to my knees.

"Do you know the first rule of obedience?" When I don't answer, his eyes darken and he heads for the dresser, wrenching open the only drawer left intact. From it, he withdraws a length of black material and what looks like a plastic pouch. Carefully, he places the pouch around the stoma and then wraps his entire abdomen in the black material: the binder I noticed before. "The first rule," he says after a moment, "is to never question. You submit."

He paces, seeming to grow larger with every step. Angrier. When his hands go to his belt, I assume he'll channel his rage into sex, make me suck him off. My mouth is already open when he yanks his belt free and curls it around one fist.

Then he lashes out with the loose end.

Crack! The flat edge hits my knee in a fiery splash of pain. I can't even attempt to hold back a gasp.

"The second is suppression. You feel nothing. You *are* nothing. Turn." He grits the word out and I have no choice but to obey.

I face the bed on my hands and knees as he comes up behind me. Rough fingers seize the back of my nightgown, yanking it over my hips, and the next blow strikes my ass. I see white—he didn't hold back.

"You fall and I will make this worse for you," he warns as my body sways, sweat beading over my skin. "Do not move."

The whip cracks again. Another burning sting assaults my system. Again. Again. My arms shake, fighting to keep me up. *Keep me up. Please. God.*

Another hit to my lower back draws a cry from my lips, mingling with the drool dripping from my mouth. A lower strike. He lashes away at my calves before finally nudging me with what feels like the toe of his boot.

"Spread your legs."

The carpet bites into the skin of my knees as I wiggle them apart before I sense the next rush of air. I feel nothing at first. Maybe he missed?

Then *stars*. One by one, they float across my vision. My pulse surges through my skin, drowning out whatever Maxim is gritting out above me—it's that damn loud. I can list off every single searing welt on my body: twelve. My thoughts are *that* goddamn clear. It's terrifying to float this high. An overdose of agony.

"Don't move." He hits me again, this time growling out words with every blow. "And finally, the last pillar is honesty. So admit it. You're toying with me. Why? Do you enjoy it?"

Thwack!

"Did you like mocking me?"

Crack! Crack!

"Answer me!" His next blow hits me so hard that I taste blood.

"N-no—"

"*Nyet!*" A string of Russian cuts me off, followed by another hit to my back. "Maybe he planted you, huh?" Maxim growls, switching to English. "Anatoli. Another test. You are just like the rest. Selfish." *Thwack!* "Reckless." *Thwack! Thwack!* "Careless! I've always seen through you. Fuck him. Fuck *you*. Fuck! FUCK!"

He strikes my shoulder and both arms give way, pitching me facedown into the carpet, my ass in the air. I don't know if it's part of my punishment, but he doesn't slow. I hear the whistle of leather. Feel the bite of pain. Over and over and over.

It's all I am. All I fucking know. It will never end. I'll die like this. My eyelids flutter as the blows trail off. He's done. He has to be done.

I've barely taken stock of the damage he's left behind before his fingers dig into my hair, tugging, pulling. He hauls me upright and shoves me forward, onto the bed. I hit the mattress face first, jostled by the shift in weight as Maxim climbs on behind me. His fingers find the back of my collar, tugging it tight. Too tight. Choking.

Blood rushes to my head. My arms jerk, weak and useless, clawing at whatever they can, trying to reach his hands. It's too much. Too much pain. Too raw.

I'm dying.

And he's inside me, thrusting deep and hard, manipulating my body like a rag doll. I'm only conscious for the first three thrusts. I feel them all the way up to my throat, suffocating me from both ends, but I lose myself after that. Clarity comes only in bits and pieces before I go under again. I hear him grunt. My airway closes. The world goes black. Gray. He groans. Climaxes. I breathe.

The ordeal doesn't end, even when he finally climbs off me. I hear him pace, still throwing off rage like heat from a bonfire. I know the moment he picks the whip up again and the last coherent thought I have is of the safe word. Remembering it.

My lips tremble, fighting to say it. "I'm hap—"

"Shhh." The mattress vibrates as Maxim finally collapses beside me. And the world goes black again before I can say a damn thing.

CHAPTER THIRTEEN

"She's alive."

The voice is familiar. I recognize the accent, but it isn't Maxim's. Shadowy features come to mind instead: dark hair, imposing build.

"She'll heal," the man continues. "There doesn't seem to be any internal bleeding. You must have held back."

"Good."

My body reacts to that gruff, raspy tone. *Maxim.* He sounds close. Maybe his fingers are the ones I feel on my lower back. My mind loses track of the conversation as I register the pain. It hurts—all of it. My skin. My muscles. My arms. My legs.

"You seem concerned about this one. It's not like you to lose control," the other man says, but it comes out more like a question. "Though something tells me that you aren't worried about the money—"

"Thank you," Maxim says, sounding farther away as the touch on my skin disappears. "I'm sorry if I interrupted your fun tonight."

"*Fun*," the other man echoes with a chilling laugh. "You're not the only one who wants to kill, dear friend. I'll be having my fun later. Anyway, while I'm here, how are you on supplies? Has there been any bleeding? I would usually warn most patients in your condition against heavy lifting."

"It's fine," Maxim growls.

"*Right.* Just so you know, I disposed of the body," the other man adds. "And you don't have to worry. Any witnesses were *persuaded* to forget. But your grand—Anatoli will be another matter. You know this."

"You should have strung the bastard up on the wall," Maxim growls. "Use him in any fucking way you wish. As for *him*? I'll handle it."

"Well, just promise me that, next time someone crosses you, you'll leave the poor fool alive. I'd have more use for them then."

They laugh, two dangerously beautiful sounds that chase me as my thoughts scatter once again.

"CAN YOU HEAR ME, *KOTYONOK*?" Maxim's voice trickles around the edge of my consciousness, mingling with the fingers running through my hair. The caress is a mocking omen of the pain seeping through my veins.

Too much. The moment I regain feeling in my limbs, I groan. But that isn't enough. I have to suck in air and cry out. Scream.

My back is on fire. My legs. My pussy.

I've never felt this sore. This swollen. This broken.

I've never felt so painfully clear, either. It's like my thoughts are jagged glass, hurtful and sharp. What do I remember? Maxim pacing. Another voice. Bits and pieces of a hushed conversation: *distribution, Anatoli, the States, Maxim's "condition," pain.*

There's too much in my skull to decipher. Is this better than fog? I don't know. I don't want to know.

"Look at me." Maxim is sitting on the opposite side of the bed when I finally peel my eyes open.

I can't see his face, but I don't have to in order to picture it. Stern, cold expression. Haunting, soulless eyes. He brushes the hair back from my clammy forehead with his thumb, dragging the pad of it along my skin.

"Do you want to say your safe word, *kotyonok*?" He eases his finger beneath my chin, turning my face up toward his.

I flinch at what I see. The rage has drained from his system, leaving his eyes a steely shade of coal. I'm not sure which is worse in him: fire or ice?

My throat jerks to swallow. Spit and blood, according to the taste. Every inch of my body begs me to do it now. Say the damn phrase. As if to make it easier, Maxim's thumb traces my lips, nudging them open.

"I will let you go now," he promises. "If you ask."

Ask. I only have to breathe out enough air to bring life to the words. *I'm....*

The seconds pass. Too long. His hand slips from my mouth, falling somewhere within the twisted sheets that drape my body. *He* must have done it, covered me.

Out of concern? I can't tell as his gaze takes me in. He grabs my hand, unfurling the fingers, and raises a single digit to his mouth, running his tongue along the ruby smear coating the pad of it.

"I misused these tools, *kotyonok*," he tells me, setting my hand aside to lift the leather belt for me to see. His jaw clenches when I flinch and he runs his free hand down my side, bringing bruises to life. "I've used them before you were ready. I've conditioned you to associate them with fear." His searching hand fans out, stroking me from hip to navel. His eyes follow the motions of his fingers, his pupils swollen and hungry. "There is so much more to it than that."

He manipulates me so that I'm on my back. I see white. My lips flutter apart. "I...I'm ha—"

"Relax," he scolds, twisting his body so that he's hovering above me, all I can see, all I can breathe. He drags the sheet away, revealing my bruised, battered skin.

I only catch glimpses of it before I settle my gaze on the ceiling instead. Dark, purple splotches. Angry, red welts. He fingers one and the sharp, burning pinch warns me that part of the mark is gaping. Open. Bleeding. I don't know what I expect him to do…

Pet me isn't it. His heavy palm explores the length of my battered skin. Touching. Claiming. Comforting?

I shiver, too weak to move. I suffer. The softer his touch becomes, the more featherlight brushes of pain I feel. It's like being cut by a million razors all at once in the same damn spot. My thoughts grow fuzzy with every sweep of his fingertips, drugged on the agony he delivers. To my breasts. Between my legs.

I moan when he eases the tip of a finger inside.

"You had your chance to run. You didn't," he says, his voice thick with that lethal emotion I've come to dread: confusion. "So trust me." It's not a command. It's a request: the most dangerous one he's made so far.

My body shivers beneath the weight of it. Trust.

I won't.

I can't.

As if to prove me wrong, his fingers dance over broken skin, capturing my left breast and squeezing until my back bows.

LANA SKY

It's like pouring sugar over wounds packed with salt. I still feel the pain—all over, everywhere. But he's relentless, stroking and teasing my nipple until it has no choice but to react to him. My hips shift, captured beneath his palms as he moves lower, positioning me so that I'm flat beneath him. One of his big hands cups me beneath my legs, and I gasp, still sore. Still on fire.

"Look at me." His eyes, dark and narrowed, capture mine, pinning me in place as his free hand finds his belt, cinching the leather. He lifts it, letting the very edge drag across the flesh of my stomach.

I go numb with fear. Paralyzed. But then his hand starts to move between my legs. Back and forth. Deeper. Harder.

I don't feel the first pinching slap—not initially. It isn't until I actually *see* him bring the end of the belt down, striking the flesh of my hip, that I connect the two sensations. I don't even have the time to flinch before he slides a finger inside me, slowly, savoring the achingly tight fit.

"Fuck." He breathes out between clenched teeth. "You're hungry for me already."

He flicks the belt again, letting it hit my hip almost gently as that searching finger curls to rub my inner walls.

Shit. My head swims. Thoughts splinter. He hits me again: softer, harder. Harder. Softer. The entire time, his thumb fingers my clit, grinding it into my flesh. It's pain. It's something else. Raw. Hot. Molten.

He strokes the reaction out of me, not even retaliating when my eyes drift shut, disobeying his command to watch. I just feel. He rocks into me with one hand. Teases my flesh with the other. Hard leather. Thick, beautiful callused skin.

More. More. More. I don't even know which one my body craves the most.

"Trust me, *kotyonok*."

I feel his hand pull away. Something needy and broken rips from my throat: a moan.

"Greedy," he scolds, his voice tight.

I feel the mattress shift beneath his weight as he nudges my thighs apart, far enough for his body to fit in between. Something larger than his fingers bats at my entrance as his breath bastes my throat.

"Open your eyes."

My eyelids drift open until I see his face, inches from mine, while his fingers trace a path up my torso, gliding over my neglected breast, reaching for my throat. I'm still wearing the collar, and something about the way my neck must look makes him change tack.

"Hold your breath," he tells me as his hips jerk, his cock sinking in. "Don't let it out until I tell you to."

My cheeks fill with air as my body becomes full of him. I fight to hold it in as he starts to thrust. Slow. Hard. Harder. Harder.

"Not yet," he warns when I gasp, swiveling his hips, making me choke.

My head buzzes. My thoughts blur. My lungs are screaming. My body is on fire. Tightening. Clenching.

When his thumb returns to my clit with devastating strokes, my eyes roll back in my head. I see lightning. I feel it.

"Now."

I gulp at the air while my body comes, riding his length as a million sensations hit me at once. And all the while, he just keeps thrusting.

"Fuck."

My eyes flutter open the moment he throws his head back, blond hair streaming out behind him, his eyes heavy-lidded. His hips roll, grinding his cock into me. I'll feel him for days. For weeks. Forever.

It seems like it will never end, but the next second, he collapses, pinning me flat with his weight. His mouth clamps down over my ear as my body rides the final wave of his release, delivering another dose of agony.

"This is pain, *kotyonok*," he tells me gruffly, releasing the lobe. "This…is all I will ever give you. This?" He grinds his deflating cock into my clit, sparking off another scorching chain-reaction. "This is all you will ever need."

At least the first part is the truth. I know that as my body screams the moment he rolls off me and moves to sit at the edge of the bed. This is pain. This is what I signed up for.

But it shouldn't be what I want.

And it definitely shouldn't be what I *need*.

Pain is the only thing I'm sure of when I regain consciousness—that and a featherlight touch against the back of my neck. A finger? No. Goosebumps prickle my skin in recognition of the callused, rough surface. *His* finger. My heart is already pounding against the wall of my rib cage by the time that guttural voice trickles into my ear.

"I know you are awake."

I feel the heat from another body first, before I even sense the hulking shape stirring beside me. *Maxim*. In the dim lighting, he barely even looks human: just a beast glistening beneath blood and sweat.

I'm hypnotized by the predatory way he moves as he stands and approaches a doorway that I assume leads into his bathroom. I hear water running for a few minutes before he reappears with his entire torso bare.

Drool slips between my dry, cracked lips. What was that saying? *Be careful what you wish for.*

If, even for a second, I wanted to sneak a peek at what lies beneath Maxim's shirts, I've learned my lesson. He's grotesquely beautiful, adorned by countless scars that riddle his skin. Some look clean—surgical maybe, like Melanie's C-section scars. The rest are jagged. Broken. Sloppy.

Like mine.

The crowning jewel of his injuries is the circular stoma on his abdomen: a bright, beefy red. Maybe this is why he uses that color as an accent so much? Taken altogether, he *is* one giant contrast of red and silver—with those eyes filling in as the signature black.

Ignoring me, he approaches the ruined dresser and withdraws a clean plastic pouch that he secures around the stoma before wrapping another binder around his waist.

"More than twice," he says, breaking the unnatural silence as he finally turns to face me.

"Y-yes?" The reply instinctively sputters out of me. Though, to be fair, I don't know what he means at first. More than two times that he's rendered me unconscious?

"I've never fucked the same woman more than twice." His shadow flickers over the sheets as he advances on my side of the bed. When his face comes into view, he's frowning. "Rarely more than once. Most void the contract by then. To them, the money isn't worth the pain or inconvenience of staying with me." He sits, and as the mattress dips beneath his weight, I register for the first time how *heavy* he actually is—like those blocks of stone he likes to beat the hell out of. "You're bleeding." Before I can react, his hand hooks beneath my thigh, flipping me onto my back.

Shit. That simple motion triggers an avalanche of pain. I gasp, but he doesn't hesitate to take an ankle in each hand, baring every inch of me to him. My cheeks heat up at the thought of what I must look like.

As if reading my mind, he jerks his chin toward my splayed legs, his mouth slanted into one of those dangerous frowns. "Look."

I crane my neck on command, gazing down at the dark curls between my legs and the slick wetness along my inner thighs. His seed. My *blood.* A deep, searing burn inside me warns that he was right.

Without taking his eyes off the mess he's made, Maxim lets me go and rises to his full height. "Get up."

I try to move—*try* being the operative word. My body is mush. I barely make it an inch before my brain forgets how to communicate with my muscles and I double over. My eyes stream, my nerves throb, but I'm not stupid enough to admit as much out loud.

"Come," Maxim repeats. The warning in his tone is crystal fucking clear and every nerve in my body registers it: *Get up.*

I swing one of my legs out in a desperate bid for balance— and wind up on the floor. My knees smart, bitten by the carpet, but before I can move, a firm hand grabs my arm and hauls me upright. Off my feet, into his arms. Without a word, he carries me into the larger bathroom himself.

I shudder at the icy contrast as he sets me on the edge of the tub with my feet dangling inside it. Without saying a word, he runs the water, warm this time, and leaves me to grab a rag from the counter. As the water rises, he wets the cloth and swipes it across my shoulders and then down between my breasts. It's such an intimate motion, but he doesn't even ask for permission. Though why should he? I'm the bitch who signed the contract, after all; here, I'm just property, his to bathe as he sees fit.

His hands move slowly, carefully, brushing over every bruise, every single cut—taking stock of how much uninjured skin I have left. While he works, a smell floats up to tickle my nostrils: more of that rose-scented soap. It's strange how much he seems to like that scent on me. Maybe it's the combination: floral and blood.

Anticipation chokes me as he sets the rag aside and his fingers sink into my hair next. I wince, expecting him to grab and pull. Instead, he lathers. More rose scent scatters on the air as he guides my head back into the water in order to rinse, and then he works his fingers through the damp strands again. I don't believe it until I feel the result slap against my shoulders a few minutes later—he braided it. Afterward, he drains the tub and dresses me in gray fabric. It's too soft to be one of the day dresses and too light a shade to be one for evening. Another nightgown.

I'm in a daze as he leads me back into my room, sets me on the bed, and tucks me beneath the covers.

Lying there, I feel like one of Ainsley's dolls again, rescued from my torment for a brief moment. The crayon and dirt have been scrubbed from my hair. My head is screwed on correctly again. But both my owner and I know the truth, even as he carefully puts me away: I'll just get broken all over again tomorrow.

"Sleep, *kotyonok*," Maxim tells me before leaving the room. His parting words drift back to me from the hall, both a promise and a threat. "You will need it."

I WAKE up choking on a scream, but the image in my head isn't one of Maxim, go figure: just an empty room. No razors. No pain.

Just silence.

Always.

"You're in my suite," a cold voice reminds me, jarring me back to reality.

My eyes fly open and I find Maxim in the doorway. Any fear lingering from the dream is instantly demolished by something stronger. Harsher.

Confronting his toys in the throes of a nightmare must be a normal occurrence for him, because he waits until I stop gasping for air before jerking his chin in a silent command. "Get up."

I contort my sore, throbbing limbs so that I'm sitting upright by the time he reaches my side. He pushes the rest of the blankets back from me, hissing at the sight of the welts on my legs. His thumb grazes one, his eyes glowing brighter with every strangled cry I fight to swallow down.

I'm starting to recognize his few, if signature, emotions: lust, rage, malice.

"Keep making those noises, *kotyonok*," he says in a warning tone before I can hone in on which one he might be feeling now. "You will not…you will not make this quick."

My pussy twinges as my eyes drift to the front of his pants. He's straining already.

"Come."

I limp after him into the adjacent bathroom and cling to the rim of the tub. This time, I'm allowed to wash myself while he watches, directing with his eyes as to which part of my body I should clean next. My arms. My stomach. Between my legs. There again. I can't shake the feeling that he's not just watching—he's *teaching*. Making sure I'll remember what he likes. How to scrub myself clean so that his scent always remains. For the next day, and the next, and the next.

When he seems satisfied, he takes the washcloth from me and sets it aside. My throat contracts instinctively as he unhooks his belt and lowers his pants. God, he's steel already, jutting into the air. Before I can even mentally prepare myself, his fingers come to pry my jaw apart.

"Open."

I hollow my cheeks around him and fight the urge to gag as he thrusts in. Once again, his sheer size catches me off guard. It doesn't even seem possible that I can take him in all the way. So deep. Over and over.

With a grunt, he pulls out, sending drool down my chin. One of his hands captures mine and guides me to his shaft as I sputter, my eyes streaming. He's rock hard and pulsing at the same damn time. My spit makes him slick and my grip moves easily as his fingers encircle my own, guiding just how hard I squeeze him with every stroke.

Once again, I'm learning more about him without trying. With this method, he likes it hard. He likes it slow. Within minutes, he's pulsing against my closed fist, and only his grip keeps mine intact. Harder. Slower. Fast.

I don't know what does it in the end—maybe the way I swallow hard as his stare reconnects with mine. The next second, his jaw clenches. His eyes flash. My only warning is a low groan before his cum spills onto my lap, dripping down between my spread thighs. One burning spurt. Another. Each lash feels like a blow from his belt. Violent. Painful. Addictive.

"Get dressed," he tells me after he cleans himself off and returns to my bedroom. Once again, he picks every item for me to wear himself, handing me a white, lace pair of panties first. He doesn't offer me the rag, and I'm not stupid enough to reach for it myself. Then again, in his eyes, I guess I'm *clean*.

"Put them on," he prompts as if reading my mind.

I obey and pull the panties up, trapping part of his seed underneath. I don't even question as he hands me a matching bra and then a simple white dress also made of flimsy lace. I just suffer his possession and push every other logical thought out but *this*. My shoes today are cream-colored heels. To complete the look, he unbraids my hair and arranges it into loose waves that drape my shoulders.

Finished, he beckons me down the hall and into the sculpture room, where he snatches a chisel and a hammer from the wall. I stand in the corner while he returns to the half-finished block of stone and channels his rage into something other than me—whatever still lurks within him since the other night. The edge of the blade gleams as he swipes it through the air. The hammer follows. It's not long before he's grunting with the effort, throwing his weight behind every single blow.

Wham!

Wham!

Wham!

The only time he stops is to enter the kitchen and prepare dinner while I watch: chicken, which he seasons before placing into the oven. Then he returns to the sculpture room. An hour later, the baking timer sounds just as the door to the suite opens from the outside.

"Who is it?" Maxim keeps a tight grip on the chisel as he storms to the doorway to meet the intruder. Lucius. The tight expression he wears chills me almost as much as the way Maxim stiffens at the sight of it does.

"It's urgent," he says.

"It can wait until after you explain," Maxim counters.

Lucius squares his shoulders and faces him, sighing. "The east warehouse was torched. Everything lost. It appears that someone else in the syndicate felt the same way that Malkov did. The heads request a meeting with you. *Now*. And that's not all."

Maxim cocks his head, his eyes radiating fire. "Oh?"

"Anatoli is on his way back to the States," Lucius says, frowning. "I tried to request a timeline, but I was blocked from every attempt at communication. However, I assume that he will want to meet with you the moment he arrives."

"Will he now?" Maxim laughs: a broken, harsh sound that trickles out of him, softly at first. Then louder. Eventually, he throws his head back, bellowing out each chuckle. When the sound finally trails off, his teeth flash in a feral smile.

"Eat alone," he tells me, stalking toward the door. "Then get to your room. And I suggest you stay in bed tonight, *kotyonok*."

Without another word, he follows Lucius out into the hallway, slamming the door behind him.

CHAPTER FOURTEEN

I don't hear Maxim return to the suite this time. When I wake up, he's already standing at the foot of my bed, casting a shadow that swallows up every ounce of nearby light. He's wearing black from head to toe today, his hair hanging loose and unbrushed around his face. For some reason, my first instinct isn't to scream when I see him.

It's to wait, my heart pounding, my breath trapped in my throat. Already my thoughts solidify, chasing away the incoherent nightmares that haunted me all night. Is that a *good* thing or bad?

The question remains unanswered by the time I fully wake up. After a long minute of silence, Maxim commands me to dress and then leads me to the sculpture room, where he spends hours beating the hell out of the block of stone. He's so brutal that he winds up cracking it, ruining the half-finished sculpture, and I spend the entire day waiting for his inevitable cue to open my mouth or strip. Maybe he'll fuck me raw? Beat me with a leather strap again?

Something.

But he storms about the suite instead, shouting orders into a cell phone—mainly in Russian. What little words of English he sprinkles in stick out to me like jagged shards of broken glass: *Find them, any means necessary. Now.*

Afterward, he commands me to bed, and the next two days play out the same way. Apart from washing me in the morning, he never fucks me—and the anticipation is somehow worse than anything he's dished out so far.

Waiting is a brand-new torture he seems determined to inflict.

By the time the final day comes to an end, the only break in the relentless routine is when Lucius comes to take me home. I'm in the corner of the sculpture room, watching Maxim work. When Lucius beckons me toward him, Maxim's only form of acknowledgment is a single command that chases me on my way out. "Have him give you the bonus payment."

It's a second before I realize what he means. A quick glance over my legs alone reveals numerous welts, way beyond the scope outlined in his contract. *Ten inches. Twelve...*

I try to mentally tally up an estimate and choke. Too goddamn much.

"The rate will stay the same if," Maxim adds, turning his back to me, "*when* you come back."

I wait, paralyzed in the doorway, but that's it. He doesn't say anything else, and Lucius has to touch my shoulder to get me to move again. It isn't until after I've stumbled through my own front door sometime after midnight that I realize just what this means.

I survived another week with Maxim—with a few extra thousand padded to my paycheck, too. I only have to last two more in order to make it a month. After that, I would earn my sixteen thousand dollars.

The number is my lullaby as I fall asleep on the couch and wake up to find Ainsley climbing onto my chest, demanding to know why I have so many booboos.

Sixteen thousand dollars: It's a fitting price tag for any whore.

Two days home should have seemed like a godsend. A break from hell.

In reality, they felt more like that sleepy twilight between dreams and waking. When your thoughts are all jumbled and it's nearly impossible to tell up from down.

So you float.

Maybe it's the love that leaves me so disoriented. It tugs at my chest every time Ainsley or Daisy fusses over me. Every time Mikie slips me a beer once the others have drifted off to bed. When they hug me. Climb onto my lap. Drag kisses over my cheeks.

It's such a contrast to Maxim's cold darkness, and ironically, it's harder to bear than the pain. *Love* just feeds on my fear, dragging up that worn-out mantra.

Money. Money. Money.

I can't escape it, but ignoring the cold reality seems easier now than ever. I'm too tired to ask if Melanie came back or brought along her new husband. I just restock the stash, refill the fridge. Enough to last. Enough to replace me for five more days.

When Lucius comes for me on the morning of what would be the third day, I leave the house without looking back. I don't even bother to pack a bag.

There's no point.

It's not like I have a single thing to my name anyway.

I REACH the penthouse through a haze of rain. Without a word, Lucius drops me off near the front of the building, and I ascend to the suite by myself. I'm only yards away when the door swings open on its own.

Dark eyes rake me over from the shadows of the interior with every step I take, and I instantly know that something is different. A shiver runs down my spine, chased by a single realization that makes me swallow hard. Just by coming here again, I've crossed some sort of invisible line that can't ever be undone.

Not with money.

Not with a signature.

Not even with some stupid safe word.

"Get in," his gruff voice commands when I'm only a few steps away, sealing my fate. Impatience laces the air like the scent of roses, and he doesn't have to say the second part of that statement out loud this time: *Strip.*

Without daring to take my eyes off his shadowed silhouette, I remove my clothing piece by piece: sweatpants of Daisy's and Mikie's old shirt. When I finally reach my panties, sliding my fingers beneath the waistband, he steps forward and a tendril of light from the hallway reveals how he shakes his head.

"Not yet. Come."

He steps aside, and my heart jumps as I follow him deeper into the suite and directly into my room. It looks the same: a haven of white in a world of shadow—but a few key changes stick out, impossible to miss.

The air smells like roses this time. Nothing else. No *one* else. I can tell at a glance that the bed hasn't been touched, either. He hasn't had anyone else in here while I've been gone.

In fact, he's been waiting for me. Two sets of leather cuffs have been neatly laid out over the white duvet.

"Sit," Maxim commands, pointing to the bed.

I obey, folding my hands on my lap to hide how they're trembling. I'm still sore from the last time leather came into play; my legs are purple with bruises. I've felt him every second I've been away: sitting, standing, walking—nothing brings relief.

"Behind your back, *kotyonok*," Maxim instructs without a shred of empathy, reaching for one set of cuffs.

When I contort my arms, he circles my position and fastens the cuffs tightly over each wrist. Once I'm bound, he drags my panties down my legs, allowing his fingers to dip inside me. One, two, three all at once. *Shit.* I'm nowhere wet enough; it burns, and he goes deep as if to make sure of that. Feeling. Searching. Whatever he finds makes him…frown.

"How long were you a prostitute?" he asks, drawing his hand back while I cringe.

I'm no shrinking violet, but call me old-fashioned—I'm not used to being asked something like that at point-blank range. The sad part? I don't even know the right answer. Did he mean in the sense of selling my body or selling my soul? Is one even worse than the other?

"*Kotyonok*—"

"Um, six months," I stammer, rattling off the timespan that I guess is nearest to the truth. Six months ago is when I started working for Benny almost every night. "Just to pay the bills."

I can tell from Maxim's icy, uncaring stare that he's heard it all before. Every fucking excuse under the sun. I could play up the sob story, but something makes me match his honesty with a bit of my own.

"It pays the bills."

"You haven't had many." He swipes his finger along my entrance again to prove it, but I'm too sore, too exhausted, to hold a cry back. If anything, his jaw clenches at the sound. "And still, you're already broken in," he adds softly. "For me."

A single question escapes my doped-up brain. "Huh?"

There must be another term for whatever he means in Russian. Something that doesn't make the person on the receiving end feel like a pair of worn-out jeans. *Broken in.*

"You will never feel tight to a smaller man." He sinks into a crouch beside me. His breath fans my bare thigh as he rams a thumb in beside the first finger, stretching me further. "How many have you been with?" he asks, sounding miles away as his fingers keep tweaking bruised, battered flesh. A pinch here. A swipe there. Then a *brutal* pinch that drives the air out of my lungs.

My blood runs cold at the thought of coming up with a solid number. It's definitely higher than three. "Um, thirty."

Maxim chuckles at the amount as he perches himself between my outstretched legs. He's too big. I have to lie back and fling my thighs apart for him to fit, which stirs an ache that travels through my entire body. Being trapped beneath him like this feels different than anything else. He doesn't even have to touch me; my body stiffens, paralyzed by the sting he dishes out.

"Who was your first?" His palm returns to my hip and I know he feels how I flinch at the question.

My first. That title is supposed to hold some kind of honor, isn't it?

As far as achievements go, *Maxim* takes that crown, in a sense: the first man whose name I actually remember.

"Some guy my mom was dating," I blurt out, not bothering to sugarcoat it. "Climbed into my bed when I was fifteen. They ran off to Vegas the next day. By the time she came back…he was gone."

There's no emotion in my voice. There are no memories in my head. Yet. I dig my nails into my palms, as I much as I can despite the bindings, to make sure. I've only just broken the skin when I sense a deeper, harsher burst of agony along my thigh. It's too sharp to be from one of the previous cuts. Sure enough, I look down and find his thumb nearby. He pinched me.

"Never be ashamed of your past, *kotyonok*," he scolds.

"I'm not." The words are already out of my mouth before I realize what I've done. *Argue.*

His eyes flash and my punishment comes swiftly; he leans forward, hovering above. The soft cotton of his shirt teases my stiffening nipples and chilled skin—but his aim isn't sex in this moment. My only warning is a dangerous, creeping heat as his mouth latches onto my shoulder. I feel teeth next. Teasing. Warning. *Biting*. Deep. Air squeezes from my lungs in a gasp. God, he broke the skin.

"My first woman was a prostitute," Maxim says as he pulls away while wiping at his mouth with the back of his hand. That one word catches me off guard as my brain attempts to reboot in the aftermath of his assault.

His first *woman*—not his first time having sex. Maybe it means nothing. Maybe my head is too fucking clear, jumping to conclusions: anything to humanize him.

"She was older than you are," he adds, fanning his fingers out to stroke the site of his bite, mingling comfort with pain. "I was even younger. My grandfather hired her, you see. To make me a man." He chuckles. It's a chilling sound. *Ha. Ha.* "She reeked of cologne and the several other men she'd been with that night. I was…untried. Untested. The entire duration, my grandfather berated me. He made sure to watch from the end of the bed, you see. To judge."

The darkness in his words shatters even the clarity his touch delivers, making everything too sharp. Raw. Revulsion churns through my stomach. He's lying. He's joking. He has to be.

"When my actions did not satisfy him, he hired more women," Maxim continues without revealing the butt of the joke. "Sometimes he would 'demonstrate' on them. How to make them scream. He only ever completed if they screamed…" He trails off, glaring into his fucked-up past even as his fingers continue stroking me. Soft. Softer. All at once, the nails return, drawing blood when I least expect it.

I jump as pain floods my system, but just as I start to lose my mind, Maxim drags his fingers between my legs again, staving off another trip over the edge.

"I learned then that fucking is just a game, *kotyonok*. But you do not seem to comprehend the rules."

My head continues to spin, even as my heart stops beating at the tone of his voice. Low. Guttural. Confused. It's like he can't grasp the concept of it: that it was possible to get off *not* at the expense of someone else. Suddenly, he reaches down and seizes my chin in his grip, forcing me to face him directly.

"Understand, that even in a game as twisted as Russian Roulette, there can only be one winner."

He doesn't reveal just what he means, but my intuition is more than happy to fill in the blanks as he lets me go: At the end of the game, there is only one survivor. As far as this round is concerned, the odds aren't even slightly stacked in my favor.

Yet Maxim still seems determined to play.

His hand returns between my legs again, and a searching thumb slides along my inner walls as if in punishment for making him feel even a shadow of human emotion—even one as primal as greed. Finally, he pulls away, but I don't even have the chance to feel relief before he flings another command my way.

"Get onto your stomach."

His voice alone affects me like nothing else—not even the pain. I scoot back over the mattress and roll onto my belly, my ass in the air. When I look up, Maxim is holding another strip of leather I instantly recognize: the collar, its chain winking in the daylight streaming in through the windows. All this time, he must have had it in his pocket.

"Lift your chin."

Once I've complied, he fastens the strip around my throat, this time so that the chain dangles against my back rather than my front: an icy reminder of the power he holds over me.

"Lift your legs," he commands next, "so that your heels are near your head."

The moment I do, the tension in the chain becomes unbearable, forcing my head back farther…farther. Going off his calculating expression, I know instantly what he's done.

If I try to lower my legs, my head follows. Just like that, he's turned me into a spit-roasted pig. The only thing missing is the apple shoved into my mouth.

Apparently, he intends to improvise on that detail. "Open," he grits out, coming to stand before me.

My lips spring apart as he finds the clasp to his jeans and rips it open, revealing his cock, pulsing and straining, underneath. Before I can even begin to imagine how this will work, he nudges my lips farther apart. Farther. Only now does the reality sink in.

He planned this, with only one goal in mind.

"Open wide, *kotyonok*."

He doesn't even have to try to deepthroat. He slides right in and there is no way I can move to even try to regain leverage. If I throw up in this position, I'll choke. So I stop breathing. I stop thinking, and the tugging of hungry fingers on my hair is my only tether to reality.

"Fuck," he growls.

His thrusts become faster. Harder. I have to breathe in through my nose in order not to suffocate. Which is fucking impossible. He's reckless. Rough. With every thrust, he tilts his hips to explore another crevice of my mouth or to plunge deeper down my esophagus. There is no mercy. Just pain.

And I can feel every single drop of it.

All at once, he pulls out, leaving a trail of drool over my chin just as my muscles sear, white-hot. I vaguely see him twisting around to mount the other end of the bed. The chain is suddenly loosened and I'm shoved onto my back, both of my hands still tethered behind me. Maxim hovers above, positioned so that he's facing the opposite wall, his cock near my mouth, his head dangerously close to my lower body. In one frantic sweep of my eyes, I take him in: rippling muscle covered in golden skin. I know this position...

"Open," he commands, his breath scorching the inside of my thighs.

Wait…

"Take me in, *kotyonok*," he grates when another second passes and my lips remain shut. I don't think I've heard this edge to his voice before. Broken. *Unsteady.* "Open and I will show you how to use that greedy mouth."

Impatient, his cock nudges my lips, seeking entrance. When I open wide, Maxim rolls his hips, teasing the back of my throat with his length in one stroke. At the same time, his fingers drift between my spread legs, roughly rubbing me open to make way for something wetter. Warmer. Thicker.

Oh! His cock muffles any sound I might make. All I can do is swallow, stroking the underside of his shaft with my tongue. He returns the favor, sinking his own inside me. Hard. Soft.

Shit.

"You like that, *kotyonok*," he mutters into my skin when I stiffen in shock.

I stop sucking, desperate to catch my breath. And my punishment comes swiftly. He seizes a bit of flesh between his teeth and bites down so hard that I see stars.

"Do not stop."

Left with no choice, I hollow my cheeks around him, taking him in as far as I can, while he copies every action with his tongue. Ramming into me. Fucking me.

Driving. Me. Insane.

I've only just gotten the hang of the motion when he comes, spilling himself down the back of my throat. The moment I feel the initial hot spurt, my thoughts drift apart and scatter. I lose my sense of fucking gravity—the climax hits me that hard. I feel it in my chest. My stomach. My fucking soul. Like a freight train.

I expect him to stop, let me come back down gradually, but his tongue only moves faster. Swallowing. Licking. Taking. Swirling, consuming.

All the while, his hips buck, driving every ounce he has left into me. I taste blood when he finally pulls out and slides off me while I blink up at the ceiling and try to remember how to breathe.

My lungs heave for air, but nothing trickles in—just out: gasps riddled with moans.

I vaguely know when Maxim leaves my room without a word and closes the door behind him. But I can't do anything but lie here as the pain in my throat mingles with the icy-hot, ravaged ache of my pussy. I don't know which one is worse to bear. Or which one pushes me closer to the edge of sanity first.

I can taste the first hint of madness when Maxim finally returns. Shadows paint the edges of my room now, making his hair stand out like a halo.

"You may eat, *kotyonok*." Heavy footsteps approach the bed, and when I crane my neck, I find him holding a tray. He lowers it, allowing me to make out the bowl of soup and crackers on it.

It's a trap. I'm sure of it; those haunting eyes are far too soft.

"Sit." Without revealing any sinister motive, Maxim unhooks the cuffs on my wrists and hands me a spoon. I hesitantly feed myself as he watches, but halfway through, he drags my bowl away. "That's enough."

I know better than to ask questions as he fastens my ankles to opposite bedposts before picking up the tray and leaving my room again. When he returns, my heart stops.

He brought me a present: a single flame flickering on the wick of a long, white candle.

CHAPTER FIFTEEN

As if taunting me, the flame dances on the wick while Maxim approaches the bed and sets the candle on the bedside table. The single bit of light serves as the sole source in the room. Hell, it would almost make for a romantic touch, if it weren't for the tension lacing his body. Stiffly, he steps back, and the orange glow spills over his silhouette, throwing his shadow against the wall.

God, he seems bigger now. Huge. Strands of golden hair fall across the chiseled planes of his face, clashing with the darkness clinging to him as he moves to stand before my spread legs. While I watch, he places something else down between them, but I can only make out the vague shape of it once I crane my neck.

A bowl?

"How do you feel, *kotyonok*?" he asks, drawing my attention.

My heart lurches at his tone—it's too soft. From this angle, the firelight illuminates the cold gleam in his eyes. I *know* that look, and I can only lie still as ice runs down my spine.

It's the same subtle change in him I saw the other night. Like something broke inside him. Inside his head. His *soul.*

"I…" Any words die in my throat as he runs a hand along my outstretched calf. His fingers feel callused yet insanely soft. Like silk and sandpaper all at once.

"Sore?" he asks.

I force myself to nod. "Y-yes."

His hand slides between my legs again, lifting something that makes a delicate clinking noise… Something shiny. He lowers whatever it is to my skin and the first brush of it hits me like a jolt of electricity. Cold. Frozen. Like ice.

Actual ice.

Shit! I react out of pure instinct, clawing at his fingers.

He only has to say one word. "Stop."

I do, just like that, lying back against the mattress. My hands go limp and he continues his assault. Almost lazily, he slides the ice along the outside of my pussy first, pressing so that I feel every firm, curved edge. My knees buckle, and I can't keep myself from shaking. Both hands clench, my nails digging into the duvet beneath me with every swipe. Just when I think I can't bear it for a second longer, he begins to thrust his fingers, working the ridge of ice inside me.

All. The. Way.

"Trust me, *kotyonok*," he growls as the world falls to fucking pieces around me. The room is a blur, and his face is the only thing I can make out clearly. Pink lips move slowly, stretched tight over ivory teeth. "You will thank me for preparing you."

Prepare... The ice is still inside me when he steps back. I know that much. My muscles tighten, numbed by the frigid chill. My stomach cramps. I have to shove my fingers into my mouth and bite down hard just to keep from reaching down again.

From the corner of my eye, I see shadows dance across the room, flickering. I blink once and realize why: The flame is in his hand now.

"Look at me."

The moment I do, he extends his arm over me. Slowly, he tilts the candle, sending a stream of hot, clear liquid onto my stomach. Fire. Ice. I'm drowning between two consuming sensations.

"I want you to ask me something, *kotyonok*. One of those questions I see burning in your eyes." His fingers return between my thighs, sliding the ice back and forth. Deeper, harder. "But in return, you will relinquish something to *me*. There is no choice," he adds before I can choke out a refusal. "You *must* participate in this."

Why? My heart hammers out a warning. Talking with him is just as dangerous as fucking. But still, self-preservation wins out. I know better than to refuse.

"Ask me something," he commands. The words seem bitten out. Impatient.

Okay.

"Why do you call me *kotyonok*?"

It seems like a harmless question. To me. However, Maxim's eyes narrow.

"It means kitten," he admits. "It is simple."

Simple. I take it that it's not a unique nickname, either. What number "kitten" am I on the spectrum of the countless toys he's played with? My tongue twitches, unwilling to travel down where that question might lead.

"But that is not the question you want to ask," he adds.

Shit. He caught onto my trick. No harmless topics. He wants me to ask him something real. Personal.

This time, I think I know what.

The moment my gaze drifts down to his torso, his posture changes, stiffening. Tensing. *Bingo.*

"Ask," he grates when the seconds pass in twisted silence.

"I..."

His hand returns between my legs. One thick finger rams its way into my pussy and then curls at the last minute, hurting me. *Waking* me. My thoughts spark, way too sharp.

"Y-your stoma," I croak, using the actual term. If he's surprised I know it, his expression doesn't reveal it. "How… Do you have cancer?"

"No. Intestinal. Damage," he says finally, chewing on the words. "I've been this way since I was a child."

Before I can even start to wonder why, he has the candle again. One flick of his wrist and more hot wax drips onto my belly, throwing me off-balance. "Next question."

My brain scrambles to process his words in addition to the searing pain. *Next question.* But what the fuck are words? It's all I can do just to clench fistfuls of the duvet on either side of me, if only to keep from reaching down.

The longer I wait, the more impatient Maxim becomes. He lowers his hand, making the flame dance through the air. I feel that dangerous heat draw close, kissing my hip. Closer.

My only warning is a stinging warmth across my side before skin actually sizzles and burns. It *hurts*.

He's ruthless.

"Ask."

"How did it happen?" I stammer, struggling to phrase something coherent.

"Punishment," Maxim says, withdrawing the candle from my skin. His tone is flat, his eyes distant. In this moment, he's colder than the ice he tormented me with.

And I prefer the first torture.

"To teach me." Suddenly, his hand lashes out, spilling wax onto my inner thigh. Too much. Too close to my entrance.

A scream tears its way out of me, too broken to hold back, even as I slam a hand over my mouth. But it doesn't seem to irritate him. Rather, Maxim's features freeze over at the sound. And just like that, I know why he's doing this.

Something upset him again, and for whatever fucked-up reason, my agony is his drug of choice to numb the pain.

"Another," he grits out, sparring the use of wax this time—but it's not a reprieve. He's saving up for one brutal punishment.

And I have no choice but to dig deep and find something else to ask. Something easy again. Simple. *Why do you live here? Why do you like black so much?*

I try to phrase one of those softball questions, but a different one trickles out over my tongue in the end. "Why me?"

He frowns, still holding the candle at enough of an angle for fresh wax to drip down, splattering the sheets inches away. Searing-hot backsplash speckles my skin, and I can't stop myself from straining my binds, scooting away.

One heavy palm over my stomach pins me in place before I get very far. "Explain."

"You don't like it when I come," I stammer. "So why—"

"I never said I didn't enjoy it," he says over me. "But it is offensive. *Everything* about you is offensive."

As crazy as it seems, that doesn't sound like an insult. Just fact. Fate. He may be the tormentor in this equation, but he makes my sins seem so much worse. Unforgivable.

"There is something broken in you, *kotyonok*. Something damaged. Most men have no trouble leaving out food for a stray kitten every once in a while," he says—a terrifying analogy, given his own nickname for me. "The creature provides him a companion. The beast eats the mice. Both benefit. But when the cat keeps returning..." His hand drifts above me, delivering more droplets of wax. Hotter. Higher.

Shit. I whine when heat sears through my nipple. I can't move. Can't breathe. Everything glows crystal fucking clearly.

"The master forgets his end of the bargain, *kotyonok*," Maxim continues, his gruff tone driving the severity of the warning in—like a hammer. "He forgets that the kitten was always meant to be free, no matter how briefly it might reside in his barn. It isn't long before his new possession receives a collar. A name. It will never leave the prison it's so innocently wandered into." He shakes his head, and I don't even want to fully name the emotion shooting down my spine. It's become a familiar friend lately: *terror.* "But do you want to know the worst part, *kotyonok?*" Maxim wonders as his eyes meet mine again. "The silly little kitten still believes that it is free."

I jump as he reaches for me, but he only grabs one of my ankles and undoes the cuff. After setting the candle on the end table, he lopes around the bed and uncuffs the other. Then he kneels, both of his hands reaching beneath the bed to drag something out from underneath it. A box, I see as he sets it beside me on the mattress.

"And now it is time for *you* to be taught a lesson, *kotyonok.*" With a wave of his hand, he commands me to sit upright, though I'm still spread eagle and bound by both ankles.

My eyes burn. I can't tear them away from his chest—no, his stomach. The twisted hints from his childhood circle my brain on an endless loop. That word he used. *A lesson. A lesson?*

Slowly, he angles the box toward me so that I can observe the tool arranged on a pillow of black silk. Sharp. Glittering.

A knife.

It's beautiful in a way: long, with a slightly curved edge. It's not designed for cutting—it's made to *carve.* When I don't reach for it myself, Maxim picks it up and hands it to me, forcing the hilt into my grip. Nothing has ever felt heavier. Not even him.

"You seem determined to keep coming back," he says, frowning as the words leave his mouth. Like the thought of it is so offensive. So wrong. It requires a punishment. "Perhaps I should make sure that, even when you are gone, you will never forget for a second…"

"Forget what?" I rasp when he trails off. My vision is a blur now, and warmth trickles down my cheeks. How fucking hilarious—I never cry. After everything I've been through, I thought I wouldn't have any tears left.

His hand falls over my shoulder, anchoring me to the bed. To him. That simple, possessive touch echoes the words he growls into my ear. "Who you belong to."

My head jerks in a refusal. I can't control it or the words that slip from my throat. "I…I don't."

I don't want anything from him. I *don't*. Just money. Only money. My fingers shake as if to betray me, threatening to drop the knife altogether.

"My mistake," Maxim corrects. Hot breath trickles across my bare shoulder, closer than before as one of his hands captures mine. As if to prove me wrong, he flips my hand over, revealing the scarred palm. All those cuts. Those "accidental" wounds—some are still open and bleeding. His thumb finds one, stroking the raw flesh. "To you, this wouldn't be a punishment, would it? No." He nods to the weapon in my hand. "*This* is what you want."

Want. Too much power lurks within that single word. My brain short-circuits. Whenever I blink, warmth spills down my cheeks. I try to wipe whatever it is away, only to have my wrist seized in a stronger grip.

"Like this…"

One minute, the knife is clutched in my fist. The next, its sharp edge grazes my skin, creeping across my inner thigh. The slightest bit of pressure sends the tip right through the skin. I jump at the feeling, even as my wrist flexes, extending the damage. Two more sharp lines. More. More. *More.*

His hand guides me, but I'm the one doing it. Me. Bit by bit, he makes me sign an entirely different kind of contract. In blood. In pain.

M

A

X

My fingers tighten over the handle of the blade and it's like I can feel the heat of the flame from across the room, scorching my skin. My hand slips—the edge cuts deeper. Harder. More. The room spins. I have to squeeze my eyes shut to keep from going under and focus on breathing in. In. Out.

Maxim grits out a harsh sound between his teeth before growling something else in Russian. Somehow, I know it's not an admonishment when he sprinkles in two guttural bits of English. "Fuck…fuck."

One more mark. Another. Two more. Only one thought flutters across the murky landscape of my brain: *More.*

"Enough."

The knife is snatched away and my eyes flutter open to reveal the monster staring back. His eyes glow, tinged dark with bloodlust. There isn't a shred of humanity in them.

And a part of me—some sick, twisted part—sighs in relief. *Finally.*

He tosses the bloodied weapon back into the box and then stares down at the mess we've made. My vision is too blurred to focus. I just see red when I crane my neck, tiny strips of it seeping in a perfectly straight line. M A X I M

"On your back."

I let my body go limp, leaving me at his mercy as he brings the candle directly over my fresh wounds. *Drop. Sizzle. Drop. Fuck!*

Each sensation is too violent to comprehend. I have to close my eyes and ride it out: every searing lick of fire and every salty, burning bit of blood cementing his name into my skin.

My teeth chatter. Sweat slicks my inner thighs. Too much. Too much.

The heat from the wax sinks into my veins, creating an entirely different brand of pain: hellish heroin. I'm barely conscious when I feel another sensation against the searing wounds on my thigh: ice. For what feels like hours, he runs it along my skin, numbing me.

Without warning, he blows the flame out, leaving hot wax to dry on my inner thigh. I hear the sound of a zipper being undone. The bed moves. His weight crushes my body into submission as one of his hands circles my throat. Tightens.

In a sinking, icy panic, I realize I can't breathe. Dark eyes stare into mine as the seconds trickle by, daring me to react. One. Two.

Five.

The world blurs; I can't see. I just feel. Him. Heat. Pain. Agony. In one fierce thrust, he's inside me, fucking deep and hard until I forget everything but the sensation of being filled. I forget my name—and just like he promised, he gives me a new one, grunted into my ear.

"*Moya.* Mine."

I forget my fear.

Every goddamn thing.

When he comes, I'm barely conscious. Just a shell, used and filled up.

Only by him and the air he finally allows me to breathe in.

CHAPTER SIXTEEN

The next four days are a whirlwind of fucking and tension. It's like he *knows*. My own, internal deadline is a blown secret, and Maxim Koslov is determined to rub whatever emotions he can into my skin before then. If I leave, he'll make sure there's nothing left of me to walk out the door.

I bathe only with his permission. Eat. Sleep. Breathe. We rarely leave the penthouse—and if we do, he only takes me to the club, making me sit at his feet while he holds court like a self-proclaimed prince in a kingdom of his own making.

In a way, he makes it easy to feel. To exist. He makes it *terrifying*. What used to take multiple slices of a blade to find, he gives me in one brutal dose. An *overdose* I don't even have to ask for.

I beg.

But the most terrifying piece of the puzzle is for how long?

That's the kicker, as they say. Hell, Maxim all but warned me himself, and as the days trickle by, the final clause of the contract is beginning to feel less like a safety net and more like a promise.

In the case of accidental death.

"Did you hear me, *kotyonok?*"

I wince as a chunk of my hair is yanked, my head jerking back so that my gaze connects with the figure looming above me. Reality returns with a whisper of cool jazz that reaches the farthest edges of the room, contrasting with the gruff voice resonating through my skin. I'm crouched on the floor at Maxim's side, but how long have I been here? Two hours? Longer?

"I told you to come." Using my hair like a leash, he hauls me upright, dragging me backward so that the tip of his knee digs into my ass—a violent invitation.

I have no choice but to lower myself onto it, sinking back against his chest. He feels like stone beneath the soft fabric of his gray cotton shirt. He's dressed casually tonight, even though we're at the club and he made me wear a dress. Oddly enough, he doesn't stick out like a slob among all these well-dressed people.

Wearing jeans and a shirt, he's more magnetic than any other man could ever hope to look in a suit.

"Your mind is wandering tonight." Warmth clamps over my right earlobe, setting every nerve in my body on edge: his teeth, nipping just once. "You were thinking about something," he growls, leaving out the obvious crime: *something other than him.*

"I…" Any pathetic attempt to save my ass sticks in my throat. There's no use.

The people watching us from every corner of the room seem to know the inevitable. They glance away. I think some of the bastards even smirk. It's a full house tonight, but the rest of the club seems to hold more interest for the guests; I guess they're all used to Maxim's quirks.

I don't feel so lucky. It's late. Darkness paints the windows black and the only source of light comes from those blood-colored sconces set into the wall. Across the dark marble, shadows and reflections glimmer like flames of hellfire. Once again, the club has come to life around us—and I didn't even notice.

"There you go again."

This time, my hair is pulled hard enough that I see stars. My head falls back, leaving me no choice but to meet his gaze fully. Two empty eyes track my facial expression, glowing brighter every time I wince. Suddenly, I'm shoved off his lap and hit the floor on my hands and knees. The marks on my inner thigh burn, ripped open, but before I can move, my dress is hiked up by a firm hand, leaving my ass bare—he didn't give me any panties today.

"I called your name *three* times," he tells me on the cusp of a sigh. He stands, his boots thudding against the floor, and the hiss of leather edges his words: like that of a belt being ripped from belt loops.

"Do you understand?"

I can't see his face, just the boots of someone walking past, but they're shiny enough to make out my reflection: wide-eyed, dazed, *pathetic*.

"Do you?"

I nod frantically, clenching my teeth even before the first thwack of something hard strikes my ass. It's flat. Unyielding. His palm? Whatever it is strikes me again so hard that my teeth clatter together. Again. Harder.

It's a warmup, I realize the moment the telltale crack of leather hits the air in the wake of the blow. The first sharp hit to my thigh is merely a warning. The next is the real deal. *Shit!* I barely manage to choke a cry down, but the brief sound acts like a lit match struck against a pool of gasoline.

With the next strike, he goes to town.

Two lashes. Three. Each one sets my body on fire, rocking me down to the goddamn core. Mangled cries slip out before I can even think to bite them back, and I'm punished for every last one.

But, even as my eyes water at the sting, I know it's not the brutal, ruthless beating he dished out in his suite. He's careful, almost methodical. None of his blows break the skin. I'm painfully aware of that—*too* aware. It's like being given drips of water from a bottle but never the whole thing.

"I do not hear you counting."

My teeth clatter together as I struggle to catch up. "Ten…f-fifteen—" *Thwack!* I see white and lose track of the count for a few precious seconds. "Eighteen. Nineteen—"

"Twenty," Maxim finishes off for me after the final violent crack.

Panting and breathless, I look up through a messy fringe of my hair. I was wrong—the others *are* watching. The blood-red lighting shields their faces, but the sudden hush beneath the music gives their attention away as I suffer every blow.

My ass is on fire, my knees rubbed raw, my palms so slick that I can barely keep myself upright. In a desperate bid for leverage, my nails scrape against the marble flooring—but nothing can save my soul from a brutal fall. It crashes through the floor. Breathing heavily, Maxim lords over me, still holding the belt. I can see the shadow of it swaying across the marble. Close. Away. Closer.

"Look at me."

I have to twist around in order to be able to. Our gazes reconnect and my heart stops beating. I know that look: *confusion.* It twists his cold features with every second that passes. My chest constricts, clinging to what little air I manage to suck in. Some deep-down instinct warns me to look away. *Now!*

But I can't. And the eye contact only seems to confuse him even more. Frowning, he clenches the belt tightly, the other hand curled into a fist. His eyes are glowing, his breathing heavy and ruffling the strands of hair that fall across his face.

God, he looks insane: an angel in his very own fucked-up corner of hell.

The muscles in the arm holding the whip jump and something inside me flinches in response. But it *feels* all wrong. I don't shy away. My hips arch instead, my sore body preparing itself for another round. The tendrils of pain encase me, flickering white hot. I almost can't stand it; it's *that* fucking intense.

At the same time, though, I've never felt this fucking clear in my life. There's no fog—just *him*: clarity in its rawest, most twisted form.

And I crave it.

"Turn over," he grits out, nudging me with his foot when I don't comply fast enough.

My gaze falls to the floor, my hips rising to meet the next blow he dishes out. And then another.

Tears sting behind my eyes, but for the first time all damn day, my mind is open. I can't think about anything but him. This. Submission. I surrender to my punishment, and he doesn't let up until a brutal lash draws a cry from my lips and my hands buckle beneath my own damn weight.

"Come here."

It takes me too long to contort my throbbing limbs in order to turn around. He already has his belt looped back around his pants when I do. His hands hang at his sides, clenching and unclenching with every second it takes my eyes to drift up to his. They're swollen in blackness, both pupils dilated and endless.

Something wet dribbles down my lip and my tongue attempts to chase it, licking at the edges of my mouth. His gaze tracks every single motion and his eyes narrow before I even manage to snap my jaw shut. Too late.

"Come. Here." I've never heard this tone from him. Guttural. Gritted. Primal. "Now."

He waits until I stagger to my feet and then grabs my arm, dragging me after him down the hall behind the bar that leads to those closed doors. He picks one somewhere in the middle and shoves me inside it. Then he slams the door behind us.

It's too dark to see anything clearly. My hands fly out in front of me, my fingers grasping for something solid. Before I can take note of my surroundings, my back strikes a hard surface. Then I smell him. Feel him. His body forces its way between my legs, grinding his erection into my pelvis. I taste him as something warm nudges my lips, coaxing them apart. Something wet. His tongue? His *teeth*, biting down brutally hard as he shoves me back farther. The cold surface behind me is a shock against my searing skin and my brain doesn't know how to process it. So it short-circuits, and I can only stare as Maxim wrenches my dress up to my waist and tears the fly of his pants open. I see the head of his cock, rigid and straining. Then I take him: every fucking inch, slammed inside me. No mercy. No restraint.

No *control.*

I can't even think. I just arch my hips to let him in instead, feeling my body struggle to register his length. His first thrust alone triggers a million little explosions: raw, bitter friction. He's never felt like this...

My eyes roll back in my head once I process just how deep he is. *Fathomlessly.* He dominates every fucking inch of me. Everywhere. There is no separating the sensation from reality the way I could with anyone else.

He is *everything*—squeezing out even the air to make room, drowning me in his scent. It's too raw. Animals fuck like this: mindlessly. Hard fingers dig into my ass, holding me in place for every punishing thrust. His teeth rake my neck, sink into it before a guttural growl revs up in his throat and I'm flooded with his release.

He should pull out now—but he doesn't. He lingers inside me, reaching down with his thumb to stroke my clit, setting off sparks. Fireworks. A goddamn explosion. I'm already on another fucking planet when his thumb drags over my open wounds, using fresh blood to add even more wet friction.

Holy shit. My toes curl. My feet lose contact with the floor, which forces him to support my weight as I lose my fucking sense of gravity. It's only when I finally come back to Earth that I register what kind of room we're actually in: not a bedroom, but an office, just a few feet from a polished wood desk that gleams in the light drifting in from the crack beneath the door.

Is this room his? When I finally look at Maxim, I can't tell. His expression is closed, his eyes flashing. All at once, he withdraws from me, wrenching up his pants and turns for the door.

"Come."

My cheeks are red when we finally reach the main room and Maxim returns to his seat at the table. Knowing eyes track our every movement. I can't stop my gaze from straying over to the stage, where a naked couple is currently going at it in plain view. The man fucking the hell out of a busty blond is a pale imitation of what I now understand no-holds-barred sex to be.

"*Kotyonok*," Maxim snaps.

I know without him even having to say another word to kneel beside him, lowering my eyes to the floor.

He doesn't acknowledge me again, not even as my inner thighs ache and something warm trickles down my left leg. It isn't until nearly an hour later that I realize why. It's a dangerous thought, but it trickles into my brain anyway as a new man joins our table.

Every other encounter we had contained some element of control. Every one but what happened in that office.

"It's a rare night when you want to talk business," a man says, his voice thick with amusement.

The back of my neck prickles at the sound of that accent. It's familiar. I lift my head as much as I dare and make out the dark hair of the British man from last time. I don't see the pretty blond around anywhere, not that I'm stupid enough to scan the entire room to be sure.

Beside me, I sense Maxim stiffen. All at once, his hand is in my hair, grasping, feeling. This time feels different than the brutal tugs I'm used to. Like the absentminded way someone might pet a cat that has crawled onto their lap. He *pets* me.

"I need your help," Maxim says, his voice cold. "It will require one of your more specialized talents—"

"Done," the man replies without an ounce of hesitation. "Tell me who, where I can find them, and what you need to know."

Maxim sighs. "Anatoli is returning to the States—"

"Your grandfather," the man cuts in, his tone knowing.

Somehow, I manage to bite my tongue rather than gasp out loud. Anatoli is his grandfather. Going off everything he's already told me about him, I doubt this return has the makings of a happy family reunion. As if to prove it, Maxim's nails graze my scalp. *Hell no.*

"I think you'll understand that it is imperative that I find out who is behind the attacks on my distribution before then," Maxim continues without acknowledging anything else about Anatoli. "Lucius will tell you which man to target. He's a mutual enemy, so you might be able to get something out of this exchange."

The other man laughs. "Always the multitasker."

He leaves, and not long after, Maxim stands as well, beckoning me after him. He doesn't say a single word as I follow him out to the car, and the drive to his suite is just as silent. The moment the car comes to a stop, though, his hand lands on my thigh, every finger clenching tight, his nails piercing my flesh.

"You." He grits the word out on a ragged exhale. It's laced with an emotion that makes my hair stand up: confusion. "You wouldn't be stupid enough to try and deceive me, *kotyonok*? Would you?"

My heart rams itself against my rib cage. This time, I don't even know what I could have done wrong. So I shake my head and say nothing while my racing heartbeat counts the seconds. One. Two. One Hundred.

Finally, Maxim sighs. "Come here." He barely allows me enough time to unbuckle my seat belt before he hooks his hand around my wrist and drags me over the center console and onto his lap. The steering wheel digs into my lower back, and I have to slump against him to keep my head from smacking on the roof of the car. Hot breath trickles between my breasts as his hands grab my waist, anchoring me to him. "Look at me."

When I do, his eyes are cold. Thoughtful. Calculating.

"I never ask where Lucius finds the women," he says softly. One of his hands drifts up my back...higher... Thick fingers settle over my shoulders and inch toward my neck. "I only know what little he tells me about them or whatever I care to find out on my own. But you—" Pain jolts up and down my spine as his hand encircles my throat from behind, tightening. Squeezing. "You will tell me everything."

Somehow, I manage to keep breathing. Air wheezes in and out of my lungs, propelling my heaving chest closer and closer to his chin. He could open his mouth and bite me if he wanted to.

"Like what?" I choke out when the seconds have passed without him saying anything.

His free hand reaches for the lever that operates the height of the chair, letting it fall back a few inches and sending me sprawling against him. "Everything," he tells me. "How did Lucius find you?"

The question is laced with suspicion, and my instincts go haywire. My thighs twitch against his lap, desperate to follow the only command my brain seems capable of issuing: *Run.* "He asked my"—my tongue shoots out to moisten my dry lips—"my pimp B-Benny and he said he had a job."

It feels so fucking strange to refer to Maxim like that now: a job. Was this ever really that simple? Deep down, a part of me knows the answer: not since the first moment he ordered me down to my knees.

"And that is all?" His fingers loosen their grip on my throat and creep up into my hair, seizing chunks, pulling tight.

"Y-yes."

"Why sell your body for sex?"

I flinch. "I need the money."

It sounds so pathetic when said out loud. I've told him this before.

But his mouth twitches into that dangerous frown; *this* time, he doesn't believe it.

"And your clients?" he demands next. "Were any of them recurring?"

In the blur of faces, a few stand out. "Yes," I admit.

The fingers in my hair tighten, causing my eyes to water from the sharp, pinching pain. "How many?"

"I…"

He tugs once and my scalp erupts into flames.

"Three or four."

"And none of them mentioned me? *Koslov?*"

I shake my head as much as I can despite his grip. Every tiny inch earns me a brief bite of pain. "N-no—"

"And you…" He tilts his head to observe me, his eyes glowing in the shadows of the car's interior. "You have been a submissive before."

Alarm prickles through my skin. "N-no." *Bad idea,* a part of me whispers as the words leave my throat. Challenging him feels like straddling a lit stick of dynamite. One wrong move and *kaboom*!

As if to prove it, his free hand moves to my hip, every finger clenching tight, daring me to flinch. "No." He seems to taste the word, digesting whether or not it's a lie. "Never?"

I shake my head a little easier this time. "Never."

He scoffs, shifting beneath me so that our bodies are more in line. He doesn't have to crane his neck back to meet my gaze anymore—I'm swallowed up by the dark, gaping irises. "Are you sure, *kotyonok*?" His tone sinks into my veins like the foundation of a trap; one wrong move will spring it.

Over my body or my soul? Who knows. That's the risk of playing roulette.

"You've never been trained?"

I see his hand move from the corner of my eye, and a sharp tug on my hair draws my head back, baring my throat to him fully.

"You've never been taught how to turn your pain into pleasure?"

My heart sputters as his teeth graze my neck, preceded by a warm burst of air. One lick. Another brief taste. My skin is still damp when he finally draws back.

"You've never had a man whip you senseless, only to turn around and look at him *in a way that begs to be fucked*?" The words end in a growl, bitten off and coarse.

I don't expect the first bite—not even the second. It's a primal assault. He sinks his teeth deep into my collar, biting down hard when I whine. I see stars. A fucking million of them. My only conscious thought is to scream as searing heat floods my veins, spreading.

Suddenly, Maxim draws back with a guttural hiss. "Even this gets you off." His gaze is aimed between my thighs; they're clenched.

Still numb with shock, I can't even defend myself. I can't muster up an excuse. I can't deny it. I just breathe, and he watches me, trailing his gaze over my heaving chest.

After what feels like an eternity, he wrenches the door on his side open and jerks his hips to buck me off. "Get out."

My trembling legs can barely support my weight as I scramble off him—not that he bothers to wait for me to catch up. I'm forced to follow him all the way up to his suite, where he slams the door, making me answer one question without ever having to mention it out loud.

Do you still want to do this?

My fingers shake as they form a fist. I can make out my reflection in the door's polished surface, but I don't recognize the girl gaping back at me. She's a shell of her former self, too desperate to give a damn as to how she might look.

For money. It's only about the money.

In the end, I only have to knock once before the door is opened from within.

Then I step inside.

CHAPTER SEVENTEEN

Muttered voices draw me out of a pathetic excuse for sleep. The moment I peel my eyes open, pain returns with the grace of a one-two punch, flooding my veins like blood.

I'm alone; that's the first thing I'm sure of. I'm also bound—something I notice second. Going off the tension in my arms, they're stretched above my head, my wrists linked together and fastened to the center of the headboard. I flex my hip and remember that my ankles are splayed, tethered to opposite bedposts.

It's a grim bit of *déjà vu*. He left me like this all night, trapped in the perfect position to feel his aftermath. Inside me. *On* me. My inner thighs are sticky with his release. His sweat still bastes my skin, and the right side of the bed—below my calf to be exact—feels warm.

Like he watched me afterward, lingering beside me until dawn.

All things considered, this encounter was tame compared to the rest. He only tied me up.

But I don't have to wait long for him to return for round two. From beyond my room, the hushed voices trail off, closed by a single statement that sounds as if it were growled into a cell phone. "Give me time."

The gruff accent sends panic surging beneath my skin. *Shit.* Just like that, I'm fully alive, electrified into awareness. My muscles tense as I lift my head from the pillow and my heart pounds out a frantic soundtrack against my rib cage. Through the shadows painting the room, I watch the door just in time to see the knob turn. Slowly.

When the door finally opens, a monster is revealed lurking on the other side. His body feeds off the shadows as he stands beyond the doorway, surveying the damage of me he left behind. There's plenty to take in. I'm sore. I'm bleeding.

He smells it; I hear him inhale, and it's a long time before an exhale follows. Without a word, he crosses the threshold and approaches the bed, letting the weak daylight wash over him. I suck in a breath and blame the reaction on lack of sleep. Today, he's dressed in shades of gray. His hair is wild, barely tamed by the brush I assume he ran through it. His eyes are narrowed again, prowling my bare body to seek out the bruises that mark it. On my hips. My ass. My back.

The cuts on my inner thigh sear, on fire. It's been longer than twenty-four hours since he made them, but they still feel open, unwilling to heal—his name branding me for eternity.

While I'm trapped, Maxim takes his time. A part of me expects him to leave again when he's finished. Make me wait. Make me suffer. Instead, he comes closer and unlatches every cuff, watching on in silence as I rub my sore wrists once they've been freed.

His hand lashes out, the rough palm grazing the length of my ass, making me shudder. When I look up, he's staring down, his eyes fathomless shadow. "Can I trust you to bathe yourself today, *kotyonok*?"

It's not a question. I know better than to let him see me flinch. Nothing unnerves me more than when he changes his rigid schedule—and *washing* me seems to be his favorite pastime, right after fucking. He shows my body the same care he does his tools in his studio: wiping them down, rubbing his ownership into every new scratch and scar. He's the hammer. I'm the chisel, at his mercy. Always.

So what changed?

"Go," he tells me without explaining his reasons why. He just nods toward the open bathroom door.

I scramble to my feet and stagger into it, running the bath water first. Moving on autopilot, I grab the rose-scented soap from under the sink, along with a washcloth.

By the time I finally look back, he's gone and my bedroom door is closed again. Another bad sign. My stomach clenches in that familiar, terrified feeling of being caught in an instructor's crosshairs. This is a *test*.

Failing isn't a fucking option, so I do my best to remember the method he likes: washing myself down with the rag in a way to preserve his scent before braiding my wet hair. From the closet, I play it safe and pick a gray dress with white lace trim. My shoes are black flats, and I've only just pulled on the second one when I hear him.

"Come here."

His voice beckons me down the hall—all the way down to that infamous black room. The door is slightly ajar, gray daylight spilling out over the ebony marble. I have to push it open with my palm in order to see him standing before the bed, his hair loose and untamed, his body shirtless.

"Come." He never looks up. Not once as I creep over toward him, wringing my hands together over the front of my dress. He's had the place cleaned since that infamous night. The furniture has been replaced, the carpet cleaned.

God, I hate the way my gaze skips the warning signs—like those flashing, dangerous eyes—and goes right to his body instead. He's showered. The binder is wrapped tight around his abdomen, but lying on the bed are what look like a fresh pouch and a cloth. The moment I reach his side, Maxim just waves toward the assembled objects, no orders given. I have to interpret what he means.

Clean me.

And it's almost terrifying how I know almost instantly just what he wants. I sink to my knees at the foot of the bed, aware of him watching my every movement. The back of my neck prickles the way it does whenever I'm prone before him. Like, at any minute, he'll sink something into it. Mark, beat, claim. My hands flutter when I finally manage to reach for him first, finding the strip of Velcro holding the binder together.

It's delicately soft. There's only the slightest resistance when I start to pull. Tug. Gradually, it comes undone and I unwrap him. Up this close, he's a collection of old scars and wounds. They paint him. Sculpt him. Every little nick in his flesh adds definition to each ounce of muscle. My aim is just to *look*. I don't even realize I'm actually *touching* him until I feel him flinch beneath me. God, he's soft. Warm, rigid.

He stiffens further, and panic locks my body into place, but he never moves. Never retaliates. And, for whatever reason, I can't tear my fucking hands away. They rebelliously trace a path all the way down to the right side of his abdomen, circling the area where the used pouch is still attached to his skin. When my fingers creep too close, he bats them away and peels it off himself before stalking toward the bathroom. I hear the toilet flush, and when he returns, his stoma is bare.

Standing before me again, he waits, and I lunge for the cloth, dragging it carefully along his skin without him having to tell me to. When he's dry, I reach for the pouch, but once again, he takes it from me and secures it himself. His movements are slow though. Deliberate. I recognize the motion; he's teaching, and I do my damned hardest to pay attention. When he's done, he makes me wrap him back up, pulling tight.

And this is when the sheer intimacy of the situation sinks in. Something tells me that this is a ritual most of his toys never see. Never take part in. The look in his eye, once I finally gather up the nerve to peek, cements that suspicion.

He's frowning again, his eyes narrowed into that terrifying expression: *confusion.*

"You're not disgusted," he says softly as he tugs the binder into place. There's no embarrassment in his tone. No shame. Just a question I'm not sure how to answer. Something tells me I just stumbled onto the reason behind this encounter: It *was* a test. To see how I'd react to this. To him.

Would I freak out? Run? I think, deep down, he *wanted* me to run. I've caught him off guard and a part of me instinctively knows that it was the worst possible thing I could have done.

So my first impulse is, like always, to lie. "I've seen worse."

"Have you?" A low sound trickles out of him, bit by bit. A laugh, I realize with a shudder. As the sound finally trails off, his fingers curl into my hair, jerking my face up to meet his gaze once again. "Do you fuck cripples routinely, *kotyonok?*" The way he says that word…

Crippled. It makes something inside my stomach curl up into a tiny ball. I know better than to let him sense the reaction—I try to hide it—but the tight line of his mouth seals my fate.

He picked up on it anyway.

His grip tightens, dragging me closer. "Or is it *pity* that keeps you near?"

"N-no." I shake my head so firmly that the damp braid clinging to my shoulder starts to unravel.

Without warning, he reaches down, curling his thumb around a loose strand. One firm tug and my head is yanked in his direction. The ice in his gaze freezes me solid. "Then what?"

"I've seen worse," I wind up blurting out. Though, this time, maybe it's not a lie. I'm thinking of Melanie and one of the many times I saw her OD. How pale she looked. How dead. The most fucked-up part of all? Each time, I'd wish more than anything else in the fucking world that she really *was* dead.

That, this time, we were finally free.

"Tell me."

My scalp is on fire, manipulated by a heavy hand. When my answer doesn't come quickly enough, he drags me upright, forcing me to sit on the edge of the bed while he stands in front of me. From this angle, he looks more stone-like than ever. Shadows dance over the sculpted planes of his face, illuminating the darkness in his eyes. They glow, daring me to deny him.

My teeth clench together. This is a story I don't want to tell. But, when his hand comes to cup my jaw, I know I don't have a choice. So I spill. Another truth, another twisted piece of my past, drips over his fingertips, more precious than blood.

"My mom was—*is*—a heroin addict," I admit. And that's the most respectable of Melanie's many goddamn flaws. "I can't even tell you how many times I found her passed out. Thought she was dead. And…"

His frown tightens. He adjusts his grip, drawing me closer so that I'm forced to drag his scent into my lungs with every frantic inhale I take. Two quick breaths and I'm the bitch overdosing this time—no amount of Narcan can ever bring me back.

"And when you realized she wasn't?" Maxim asks.

"I…"

Two of his fingers trail the length of my cheek as if he's deciphering my emotions through touch. Only he can make me feel like this: like an open book. His mouth tilts—were he a normal person, he might even yell out *bingo*.

"You were disappointed…weren't you?"

I have no choice but to respond. "Y-yes. I was."

A heavy thumb batters the corner of my lip as if testing the weight of every single word. "And why is that?"

My heart starts pounding, every nerve in my body on red alert. *Mayday, mayday.* This confession bites too deep. My eyes sting. This tiny part of me that still recognizes the creature I call my "mother" doesn't want the truth to come out.

"Tell me," Maxim demands, stroking my jaw.

Just like that, my brain ceases to hold any control. The confession is ripped out of me, dragging up old memories I don't want to face. "Because I hate her."

It's one thing to think it to yourself every minute of every damn day—but it's another entirely to fucking say it. My nails dig into the palm of my right hand, seeking clarity from the racing thoughts. Hard. Harder.

But nothing. My head doesn't clear. My body's grown accustomed to a different brand of pain, and when I look up, it receives another brutal dose. Maxim's fingers leave my face and rake through my hair, wrenching my head back as his body forces its way between my legs.

I fall back. He prowls over me, his mouth catching mine, his teeth nipping the tip of my tongue. Shock renders me paralyzed. Men like him don't kiss; he fucks me with his mouth, crushing my body into submission—tongue-stabbing, drowning, choking, lethal *submission.*

It's hungry.

It's punishing.

I taste copper when he finally pulls away, rolling off me—but his sudden grip on my braid keeps me tethered to his side. Enslaved.

"This pains you to admit," he says, grinding the words out as if through clenched teeth. I can't see his face—just his back. Golden skin is stretched taut over rippling muscle. He radiates tension. Hoards it.

Warning bells go off. I know where this emotion leads when it comes to him. My mouth waters in anticipation, even as my throat goes dry. I'm a wind-up doll, ready to unravel when he finally turns to face me, controlling the direction of my gaze with his grip on my hair.

"You loathe the fact that you hate your own mother," he tells me, his eyes piercing deep into mine, seeing what I can't admit out loud. "You think this makes you…broken. But do you even know the true meaning of hate, *kotyonok*?"

His fist twitches, winding my braid around the scarred knuckles, drawing me closer to him. Inch, by inch. Rising onto my hands and knees I have to crawl toward him as the pressure on my scalp becomes unbearable. My face comes close enough to his that I can feel his breath on my parted lips.

"True hate is being bound only by duty. By blood. It is not even being allowed to feel anything else." His free hand seizes my chin, forcing my mouth open. In a fluid burst of muscle, he raises his head, flicking his tongue along my lower lip. Seconds later, he seizes that same bit of flesh between his teeth and bites down, swallowing my gasp. "I was never allowed to feel," he growls into me: a twisted confession. "I never *wanted* to feel. And you. *You* mock me for it, don't you?"

All at once, I'm pushed back. The force of the blow sends me flying off the mattress and I land on my side. The loss of his heat stings like a slap, even as the taste of my own blood lingers on my tongue.

"In my family, weakness is smothered out," Maxim declares from the other side of the room. The broken, guttural baritone sucks every ounce of oxygen from my lungs. "It is beaten into submission, fucked, cut, killed, betrayed, sold, coveted. It is *ruined*. So comfort yourself." His gaze sweeps over me from across the length of the bed—I sense it. "Had you my father, you would have been forced to kill your mother, rather than merely *hate* her. And if *I* felt anything for you?" He laughs and I've never heard a more twisted fucking sound. "I'd pity you."

Just like that, he leaves the room, slamming the door behind him.

And I don't dare move.

Not one fucking inch.

THE WEIGHT PRESSING on the back of my neck jars me awake. I jolt into awareness, my fingers digging into the carpet beneath me. One inhale warns me to keep still because the scent filling my lungs is the first clue as to the identity of my tormentor. It's followed by the harsh breaths catching on the air.

Maxim. Anger wafts from him like perfume.

I know better than to struggle, so I wait, feeling the warmth imparted by the limb at my throat. His foot? He smells like sweat, and when I open my eyes again, darkness shrouds the already black room.

"Get up, *kotyonok*," Maxim tells me before withdrawing the pressure and walking away.

I hear him cross over to the other side of the room, each step heavy and aimless. Restless. When I finally turn to face him, he's already switched a free-standing lamp in a corner on. The harsh light contrasts with the ebony walls, illuminating the sweat glistening on his skin and seeping through patches of his shirt. He's been sculpting, I assume.

But the physical exertion hasn't helped his mood that much. His eyes fucking glow, stalking my position as I warily climb to my feet. The moment I find my balance, he jerks his chin, sending a fringe of hair across his face, obscuring whatever expression is distorting it.

"Come here."

I swallow hard and force my trembling legs to obey. He lets me come almost a foot away before his hand lashes out, shoving me back onto the bed. I scramble to get my bearings, both hands fisting into the comforter on either side of me.

"If I gave you the full amount specified in your contract tonight, would you return?" he asks.

"I..." That's right. The final day of this week is approaching fast—and the sheer amount of money combined with the insanity of the question overloads my brain. *Shit.* Logic goes to war with what little bit of sanity I have left. Do I lie? Come clean? The answer is obvious though.

Hell no. I wouldn't come back.

"I... Yes," I choke out. But it's *wrong*. I'm lying.

He knows it. With a step closer, he's able to brush my chin with the tip of his thumb, setting every nerve in my body on red alert. "And why would that be, *kotyonok*?" he wonders mockingly, humoring me for once. "The sex?"

Once again, I know the right answer.

And *again*, fear makes a fool of me. "Yes... No." I swallow hard, grappling on the edge of panic and terror. "I don't know—"

"You don't." All at once, his hand falls away, leaving my chin burning in the aftermath of his touch. That unnerving twist to his mouth returns, stopping my heart in its tracks. I've more than just confused him; I've pissed him off. "Fine, then." He backs away, turning to face me fully. His expression alone makes my stomach sink even before he issues his next command. "Touch yourself. With your *fingers*," he adds with harsh emphasis when I just blink up at him. "Get yourself off."

One of my hands dutifully uncurls from the black duvet. Reaches down...hesitates.

"Do not make me tell you again," he warns from the corner, casting a shadow that swallows every ounce of nearby light.

He's on edge again, tossing off sparks of anger like electricity. His fingers flex at his sides, curling and uncurling in and out of fists.

He's a live wire.

And I know better than to test him now. My fingers find my pussy and sink into the folds. I feel nothing. Just dry, sore flesh, throbbing and tender. It's like my own body rejects me—and I don't know what the hell he expects me to do.

After a few awkward minutes, he steps forward, his gaze fixated between my legs. "Spread them," he grits out, the muscles in his shoulders flexing as his hands clench again. "Wider. *Wider.*"

I fling my thighs apart, forced to prop my upper body back on my elbows while Maxim stalks closer, observing the motions of my fingers.

"Remove the panties," he says. "Give them to me."

When I do, he crushes them in a fist before tossing the wad of lace into a corner of the room.

"Now, get yourself off," he repeats, "but you tell me everything you think. Everything you feel. Don't fucking pretend like you don't know damn well what I mean."

Maybe I do.

Images pop into my head and I instinctively bite my lip to push them back. Away. I don't want to focus. I don't *want* to feel. But fuck, it's like he's in my head. I hear him growl, and the floorboards creak beneath the weight of two dangerous steps.

So I panic. I give in. One of my fingers drifts up to strike my clit. *Shit.* The reaction that swirls in my belly serves as a match—but the image that worms its way into my head is the gasoline. Just like that, the air gets harder to breathe: I pant.

"Tell me," Maxim growls, his tone alone warning me not to lie. "Is it the money? I know that's it, you greedy little cunt. Say it."

It's disgusting how even his hate feeds the flames. My fingers move faster. The fire grows hotter, and the image in my head? It gets sharper. More detailed. *Him. The floor. The bed. His hands. His teeth.*

"Tell me!" Two more ominous thuds snap my thread of concentration.

I blink, my vision unfocused until I find Maxim looming above me.

"What is in your head?" he wonders, his voice a tenuous rasp. Control, his favorite drug, is running out. I sense it, and suddenly, my fingers are so goddamn slippery that I can't get any leverage. His nostrils flare at the increase in arousal, his eyes flashing, demanding an answer. "What the *fuck* is getting you off?"

"You…" I squeeze my eyes shut, hating the sound of my own voice. So fucking pathetic. High-pitched, needy. If he were anyone else, I'd know the right shit to say: *You get me off, baby. You drive me wild.* It would all be fucking lies.

But him?

Maxim.

Koslov.

Drives.

Me.

Wild. Wild like a thunderstorm with deadly lightning. Wild like a fucking tornado. He rips me to shreds. Tears me apart.

And I never stood a chance.

CHAPTER EIGHTEEN

"I see *you*," I croak out again, relieved that I don't hear another cruel advance—just silence and my own frantic breathing. Does he believe me? Does it even matter?

"*Me*," he echoes in a heart-stopping undertone. "Then show me."

Alarm jolts through my skin, clashing with the building orgasm. I'm obeying him down to the fucking T: I'm getting myself off with touch alone. Something I've never, ever done in front of another person. Or *because* of another person. My head swims with the conflicting sensations. I can't think…

"Look at me."

My eyes fly open and, this time, I watch him approach. He comes directly between my spread legs, staring down at my still-moving fingers.

When his eyes meet mine, my hand quakes, presses harder. Faster.

"You're thinking of *me*?" He laughs in that sinister, awful way, slowly shaking his head. "What *about* me?"

He flings the question at me like another test, but this time, I know the answer by heart. My eyes drift shut again and I focus on the image taunting me, feeding the heat building in my blood. God, there are too many fucking answers. My mouth opens, but only a million broken words and fragmented sentences spill out.

"Your face," I hear myself croak. But there's more. "You with the belt—" My entire body jolts as if remembering the biting sting of each lash. The look in his eye. The sounds he made. "Your voice...your—"

"*I* get you off?" He phrases the statement differently this time: colder, harder.

The mattress shifts. Suddenly, my hair is in his grip, and when I open my eyes, his face is inches from mine. Those eyes are midnight, his mouth a snarl of bitter confusion.

"I get you off?" he repeats. "Or is it the *pain*?" His nails dig into my scalp, drawing a gasp and making my eyes well up and sting.

Fuck. The burning pinch alone is too much. I shiver, feeling my own finger slide inside me, desperate for friction—only to be violently ripped away.

"Do I get you off?" Maxim asks, snarling the words into my face one by one as his grip threatens to snap my wrist.

All I can do is nod. "Y-yes."

For the longest time, he stares into my eyes. Stares through me. Beyond me—maybe as far as his fucked-up past. I don't know what finally drags him back. It could be the moan that sticks in my throat when his weight begins to press into my lower half. One of his knees nudges my inner thighs. God, the friction. I can't take it.

"Prove it," he commands, his breath harsh against my earlobe. "Let me see that greedy fucking cunt weep for me."

His voice...the gritted cadence of it sets me off. Like. A. Bomb.

I explode. My head flies back, my teeth seizing my lower lip to trap every strangled cry threatening to break free. I fail. I fall. My spine curls, my back arching, my fingers thrusting in a poor imitation of his cock. Two. Three. Four. It's never enough. Not thick enough. Violent enough.

I need...I need...

Teeth. I feel them first, grazing my outer lips before his tongue plunges inside me. He swirls. Tastes. I glance down and see him on all fours, crouched between my legs, devouring me. Three brutal thrusts and I'm higher than the fucking ceiling, shooting off into orbit. I see stars, galaxies, but when I finally come down, nothing matches the sight of his eyes glaring up at me from over the ridge of my belly: two gaping black holes, swallowing me whole.

He lunges, ripping his jeans down. I go limp and find myself pressed beneath him, his hips between my thighs, pistoning... He doesn't even have to batter his way in—my body *drags* him deeper. Too deep. I have to wrap my legs around him to preserve the fit, riding every hard, sharp thrust. They start off brutal and punishing: a devastatingly timed tempo. Deep. Hard. Deeper. Every bit of raw, sliding friction makes me see stars. My mouth is open, my tongue slithering along my bottom lip in a frantic search for air—but it's a bad move. I wind up tasting sweat, salt, skin. *Him.*

I drown in his scent, and each thrust gets sharper with every taste, slamming back, back, back until my head hits the headboard—his hand flies up and slams down over the ridge of it, clenching the wood.

"Fuck," he growls, his voice gravelly. Then his hips start to roll, forsaking control in exchange for speed. Depth.

Insanity.

Mangled Russian trickles against my throat, giving way to thickened English. "Beautiful," he grits out, pressing his chest against mine with the next shove inside me, feeling my nipples graze his flesh. "So tight. Greedy...bitch. Fuck you. Fuck you. Kill you..."

His hand leaves the headboard and clutches my throat instead. Air becomes a commodity he controls: fucking it out of me, no matter how desperately I suck it in.

Fuck. Fuck. Fuck.

It's not a game this time. It's fucking survival; I cling to him, trying to breathe.

His other hand palms my ass, yanking me from the mattress, slamming me into him. Violently. Again. Faster. Nails break the skin, drawing blood. I feel it fucking up his grip. He has to kneel, propping me up with one knee, the other braced beside me on the bed, my body slammed against the headboard.

Sounds I never knew a human being could fucking make tear from my throat. Moans. Whimpers. I break his unspoken rule: I grab him; I have to. My hands cling to his shoulders while fireworks explode inside me. The orgasm starts up like a controlled demolition, but the moment I clench around him, Maxim slams into me. It's brutal, unsteady. A low growl tears from his throat—one I've never heard from him before.

It's primal. And then he bites me, his teeth sinking into my shoulder as if to prevent himself from making any more of those sounds. He fucks me in a frenzy to finish himself off. When he finally comes, the first few spurts spill inside me. Then he pulls out and flips me over. Two hot lashes strike my lower back, every bit as painful as the whip.

I'm in a daze when I feel him hovering over me, finding my ear, and nipping the lobe.

"You are a good liar, *kotyonok*," he breathes into my flushed skin. "This time…" He licks me, drawing a whine I can't suppress, before rising to his feet and heading for the door. "This time, I almost believed you. But know that, if you lie to me again—" He cocks his head back at me. Then he smiles in a dangerous array of porcelain teeth and dark, confused eyes. "I will kill you."

He leaves me here, breathless and senseless on his bed.

And I don't dare crawl out of his room until the next morning.

WHEN THE FIFTH day comes to an end, it's like being kicked out of a nightmare without being allowed to fully wake up. Maxim barely acknowledges me. The only time he does is when Lucius arrives. He stalks his way across the foyer to shove something into my hands: an envelope.

"Count it," he tells me before turning away. "Every last cent. Think carefully before you come back."

He leaves the room, entering his studio without another word. All I can do is follow Lucius out of the suite, and like always, the real world returns like a bitch-slap hello. The moment the car pulls up to my battered house and I step over the threshold, I know that something is wrong.

First off, Daisy's seated on the couch in the middle of a goddamn school day. There's a man beside her, and not only that, but the fucker has his hand on her thigh. She's too pale, staring down at the floor.

Rage washes through my body. I don't think. I just head for the baseball bat we keep under the sink. No. Fuck that.

The knife. My only coherent action is to spit out a question on my way into the kitchen. "Who the fuck are you?"

"I'm your new daddy, girlie," the man says as I wrench the knife drawer open and grab the biggest one. When I turn around, he's smiling, revealing a mouth full of crooked teeth.

"You have five seconds to get the fuck out," I tell him. "Whoever the hell you are."

The bastard laughs. He looks like the same brand of asshole Melanie usually goes for: greasy hair, dirty jeans. She must be with him for his money. He probably got a settlement from some dumbass lawsuit or money from his dead wife— something good enough to make her fuck him. A man after her own heart.

"And what are you going to do if I don't?" He looks me over, licking his lips, and I can't help the way I cringe.

I'm wearing one of Maxim's dresses. I still smell like roses. Today, he even braided my hair, leaving my neck exposed— the perfect doll.

"You want to find out?" When I lift the knife, only Daisy is smart enough to jump up and back away. "Four seconds," I tell him. "Three."

Laughing, he stands and swaggers toward me, raising his hands and flexing the fingers. *Come at me.*

Any other day, I might have called the police instead. Thought about the consequences. Today, I go at the motherfucker with the blade, swiping it through the air.

Laughing, he dodges, quicker on his feet than I was expecting. "Your mommy was right, little girl," he tells me. "You kids need a *daddy's* touch."

I see black. This time when I swing my hand out, the knife catches him deep, tearing through the flesh of his arm.

"Bitch!"

I see his fist come for me from the corner of my eye. The next second, I'm on my knees. Wham! My vision blinks on and off, but I don't let the blade go. I keep it raised, my teeth gritted, my eyes narrowed.

"You want to go for round two?" I croak, spitting out a mouthful of something that tastes like blood. "Get the fuck out!"

Clutching at his arm, the bastard finally heads for the door. "You better watch yourself, bitch."

I lift the knife even higher so that his blood gleams on the edge. "Likewise, buddy."

The moment he leaves, I toss the knife aside, hearing it scatter across the tile. Then the world starts spinning. I can't get my bearings and wind up on my hands and knees. *Shit.* Pain throbs through my skull. I reach up and run my trembling fingers over my right eye. *Double shit.* It's tender; the sucker's going to bruise.

"Are…are you okay?" Daisy's standing by the couch, wringing her fingers together. I don't see a mark on her, but she's wearing a sweater, so I can't tell much.

Still, I've never felt this kind of fear before.

"Did he touch you?" I jerk my chin to the door.

When she shakes her head, the breath I didn't even realize I was holding escapes in a rush.

"Good." It's the only thing that fucking matters. I can't waste energy on anger. I can't…

The money. That's all I focus on as I stand and stagger over to the fridge. I yank open the door and reach for my stash —but it's gone. All of it. I feel around the back of the fridge. I look under a carton of milk but don't turn up even a fucking penny.

"You gave it to her." The words stick in my throat. I have to spit them out, but hearing them out loud stings worse than the itching suspicion I've had all month. "You gave that bitch more of my money."

"I'm *sorry.*"

Sorry. It seems to be the only fucking thing Daisy can say. There are tears in her eyes when I turn around to face her. Her bottom lip trembles. She looks like Melanie now more than ever. Guilty as shit.

"You're sorry?" I can't stop myself. Can't contain the anger. I'm in front of her in an instant, my hand flying out, striking her cheek. "You're fucking sorry! Do you know what I had to do for that money?"

What I sold.

Who I became.

"Frankie—"

"Shut up!"

Think. Think. Think. I can't. Not when I dig my nails into my arm. Not when I bite my lip. I have to snatch another knife from the drawer, swiping at my wrist. Deeper.

Fuck.

"Frankie! What the hell are you doing—"

"Go pack your stuff," I snap when a hint of clarity peeks through the chaos in my mind. It's enough to help me refocus. Bright-red drops drip down to splatter the floor, but I squeeze my eyes shut rather than notice them. Breathe. Just breathe. "Now!" I add when I don't hear her moving. "Ainsley's and the boys' too. Go!"

Knowing Melanie, the bastard she was shacking up with now probably had plenty of "friends" who wouldn't hesitate to help him beat his new "wife's" family into submission. They'd come back. Take the house. Take the rest of the money.

Everything.

And.

I.

Don't.

Fucking.

Care.

When Daisy finally staggers down the stairs, carrying a pile of bags slung over her arms, I don't go through it all. I just lead the way out and hail a cab once we've reached a main road. Then I head in any random direction until I find a hotel. I go pick the other kids up from school myself, and that night, the seven of us wind up sharing one room. Ironically, it doesn't seem to faze them too much that we don't head home.

But, when the others have fallen asleep, Mikie creeps over to me and presses something into my hand: a wad of cash.

"I kept most of it on me," he whispers. "Daisy only gave Mom a couple hundred."

I swallow hard, clinging to the bills like they're the only fucking thing I have left to hold on to. Maybe they are. "Thanks…"

In the end, a part of me knows I shouldn't even care about the money. My latest envelope from Maxim is in my pocket. By the end of next week, I'll have even more.

But it's funny how money never seems to fix things—whether you have enough or too little.

It just makes them fucking worse.

ON THE DAY when I'm supposed to return to Maxim…I don't. I stay in bed. My right eye is swollen, my head throbbing, and somehow, this injury aches worse than any Maxim delivered.

I don't want to move. Don't want to feel. Don't want to have to think. I just lie here in a pile of twisted sheets while the kids watch cartoons and fight over the free shit they want to stuff into their bags before we leave.

Maybe I *forget* my deadline.

Maybe I think that, away from home, he won't be able to find me.

Hell, perhaps he wouldn't even care? I'm sure I wouldn't be the first girl who disappeared on him, given his tastes. And he all but told me to take his money. Take a hike. Leave. So I don't think much of it when one of the kids races to answer a knock on the door. I assume they ordered room service—until I hear the voice of the visitor.

"Hello," the man says in a soft, warm tone. Only the unmistakable accent gives his identity away—and my entire body goes cold. "Is Francesca here?"

"Frankie!" Ainsley calls.

My heart sinks. My right eye is too sore to even open properly…

Shit.

I crawl out of bed. My eyes cut over to the bathroom adjacent to the room. Daisy's makeup bag is on the counter, but there isn't enough time.

I feel his gaze on me before I even look over my shoulder and see him lurking in the doorway. Dressed to kill in an ebony suit, Maxim is wearing a smile for Ainsley's benefit, though his fingers clench into fists the moment he sees my face. Two words are ripped from his throat, chilling me to the fucking core.

"Hello, Francesca."

CHAPTER NINETEEN

Francesca. Nothing in the world has terrified me more than hearing my name come out of his mouth. Nothing. I rock back on my heels as every cell in my body urges me to slam the door. Grab the kids. *Run.*

But I'm drawn forward purely by the look in his eye—that dangerous gleam I've come to know so well: confusion. It's like he doesn't know exactly why he's here.

"Can we talk in private?" He's still smiling, his voice deceptively casual. For Ainsley's benefit, not mine. And a part of me feels *grateful* for that.

He can do whatever the hell he wants to me. Just not in front of her.

"Y-yes." In the end, I hesitate only a second before stepping out into the hall and wrenching the door shut.

The moment we're alone, he lunges. One of his hands circles my throat, pressing me back against the wall. I already have an excuse on the tip of my tongue when his fingers drift up, the knuckles grazing my swollen eye. One brush of his thumb and I lose my train of thought.

He doesn't prod the way he examines the injuries he inflicts himself. He just feels. Acknowledges. When he draws back, there's blood on his fingertips and his eyes reflect murder.

"Explain."

That raspy baritone… It sinks into me. Corrupts me.

It wakes me up.

But maybe it's better to remain in the nightmare.

"I don't want to go back to you," I insist, shaking my head. His jaw clenches, but he doesn't move, watching me. "I don't. I don't! I can do this on my own. I always do everything on my own!"

My voice echoes back to me like a stranger's and I deflate against the wall. I was screaming. My throat aches and I can't bite back the sob that rips from it. "Just leave me alone. Leave me alone! I don't need you." I meet his gaze, willing him to listen to every word despite the hitch in my voice. It's the truth. It *has* to be. "I don't want you—"

"Tell me what happened." His voice resonates like thunder, easily overpowering mine but it's the look in his eye that leaves me stunned. There's no anger. No hate. Just a primal, raw understanding that cuts me right to the fucking core. "Tell me."

Like a switch being flipped, my lips part. Words spill out—I tell him everything. Melanie. The money. Her stupid new husband. Everything. He drinks in every rambled truth with no reaction. No frown. No narrowing of his eyes.

Nothing at all.

When I finally trail off, panting, he uses his grip on my throat to angle my chin back, forcing me to meet his gaze fully. "Get...home—to my suite."

I suck in air. It's the first time I've ever heard him speak in anything but polished, completed sentences. His eyes widen once he realizes, and his fingers shake—and even clench—closing off my windpipe.

"Now," he commands as I wheeze. "The car is waiting out front."

I cling to the wall when he lets me go, my legs already twitching to obey. But something holds me back, strong enough to outlast even my fear of him. I can hear Ainsley laughing at the television from here, completely oblivious to the danger lurking at her doorstep.

"My family..."

His eyes darken, swallowing up the shadows in the hall. "Go. Leave it to me."

"But—"

"That wasn't a request, *kotyonok*." His posture alone promises one hell of a punishment should I dare disobey. "Unless you want to use your safe word."

He waits, but I don't say a damn thing.

"Then go." He jerks his chin toward the end of the hall. "Now!"

I shouldn't. I should stay, fight on my own, handle shit alone, the way I have for so long.

But go fucking figure, Melanie's genes kick in this time: I leave. I put my trust in a man who likes to keep me on a leash. I put my family's *lives* in his hands.

I'm a terrible sister. A terrible person. The worse offense of all?

Even as I escape the hotel and slip into the back seat of the car waiting out front, I don't feel a single ounce of regret.

I don't feel anything.

He does the thinking for me.

I just obey.

I WAIT IN MY ROOM, but he doesn't return to the suite until after midnight, storming into the foyer like a creature ascending from hell. I hear his loud unsteady footsteps over the marble flooring. Wait, make that *two* sets of footsteps.

Is Lucius with him?

"Come here."

The command draws me out of my bedroom and into the hall. I'm still wearing the pair of crumbled sweats from this morning and an oversized tee. There's no time to even consider whether I should change. Maxim is waiting for me at the mouth of the hallway, but behind him…

Rather than his trusted butler, a trail of red paints a path toward the sculpture room. My nostrils flare, recognizing the telltale hint of salt on the air.

Oh shit.

"Come," Maxim growls when I stop moving.

Dread floods my stomach. I can hear my pulse in my ears— it's *that* damn loud. The steady thump plays like a backdrop to every slow, deliberate step I take. The only other thing I seem capable of doing is watching him. He's wet, dripping moisture onto the floor. It must be raining outside. The dampness slicks his hair back away from his face, leaving every feature in stark detail. Like always, his eyes are the most beautiful, terrifying part of all: they're narrowed, his mouth tight. When I'm close enough, he grabs me by the throat, dragging my body against his chest, lowering his mouth near my ear.

"You know what I am. *Who* I am." Without waiting for me to respond, he growls, "So do you want to see what happens to someone who dares to touch what is *mine*?"

My heart shrivels up at the grated quality to his voice. He sounds barely fucking human. Before I can answer, he steers me around, forcing me to face the mess streaking the marble. Together, we follow the ruby smears all the way to the mouth of the studio.

A pool of orange light cast by a chandelier illuminates the scene before us. There's a man crouched in the center of the floor, bloodied and bound, both hands tied behind his back. His forehead is bleeding, marred by a single gash that looks fresh. Other than that, he doesn't seem too worse for wear, though a bit of red has seeped through the sleeve of his raggedy tee shirt. I guess I cut him deeper than I'd thought.

"You bitch," Melanie's Fuckface snarls at me the moment he sees my face. He spits at the floor, aiming for my bare feet, and misses. The act is all for show though; he's scared. He keeps cutting his gaze over to Maxim, watching him warily.

I take it that their introduction wasn't a pleasant affair.

"What the fuck is this?" Fuckface demands. "Do you know who the fuck I am?"

"Your mother has chosen a Skinhead as her lover this time," Maxim says behind me. His voice is a cruel imitation of its usual polished cadence. He's a wolf, barely fitting within the sheep's clothing he's trying to wear—but it's all part of the game. There is no honesty in Russian Roulette.

Like an expert player, he steps around me, cutting a breathtaking silhouette. Black and gold gleam against red: his trademark colors. I expect him to glower, as in control as always, but when he finally turns to face me, I don't know how to process the look on his face.

So I dissect it in tiny, bite-sized pieces. Haunted, empty eyes. Hollowed-out expression. He's a ghost. A monster. A demon.

I take an instinctive step back, but deep down, I know there's no use in running. I've already sold my soul to him, after all. Still... A question wheezes out of my dry, sore throat. "What is this?"

"It was easy to find him," Maxim says without elaborating. "I tracked him down but I had Lucius arrange to bring him here, just so that I didn't kill him too soon."

My heart stops beating when he laughs, each bellowed sound trickling to the farthest edges of the room.

"He belongs to an upstart MC," he adds. "The Saints. They typically run in street drugs, but lately, they've taken to rounding up young women and selling them off for sex. Pretty girls."

I think of Daisy and flinch. My mind skips ahead: her face. This motherfucker. Her eyes without their typical innocent gleam. He had his hand on her leg. If I hadn't come home then, only god knows what would have happened. But that's a lie; I know.

She'd have wound up just like me, and it fucking *hurts* like nothing I've ever felt to picture it. I can't.

"So tell me, *kotyonok*," Maxim says over Fuckface's shouted curses. Those black eyes find mine, hollow and endless. "How should he suffer? The choice is yours."

I can taste the dare lurking behind his expression. The taunt he doesn't voice out loud: *You think you can crave me? Fuck me? Accept me? Think again. This is what I am. A monster.*

I know the reaction he expects from me. Maybe at any other moment, I'd give it to him: shiver in the corner, shake my head, cower, scream. I'd beg him not to do the big, bad things I know he's capable of. I'd make a game of it.

But tonight, my mind is too damn fuzzy. I attempt to rake the hair away from my face and realize I'm shaking. From head to toe. I can't stop.

"Tell me," Maxim warns, sounding miles away. "Tell me what is in your head."

What a fucking question. My lips part on command, but a torrent of nonsense spills out.

"Melanie's done this before," I croak, hugging myself tight. "That stupid bitch. She did it before—"

"Did what?" he presses, suddenly patient. That uncharacteristic note in his voice sets my nerves on edge like nothing else. It's…*comforting.*

"She has messed with a drug dealer before," I say in a rush. "Or fucking gang member. When she cuts them loose, they never stop. For months after, they'd come by the house, looking for her, looking for payback. Once…"

I swallow hard and stagger aimlessly as the room starts to spin around me. *Shit.* My hand flies out, my palm flattening against the wall for enough leverage to stay upright. Only now does the memory descend with full force.

"Tell me," I'm commanded.

Voice shaking, I obey. "Once, three of them came looking for her and found me instead, sleeping on the couch while the others were passed out upstairs."

The words die as I re-live that moment in chilling fucking detail.

They wanted fun and there were too many of them to fight off alone. Mikie was only a kid back then, Daisy even more naïve than she is now. I had no choice but to let them in. No choice but to do whatever they wanted just to make them leave. No choice... So I shoved a sock inside my mouth to muffle my own screams. I survived. I always fucking survive.

But once again—like always—there is another threat. And I know that, no matter what Maxim does, it won't be enough. This new Fuckface will always come back. His friends will return. And considering how long it's been since I've done laundry, I don't have any clean socks left.

And Daisy...

She will never be put in that position. Ever. Not if I can fucking help it.

"*Kotyonok*." Maxim's tone sounds different now. Less mocking, more curious. Even more unnervingly gentle.

I look up and find him watching me, his eyes narrowed, his mouth twisted up in confusion. I haven't run. He isn't sure why, and this time, his question isn't a taunt.

"Tell me what to do."

After everything he's dragged out of me these past few days, there are some secrets even he can't command me to tell. I have to show him.

My hand slides up along the wall until my fingertips brush something sharp hanging from a hook. I grab it, pulling it lose, and when my eyes drift up, they meet midnight. Once again, he does that thing: seep into my brain without permission, picking apart my thoughts and my fears before I've even admitted them to myself.

He stiffens when I take a step toward him, his nostrils flaring, his fingers flexing. The moment I come close enough, he reaches out, ready to take the offering in my hand.

But somewhere along the way, I mess up. I keep going, turning my attention to the man on the floor. Obeying Maxim would be the easy way out; I'd keep my conscience intact. But then I see that motherfucker's face and he's grinning. Laughing at me.

So I think of my sister.

And then I stop thinking altogether. I do what I always do: I *survive.*

My arm flies out and the blunt end of the chisel hits bone. Skull. The sound it makes: sharp, cracking. God. Someone cries out.

Him or me? I can't fucking tell. The next blow smashes one of his eyes in its socket though. I know that much. The third hits his mouth. The next... I lose count. I lose my fucking mind. My arm throbs as I strike over and over and over. The air is thick with salt and copper. My face is wet.

But I can't stop—not until someone grabs me around my waist, dragging me back and lifting me off the floor. The chisel falls from my grip, scattering into a distant corner. And Maxim...

His mouth is on my neck, his fingers running through my hair—not tugging this time. Petting. Through blurred vision, I see our shadows flung over the wall, like one distorted monster.

"*Moya*," he rasps into my skin when I try to pull away. "*Moya angel.* You were made for me. Mine."

I don't know what he's saying, but I recognize how he says it. His voice is thick. Gritted. Strained. It's the rare bit of emotion I've seen from him other than anger, and I don't know what name to put to it.

"Shhh," he murmurs, turning me around to face him before I can try. His eyes scan my face, his fingers stroking away the fresh drops of blood and tears. Is he angry?

I wait, shivering, but he caresses me, dragging his palm over my tangled curls.

"Mine. You were made for me." He's rambling, speaking to himself more than anyone else. "I knew it. I didn't want…" He shakes his head, cutting the thought off. Both of his hands come to land on my shoulders, dragging me closer so that his mouth can hover over my parted lips. Close enough to touch. Inhale. "You are mine," he tells me, sealing the confession with a harsh, bruising kiss that leaves me gasping for air. "Mine."

When he draws back, I look over my shoulder, too numb to process any of this. I see the man lying there. What's left of his fucking head. *Oh god. Oh god.*

"What did I do?" The question spills out of me, a broken howl. I'm on my knees, rocking back and forth. "What did I do? What did I do? Oh my god, what did I do?"

I look down at my hands. They're red. No matter how hard I rub them into the cotton of my shirt, I can't clean them off. *I can't get it off!*

"Look at me."

I blink and he's there, sinking to one knee while his hand cups my chin. His grip is strong; I can't turn away. I just stare up into his gaze and drown.

Golden hair frames his features like a halo, while his shadow stretches over the floor in a way that resembles broken wings.

My devil.

My deliverer.

My doom.

"You killed him," he tells me, shaking his head when I moan in disbelief.

No no no no no.

"Yes." His grip tightens over my chin before I can turn away, forcing me to face him. "There is no denying that— you would only hurt yourself. You *killed* him. In your mind, I suppose you had to. But do you know the secret behind committing sin?" This time, he doesn't wait for an answer. "It is absolution. Punishment in exchange for release. So let me deliver it to you." He tilts my head back, exposing my wet face to his gaze. "Tell me how."

The gist of his words resonates with what little sanity I have left: *Pick your punishment.*

My eyes go to his belt, and he stands and nearly rips the damn thing in half, wrenching it from the belt loops. I'm already on my hands and knees when he gets it free. I drop to my elbow, my free hand reaching back to wrench up my shirt.

He doesn't bother with tearing my pants off. The first blow hits me through them, biting deep down into the skin. I cry out, wailing into the flesh of my wrist. The slapping pinch isn't enough, and my teeth clamp down, causing enough pain to help me ride it out.

He doesn't hold back. I'm punished, blow for blow. Sin for sin. Each lash rips flesh open, making me bleed before I'm stitched back together. With pain. With agony.

That word he chose makes crystal-clear fucking sense now — he *absolves* me. And I can think again, feeding on the burning ache, blocking out the mental image of everything else. Nothing in the world exists but *this*. But him.

I'm lying flat on the floor when he finally ceases his assault. My eyes overflow with tears, my sobs catching on the air. I've never cried like this. Never felt like this. Broken. Damaged. *Free.*

"Come here." Rough fingers fist in my hair, dragging me upright and into the living room. When he lets me go, I hit the leather couch facedown, too weak to hold myself upright.

"You have a lot to be punished for tonight," Maxim tells me, breathless and ragged. The gruff tone doesn't match the reverent way his fingertips rake my flesh though, aggravating old bruises. "Do you know for what?"

I can't help the laugh that trickles out of me and ends up smothered into the leather. I know. My heart lurches, but I don't say anything until he flattens his palm against my throbbing ass. "I didn't come—"

"You came back to me the first time," he tells me, his big body resonating with the words, driving the vibration of each one into me. Through me. "Then the second. I could have thrown you away, even after the second." He flips me over so that I'm facing him fully. "Even the third time," he says as he scans my body. "I believed the lie that I could let you leave whenever I fucking wanted."

I'm prepared when he reaches for the hem of my pants and yanks them mercilessly down my legs.

He sniffs the fabric. Growls. Tosses it aside.

"But the fourth?" His fingers dip into the waistband of my panties, dragging. Tearing. "No. The fifth? *Never.* It's too late now."

His fingers bat my thighs apart and plunge inside me. He's ruthless. My thoughts splinter, my hips jerk, and my spine curls. Even as my head detaches from my body, I hear every word he says.

"I will never let you go now. Do you hear me, Francesca? You belong to me."

There's no chance to resist. His body moves over mine, his hands stripping me down to nothing but bare skin. One thrust takes him deep. My body surrenders, letting him in, clinging to every inch of his cock. With each brutal shove, he takes me higher.

Fucking me. Biting me. Swallowing me.

Even after he finally comes, filling me up, he doesn't stop. He flips me over. Rams in with his fingers. Makes me cry out. Makes me scream.

It isn't until I'm shaking, brainless, and half-numb with pain and lust that I realize just what he wants from me. Something he can't even ask for.

It has to be given.

"Maxim." His name tears from my throat as he enters me again, sinking in to the hilt. Deeper than I ever thought he could reach. He's beyond my body. He's in my soul. "Max…Maxim."

After one last bone-shattering thrust, he collapses on top of me, pressing me into the couch with his weight, breaking in the leather surface once and for all. "You are mine, *kotyonok*," he swears into my ear. "I will never let you go. Even if… Even if they rip you from my goddamn hands. *Never*."

They? My splintering thoughts can only come up with a faceless army of enemies. Melanie and her future fuck-ups? His mysterious Anatoli?

"Mine," he says, smothering every other concern but him.

Deep down, I know this is not a heartwarming confession.

It's a promise.

A threat.

This man will never let me go.

And maybe…I don't want him to.

⁃ TO BE CONTINUED ⁃

Maxim and Frankie's story continues in **Maxim: Obey**!
And keep reading for a sneak peek!

THERE
IS ONLY
ONE
WINNER...
AND
HE'LL
TAKE IT
ALL.

OBEY

A CLUB XXX NOVEL

MAXIM BOOK TWO

LANA SKY

A SNIPPET FROM BOOK 2: OBEY...

Hours pass before the whimpering finally dies off. From my position on my bed, I hear the front door open and then slam shut, which creates a chilling prelude to the slow, steady steps advancing on my room a second later.

He takes his time, turning my heartbeat into a rapid melody of surging blood and a hammering pulse. Just as it reaches a crescendo, my door opens.

These four white walls can't contain his bulk. They strain at the seams like an overstuffed birdcage and I'm the fucking canary. The half of my prison he dominates becomes shadow, swallowed in darkness. My little corner contains the only hint of light seeping in through a nearby window, while my racing heartbeat floods the air. Only one of us can survive the impending collision.

Him?

Me?

What a stupid fucking question.

My knees knock together, but I can't move. I just wait. In a vain attempt to ground myself, my fingers flutter over my white duvet, cinching chunks of it.

"Look at me." One step brings him closer.

I smell him, choking on the scent of sweat and lust as my eyes adjust, seeking his shape out. His eyes glow, adding a chilling contrast to the bulge straining against the front of his pants. Instinct warns me that he's erect. Violence gets him off. So does fear.

So does *this*.

"You didn't run," he tells me, anger deepening the words into a guttural hum. "Not even when you saw the worst. You stayed. Do you think that makes you brave?"

I blink. The worst? He must mean torturing people in front of me, apparently—more than once.

But he's wrong.

The worst horrors he inflicts on me are what he's doing now: switching personas like hats. One man claims I was made for him. And the other? Made to spite him.

The only weapon I have in my arsenal is deflection. "Why did he say my name?"

He frowns, his head cocked. Just as quickly, he recovers, crossing over to the bed. With a well-placed swipe of his thumb against my lip, my body shivers, resonating with his possession. It's the strangest feeling imaginable—terror and need. It's like being on the edge of a high. Like bleeding out. Hemorrhaging.

"He was mistaken." His accent chops each word into several harsh syllables. "Forget him."

"What about that guy?" I croak. "The one I…" God, I can't even say the rest.

"Are you worried?" he counters. "Do you think I won't protect you?" He makes it sound so dangerous, doubting him.

A reply I can't swallow down springs to my lips. "What happens now?"

"Now…" He rolls his head along his shoulders, the closest I figure he can get to a casual shrug. "Have you consider what I asked you before?"

"What?"

"You can watch me beat a man to death…but can you give me your trust?" The way he speaks—strained and guttural —makes a part of me tremble. "Could you trust your life to me? No, I don't think you could." He shakes his head. "But the day you give me your trust—your full trust. There is nothing that I would deny you."

A dare? It's easier to focus on the mocking dip in his tone than the rest. His honesty is like a shotgun blast—lethal at point-blank range. I could test him like he said. Ask for something insane. Outrageous. Make him give me a response.

"So…" I swallow to clear my throat. "So, if I asked you for a million dollars—"

"You ask me for what you need. I will give it to you," he warns.

So, in other words, *yes*. If I needed a million dollars, he'd give it to me, in theory. The thought of that blows my mind.

He can't possibly mean it.

But the funny part is that, the longer I stare into his gaze, the more it seems like he does.

"So…how do I?" I croak. *Trust you.*

He comes to stand before me, his head cocked slightly to the side, those eyes fathomless. "Come here."

Holding my breath, I stand and approach him.

"Trust means nothing more than surrender," he explains. "I'm not asking for anything more than that. You. So get on your knees. Prove it to me."

On my knees. Prove it. He doesn't have to spell it out. My tongue slides along my lower lip, even as my instinct goes to war with logic.

Instinct wins: obey. I sink to my knees and shift toward him. He stays standing, though he spreads his legs wider when I reach for the fly of his slacks. With one tug on the zipper, his cock springs free. He's hard already. I can barely fit my lips around the swelling crown.

The moment my tongue cradles his shaft, I realize that this isn't like all the other times I've sucked him off. I hesitate for the space of a second, but he never grunts out any harsh commands. No orders to deepthroat. His hand grips my scalp instead, more for reinforcement than anything, driving the truth into my skull.

He's here. My goal is to pleasure him. Nothing else…

There are no dollar bills to mask my shame with. No salary to make it worth it. Just the slim knowledge that as long as I give him what he wants, he'll do the same.

Trust, I guess.

Slowly, I let my tongue drift up and down his length before spreading my lips around him again.

"Fuck," he grunts, the vibration rumbling through him.

With each suck, his grip tightens, pulling loose strands of hair. Ripping them *out*. It isn't long before he's pulsing at the entrance of my throat, demanding I take him in. All of him. Deep. Deeper…

For the second time, I have the same suspicion: Violence *must* turn him on. He's even thicker now. Straining. Some rabid impulse spurs me on, making me hollow my cheeks around him. I know he's at the edge when a burst of precum floods my tongue, ripe with his taste. Just when he starts to tense beneath me, his grip on my hair becomes a vise.

"Enough."

Before I can let him go, he drags me upright. My eyes flutter, taking in bits and pieces of the room—but he's already shoving me face down onto the mattress.

"Stay like this," he growls into my ear.

Drugged on anticipation, my brain struggles to interpret what he means. *Oh.* Like this: prone, at his mercy. *His.*

"Just like this..."

A sharp nip on my earlobe sends a jolt through me as his erection throbs against my inner thigh. Grasping, his hand travels down my hip to nudge my legs apart before guiding his length inside me.

One hard thrust and he's as deep as this position will allow. Fathomless. I can't even begin to silence my cry. So I don't, letting the sound ring out.

I squeeze my eyes shut, surrendering my body to the pace he sets. Fast. Slow. Slower. I come even before he spills himself inside me, and then I float back down to Earth just in time to feel the bed shift with his weight.

With his fingers in my hair, he tugs me toward him. Gnashing teeth meet my lips in a flurry, prying them apart, tearing me open. Kissing him always feels more penetrating than the sex. More intimate.

I'm breathing his air, inhaling his scent, and there is no boundary to negate the intensity.

He crushes me down, claiming my mouth with more ruthless need than he ever has my body. Harder. Deeper. I'm a writhing mass of sensation as muscle and bone react to his touch like a magnet. We're intertwined, skin on skin. Eager for more, I shift against him, sinking my fingers into his hair.

His words echo in my skull, a mocking taunt. *I can give you what you need.*

And maybe I want it: all of him.

Every inch.

Everything.

Something broken and unwarranted slips from my lips, mingling with his satisfied growl as his teeth nip at my jaw. "Maxim…"

Panting, he draws back, his gaze meeting mine, and my heart stops. He's beautiful like this. He's terrifying like this —because he's too close. My thoughts scatter and I almost forget the truth of why I'm here. Why he's kept me with him.

Necessity.

This is just a game, but I can't stop myself from dragging my fingers along the planes of his face anyway, adding more bullets to the barrel of this dangerous round of roulette. There's no pain in this moment to get me high. No thoughts of money in my head. Just him. And he's enough. I'm not just a desperate hooker anymore.

"Maxim—"

"No!" Suddenly, he wrenches back as if electrocuted. Within seconds, he's at the other end of the room. His chest heaves, muscle rippling with every breath he takes.

Our gazes reconnect and my blood runs cold at what I find in his: nothing. Not lust. Not hate.

Just shadow, dark enough to paralyze me despite the haze of sex weighing me down like a cloud.

His lips twitch, preparing to say something.

But, without a word, he turns and leaves, slamming the door in his wake.

A WORD FROM THE AUTHOR

Hey there!

Thank you so much for reading! If you enjoyed the story, please leave a review and recommend the book to any friend you think would love this twisted world. You'd have my eternal gratitude. Even a short sentence goes a long way!

Then, come join the rest of us dark romance lovers in my Facebook Group where you can get snippets, sneak peeks of upcoming books and even help vote on aspects of future novels.

Come to the dark side:
https://www.facebook.com/groups/lanasbeautifulmonsters/

WANT MORE STUFF TO READ?
Join my newsletter and get a **free book**! Plus, you get to stay updated with any new releases, random giveaways and exclusive sneak peeks!
https://www.lanaskybooks.com/newsletter

Other Novels: https://lanaskybooks.com/

Dark, Twisted Romance

ABOUT THE AUTHOR

Lana Sky is a reclusive writer in the United States who spends most of her time daydreaming about complex male characters and parenting her Cockapoo Joey. She writes dark, twisted romance across several genres. Her titles include everything from mafia romance to vampires.

facebook.com/AuthorLanaSky

twitter.com/lanasky101

amazon.com/author/lanasky

pinterest.com/lanasky101

goodreads.com/lanasky

instagram.com/lanasky101

bookbub.com/authors/lana-sky